THE CURRENT BETWEEN

by

Valerie Mills-Milde

AOS Publishing, 2023

Copyright © 2023

Valerie Mills-Milde

All rights reserved under International
and Pan-American copyright conventions

ISBN: 978-1-990496-09-7

Cover Design: Jessica James

Visit AOS Publishing's website:
www.aospublishing.com

"There's no sun there, no sense of time. Just fine white sand swirling up to the sky like pulverized bones."
Haruki Murakami

"I foresee the day when we shall read nothing but telegrams and prayers."
Emil Cioran

For my favorite sailors, living and dead,
you know who you are.

Monday November 10th, 1913
Lake Huron Shore,

After

The air outside carried the smells of woodsmoke, lake, and the slightly metallic scent of snow. Rob McNeil peered up at the ragged dawn and then dropped his gaze to the white pastureland that rose to the north, crested by the hardwood bush. The storm would have brought down trees, but that was of no matter. In the days to come, he'd haul the timber with the horses, split it, and sell what he wouldn't need. What nagged him was the erosion at the farm's western boundary along the beach, where waves and wind gnawed the edge of his fields.

A mercy, at least, that the snow had finally stopped, and the wind was dying. McNeil left his boys, Donald and Stewart, to finish with the milking and went to the far side of the barn, to where the horses were kept. Dolly, the largest, gave him a rueful look. He fed and watered her, and then lugging her harness, he led her outside, breaking a trail to the cutter.

The cutter was beside the drive shed, half-buried in drifts. Each autumn, McNeil would scrape the rust from its skids but there had been no time this year, the snow, coming as it had so early. He took his shovel and began to dig and when the skids were clear enough, he attached the cutter to the horse. He poked his head into the barn, his eyes travelling over the cows, their boney backs rising like the ridges of mountains. When McNeil saw his sons, squatting on their wooden stools, their hands steady and purposeful at the teats, a palpable gratitude ambushed him. They were already young men, although he could still see the boy in each of them. Stewart, the younger of the two, was sharp and quick-witted. "Outhouse likely got blowed off in that wind," he cracked. "We'll freeze our arses. We'll be found arses stuck to the snow."

Donald chortled, his shoulder against the warmth of the cow, his head down. "We'll die relieved, at least." Donald was big-boned and quieter than his brother, and with age McNeil felt himself lean on him more-and-more. McNeil exchanged an empty pail for Donald's full one. "Takin' a look at the beach."

Donald nodded but didn't turn; "Once we're done here, me and Stew will take Smudge and the old cutter down to the bush," he said. "Look for Blue." Blue, McNeil's bull, was a silly creature, an unreliable procreator and prone to wandering. Regardless of Blue's propagative value, McNeil, who took the notion of stewardship seriously, felt the press of guilt. He should have read the signs of a weather change earlier on Saturday – the strangely bruised sky, a blousy wind engorged with the coming snow. It was nightfall when they got the cows in, and Blue was still nowhere to be seen.

"That would be fine," he said, adding nothing about the bull, or the bad feeling he had about him.

~

McNeil stood at the end of his field, surveying the lake. The sky was an exhausted grey and a thick fog hovered over the water, a confused and jostled collision of waves on the lake's surface. The air was damp with yesterday's snow, the diminished wind still fitful. McNeil took an apple from his jacket pocket and offered it to the horse, Dolly nosing it to the ground, then *nudging it with her muzzle. She was a good horse, but she was growing old.*

"Never saw a fall storm like this one, Dolly," he muttered, glad for the horse's familiar presence on a strange and unsettling day. He scrutinized the ravine: the wind had driven the snow into every hollow and nook. Negotiating his way down to the beach would be a chore. Having reached the age of sixty, McNeil was plagued by arthritis but what he lacked in strength, he made up for in determination. He did the hike in small steps while gripping cedars and dogwood, his feet sideways to the slope, his eyes cast cautiously down. Two-thirds of the way, the ravine became concave, as though an enormous creature had sunk its teeth into it. Dropping to his behind, McNeil slid, then jumped the last four feet. Straightening, he turned to look back at the bluff. With its bottom torn out, it would crumble and take several feet of his land with it. The idea of this loss set up a rumble of complaint in McNeil, his mind jumping to curses.

Grunting, he surveyed the beach. The fieldstone he had dumped over the years had vanished and there were great craters where before there had been a wide band of sand. The breaking waves came high onshore, the water travelling up the beach in strange backward rivulets and snaking through narrowed caverns. Debris – an uncorked bottle, trees, planks of wood, an assortment of tins – all strewn in great swathes over the beach and covered in ice and foam. There was the frozen carcass of a buck, and not far from it, a narrow rubber wheel.

The storm had turned the lake inside-out and now, spread lavishly before him was a peculiar and suspect bounty. It was a fantastic sight, an utter and dark transformation, and McNeil stood dumbstruck in the face of it.

1

November 1913
Lake Huron Shore,
Out of the Blue

Connor Darling trudges to the mink shed as the wind lifts fallen leaves from the lane in a yellow whirl. An autumn sun edges through the line of his bush and catches him in a smudge of amber light. The slyness of the day dully irritates, as if a trick is being played and he is the unwitting victim of it.

He squints into a scarred blue sky where clouds trail from the direction of the lake. Perhaps later today or tomorrow there will be rain. Except for the bare limbs on the trees and the abrupt sound of gunshot that comes from McNeil's hardwood bush (can it be hunting season?), it doesn't feel like November. A strange year during which an unusually wet spring had caused the Pine River to overflow its banks and take out bridges. Now, this lingering warmth, which in early November seems stolen and undeserved.

The building where the mink are housed is set low amongst the wild raspberry bushes, goldenrod, and the purple loose strife that bristles in the nether regions of his yard. Even from the distance of twenty feet Connor hears the minks' incessant scrabble and chatter; the creatures are never still. As if sensing his slow approach, they urgently bark and shriek.

Valerie Mills-Milde

Despite his years of mink farming their sounds still perplex. Protest? Need?

Hunger, he suspects. The minks' appetites are apparently insatiable and he's running low on offal. To make do, he shorts their food, knowing full well that their skins will dry, and their coats will dull. But furriers will barely give the furs a second glance if he shorts them for too long. His care for the mink rests on a razor's edge.

He carries the animals' feed in a pail, which earlier this morning, he scooped from his dwindling stores. Over the years he's learned to parse his earnings, securing enough feed at the fish docks for a week or two, relying on his friend Macey who keeps his tug in Kincardine harbour. Ten days before, he'd found Macey crouched on the small deck of the *Grace,* a wrench in his hand. He's a big, hairless man and fat. Seeing Connor, Macey grunted and then pulled himself painfully to a stand, the remnant of an old injury from his days in the mill still nagging him. "Bloody hip," he grimaced.

"What you up to, Mace?"

"Starboard block's jammed. I'm going to replace all this rig when she's hauled, but for now, I just need the lines to run smooth." He was sweating. Mopping his forehead with his sleeve, he stepped heavily from the tug to the dock, the *Grace* riding up like a cork. "She's becoming a creaky old dear. " Grizzled as she was, Macey would never give up the *Grace.* She had earned every one of her scars and he loved her.

"You got near to a glut there, Mace, despite your troubles with the rig." Connor nodded in the direction of a silvery mound of fish glistening on a tarp.

Macey shrewdly scrutinized the heap. "Not a glut but yeah, it's good enough." His neck craned back awkwardly, his head making a big sweep toward a summer-blue sky. "So warm it don't feel right."

Connor shrugged. "Better that than the other way." He jutted his chin in the direction of the lake. "It isn't ice fishing you're aiming for, is it, Mace?"

Macey barked out a laugh of agreement. "Right about that." He eyed the pails Connor had brought with him. "Guess you're here for a reason. Unless you want me to put you to work."

"Mace, I gotta ask you for some offal. I know I owe you already." He was embarrassed to have to ask.

Macey studied him. "It's almost the end of my season and I've got farmers willing to pay for the stuff. I'm calling in credit."

"I'll pay for it too, once I've culled."

Reaching into his jacket, Macey pulled out a cigarette, offering it first to Connor, who shook his head.

"The kits aren't far off harvest. Another two, three weeks at most."

"And if that don't come through?"

Connor watched a passing tug, the fisherman at the helm in his shirtsleeves. "I dunno."

Macey tossed his half-finished cigarette, gesturing with his chin and leading the way into the shanty. He set his gaze on Connor's empty pails, his eyes a watery grey, verging on over-flowing. He's a man who often cries when he laughs and laughs when he cries.

"Four of them do you?"

"Sure, Mace. That's good."

Giving a nod, Macey took the pails from Connor. A barrel had been placed at the end of the worktop and when Macey slipped off the lid, there was the dense smell of fish gut. Using an enormous ladle, he scooped the offal into the pails, studying it as he did so, as if the sight still held a fascination for him.

"Hope they're grateful."

"Who?"

"The bloody mink."

Connor snorted. "They'd take my hand if I let them."

"Little bastards," Macey said, chuckling. "Anyway, you ought'a think of hanging it up, Con." He lifted the pails onto the worktop and slid them over to Connor. "There you are. You can settle-up with me sometime before Christmas, eh?"

The handles of the pails bit into Connor's flesh when he took them. Macey had filled them to the brim.

~

When Connor gives the shed door a push with his boot, his stomach lurches. He has never grown accustomed to the minks' peculiar odor, musky and sharper than pigs'. A sourness floods his throat and when he swallows it, a fiery lump descends. His eyes take a moment to adjust to the gloom. The building is long and low, and at each end there are two small windows that remain shuttered. The mink, although not nocturnal, prefer half-light – the same murky dimness they would enjoy if slipping nimbly along streams and rivers.

Connor blinks, sensing the heightened expectations of the animals. He takes a lamp from the wall and lights it, and then draws it in close to the nearest pen. The animal inside leaps and somersaults and then rising on its hind legs, its thick claws scrabble at the wire. As he inspects each pen, the creatures chatter furiously at him, their mouths open, their teeth glinting in the lamplight like hard white stones.

Scooping a small amount of the offal into each trough, his lamp hesitates at every pen, pausing until he gets a hint of glister on the oily coat. He'd hoped to see more. The mink are of the black variety – the most sought-after colour. The market for mink hasn't hardened in Ontario, not the way Connor believed it would when, several years ago, he'd bought the first two pairs from a farm down east. He'd read about mink farming in an agriculture catalogue – mink furs were quickly becoming popular in Europe. Soon people in New York and Boston would be spending hundreds of dollars for a luxurious mink stole or hat.

On the day of the animals' expected arrival, Connor and his son Harry drove to the Goderich train station to collect them. They'd been crated in P.E.I., shipped to the mainland, and then loaded onto a series of cattle cars for the rest of the journey. The mink farmer had sternly warned Connor that the animals didn't transplant well and that he would not guarantee they'd turn up alive. "The care that's given to other livestock won't be enough," he'd written. "They'll need fish pellets, and regular watering. I'll put a tag with instructions on their cages, and ship some food with them, but you'll have to arrange with the rail company for the extra attention." In the end, Connor paid an exorbitant livestock transportation fee to ensure the minks' survival and still, he feared the worst.

The mink had been unceremoniously dumped in the livestock yard at the back of the station, on terrain that was a mess of mud and cow shit. Cattle, filthy and glum, pressed themselves against the wire fencing and stared dolefully at Connor and Harry as they trod past. "There they are." Harry pointed at a pair of metal crates that rocked and gyrated – signs of life, Connor thought with uneasy hopefulness.

Setting himself down on his haunches, Harry peered through the wire mesh. At thirteen, the boy had a broad face and clouds of dark, glistening curls. His wide blue eyes were unafraid and curious. "I never saw anything like that," he said, puzzled. "Not in a cage, anyway."

Connor stood over his son and studied the animals. He wasn't sure what he'd expected to see. Something like a large stoat or a small beaver. The creatures were long and thin, their bodies serpentine. They hooked dense claws around the mesh, then darted back and forth, squawking like birds, chattering, their voices brittle. "Make sure those crates are well latched before you pick them up," Connor said, "and mind you wear gloves." He hated to think of the boy being torn up by one of the animals before they'd barely begun with them.

~

With the morning chores done, Connor walks brusquely from the shed, glancing toward the end of his lane where he imagines rather than sees the shoreline road, from which the lake – impossibly blue and wide – can be glimpsed. He would like to distract himself from the animals today with a trip to town, maybe have a drink with Macey. Not that he will ask for more credit from Mace, just have a laugh, a bit of talk. Instead, he turns his head and resolutely eyes the cold cellar where the offal is kept. He'll have to stretch the remaining stores. Many times, he's imagined himself walking away from the mink. *Let nature take its course.* It would be a stop to the unending problem of the food, and the prospect is both enticing and deplorable. It leaves a heat that spreads over his face, pricking his eyes. Frustration lodges in his throat, a stubborn persistence. He will keep the animals alive until he can cull them.

The steps between the house and the mink shed are precisely 42, the steps from the shed to the cellar, precisely 21, and from the cellar to his kitchen door, 19. He traipses the same circular route twice a day, alone for the last five years since Harry left. Around and around like a marble set to circling the bottom of a bowl. He doesn't expect he'll ever see Harry again. It's just as well for Harry that he not come back to the farm, the raising of mink a desultory business, grim and joyless. Harry was a fine lacrosse player and there had been the hope, for a time, that he would make a name for himself on the field. Big shining Harry, limping off a playing green, bloodied, his face ruffled with pain, but also victory and disappointment and joy. Watching him, Connor felt himself wanting to burst with pride and worry – but he would never show it, the gratification of fatherhood mysteriously thick with danger, the pleasure in it needling him. He'd stolen his delight in the boy. Now, looking back, it was as if Harry – the warm and breathing verity of him – had been a bolt out of the blue.

Too much water under the bridge now, between him and Harry. They are well past repair. When Connor thinks about what he would say to him, if Harry were to unexpectedly amble up the lane, his tongue stubbornly sticks to the roof of his mouth, a numbing bewilderment gripping him.

~

Harry helped with the mink without complaint, but Connor knew he'd have preferred cattle or sheep, and a regular barn, like the McNeils' – not one ruled by constant panic.

But in truth, it was Connor who had the harder time adjusting to them when they came, the creatures having the same effect on him as a fever. On a moonless night, soon after they arrived, Connor imagined he could hear them raking the floorboards of his room, pausing under the window, their flat eyes shining at him through the darkness: "Get out, you little bastards!" he hissed. Stalking out of the room, the door banging behind him, he'd stood breathless and sweating in the cold hallway.

After a few moments, Harry appeared on the landing, rumpled with sleep, smiling, his round eyes dreamy. (It is the unexpected that Connor misses most, the secret jump of delight when he came upon Harry rummaging in the icebox or scraping the mud from his lacrosse stick.) Harry was a big lad, with surprisingly narrow feet, almost delicate beneath his nightshirt. He waited for Connor to say what was wrong, his fingers mindlessly scratching his belly.

"One of them's got in. Maybe more than one. I can hear it." Connor was practically panting. He'd pinned Harry with a desperate gaze.

Harry's dark eyebrows lifted in surprise, his face opening, dimples winking. "Them? The mink?"

In that moment, Connor resented Harry's obstinate cheeriness which he felt as a tease, his own good humour maddeningly illusive. Anyway, he'd been clear enough about the mink. "*Did* you bring one in here? *That's* what I mean, Harry."

Harry blinked, a hint of confusion floating across his face. "Why would I? That would be a dumb-arsed thing to do."

Connor's heart thudded against the inside of his chest, a fine bead of sweat forming on his upper lip, nerves like grasshoppers gyrating in his gut. "How would I know *why*?" He sounded strangled in his own ears.

Harry's blue eyes were on him, kindness in the expression. "There's no mink in the house. Probably a mouse or bat. Besides," he shrugged, "I don't like handling them." He'd yawned extravagantly and gone back to his room.

The next day, Connor found Harry slipping blankets over the minks' wire pens.

"What are you doing with those, Harry?"

Harry shrugged. "We put blinders on horses when they're skittish, don't we? And these don't like too much light. It bothers them when we swing the lamps in their faces all the time."

Connor laughed. "Hardly horses." He'd put a hand on the boy's wide back, the broad band of muscle there warm and reassuring. Connor's heartbeat often slowed when standing close to the boy. "They aren't livestock exactly – more like something you hunt."

"But they're caged. It isn't hunting." Harry rooted himself while the wire pen rattled and jumped noisily beneath his flattened hand, his eyes clear and steady on Connor's. "And anyhow, they're too much for you to handle." It was true that Connor wasn't much for animal husbandry, and after what Harry had seen the night before – his father sweating and panicked as if besieged by the animals – it shouldn't have been a surprise to Connor that Harry doubted him.

"We could send them back," Harry went on gently.

Straightening, Connor looked away from his son, his eyes screwed down on a bit of snare wire that hung by a hook from the wall. "No, no need," he said, determined.

~

Connor did the culling himself, remembering that his own father had spared him the awful spectre of shooting a sheep that was sick with bloat. The killing of mink is a terrible task. Connor wrung the creatures' necks, his hands protected from their snapping and biting in a pair of thick gloves. There had been a merciful surge of relief as one after the other, the sinewy bodies grew limp. But later, while skinning the animals and preparing the pelts, he'd felt ashamed for how the animals, in life, had unnerved him – as though they had dug through his centre and left a hole, black and sad and close to unbearable.

Except for the mating pairs, the cages were always empty after a cull, but they soon filled. Again, and again, the animals procreated, even long after Harry was gone. Now, Connor casts his eye over the land around him, all humps and scrub. It's a useless tract – too mean for livestock and not worth the work it requires for clearing.

What is it good for, if not for the mink? He has asked himself the question again and again. There is a dearth of possibilities, or at least he is myopic in that respect, peering at his horizon as if through an unshakable funk. Besides, he isn't fully free to decide about the farm, which is only partly his. Half of the ownership had come to his late wife Essie through her mother's family, and half had gone to Essie's brother Ed.

When they'd first come, he and Essie stood in the yard, Connor giving a desultory try at the water pump, the handle coming away in his hand and leaving him with a deeply angled sliver. The place hadn't been worked for decades.

"We'll sell it." Connor's gaze hardened. "We can live better in town".

Essie pulled a blanket around the baby's head to protect him from the knife-edged wind. Harry was asleep, his cheeks flushed pink, his lips forming a tiny whistle. "I'd need Eddie's okay to do that. I'm sure he won't sell." Ed was mining around Sudbury where, Connor assumed, he was drinking himself to death, all the while indulging the pipe dream of a softer life in his home county – growing apples or raising chickens.

Essie looked at Harry, her face full-up with love for him, everything she wanted there in her arms. "If he won't let us out of it, we'll make a go. It's not bad here, Connor."

But it was bad, at least for him, having years before fled his childhood place and home – Darling Farm, a sheep operation east of Cornwall that in his mind's-eye, was not so different from here. Not by the time he'd left it. He ruefully gazed at Essie's inheritance – the scrub, the hollowed-out house, the rotting sheds and tangled orchards, all of it producing a nervous echo in him. He had a weary sense of return.

"You will *tell* Ed you are going to sell. I won't shovel up someone else's shit, Essie." His tone had been rougher than he intended, and Essie held the baby closer. She looked down at Harry and smiled distractedly. "Fine. I'll try, but he'll say no."

She'd written but it took a long while for Ed to respond, and the letter he sent was rambling and sop-filled. (Connor was sure Ed had been drunk when he wrote it.) In the end, he'd written that it was his home, that he wanted to hold on to it, and that he didn't have the money to buy her out.

"You won't see Ed again, Essie," Connor prophesized, disgusted, tossing Ed's letter into the stove. "He'll die before he comes back here."

But it was Essie who died soon after Harry turned three, and Connor was left little better than a caretaker for a scrappy piece of land he didn't want.

~

For a few years, he logged the bush, but when the last of the timber was gone, he resorted to other ways of scratching out a living.

He took on seasonal work, hiring himself out for threshing, taking up jobs hauling and splitting logs even though he is uneasy working under other men. He drove long wagons loaded with lumber the forty-five miles from north of Kincardine to the docks in Goderich, although that work slowed, the mills and the Goderich operation shutting down, the forests steadily shrinking. Many times, he thought about walking away, making no claim on the land and starting somewhere new. (Once, while fencing for McNeil, Connor had quipped that shoreline farms would be worth more if they were all under water. "Let the bloody lake have them." After all, the fisheries on Lake Huron were doing well. And the boats were a spectacle. For six months out of the year, they swarmed across the lake's surface, thick as blue bottle flies. "You ought to be grateful you have a bit of land to work," McNeil said sternly. Connor feeling chastised, had silently taken his mallet to the post.)

In all the years since Essie died, her brother hasn't shown a lick of real interest in the place, or in Harry for that matter, but each Christmas he sends a letter to Connor. *Would like to try my hand at farming. Maybe next year.* Or *don't tear out the apple trees, there might be money in them.* Without consulting his brother-in-law, Connor cut down the old trees when he built the mink shed. The trees had been overgrown anyway and broken beyond salvation.

~

The cellar is dug deep between the mink shed and the well. In the warm weather, before freeze-up and access to ice, the place is cool enough for the offal to last. When he opens the trap door and descends the steps, brash and unsparing daylight illuminates the earth floor. The cellar smells of mildew, fish, and rot. Long ago, in the autumn time, Essie had kept vegetables down there – baskets of potatoes, and beets.

He met Essie in Goderich at a Victoria Day dance in the first year he worked at the mill. The hall was brightly lit with lamps, pink and violet bunting draped over the windows, an old man sawing a fiddle. Essie was short, with dark steady eyes above a nub of a nose. Her gaze was both expectant and assured and when he asked her to dance, she didn't seem surprised.

They went to several dances over that summer. He liked to joke with her, to tease – there was playfulness in Connor then – and she told him she liked that he could make her laugh. She didn't object the first time he kissed her, her mouth open to him, his hand unobstructed as it travelled over her full breasts and into the small of her back.

On a cool Saturday evening in September, Essie took Connor firmly by the hand and led him to the house where he was boarding. The widow who ran the place had long before gone to bed, and the other residents were out drinking off the week. Essie showed no hesitation as she stepped out of her dress and underclothes. She waited for him on a small sagging settee, the look of intention on her face, unmistakable even for

Connor, who'd never been with a woman before. He'd rushed to peel away his clothes, kicking away his trousers, one hand braced on the arm of the settee as he lowered himself down. He'd flailed awkwardly, finally gasping like a dying fish when the act was done. The whole exercise had felt startling and urgent, the explosions of sensation in his body a revelation, as brief and strangely distant as watching a shooting star.

After, standing on the threshold of the square wood frame house, he kissed her goodnight with the passion and conviction of gratitude. It hadn't been love. Not for him. And when several weeks later Essie told him she was pregnant, he was struck by how level she was, how unafraid.

Soon after Harry was born, they moved to the farm, each of them attempting to put some order into the place – Essie whitewashing cupboards and mending bedding, Connor propping up aging outbuildings, fixing rusting equipment. They seldom spoke. Yet when he saw the child wrapped in Essie's absolute joy, and the boy's open gleeful mouth, his laughing eyes, Connor felt such longing he would wish he remembered how to cry.

Remembering Essie, Connor blinks into the dark corners of the cold cellar as if perplexed by the failures of his own heart. He hadn't grown to love her. Perhaps she had forgiven him for that, and anyway, for a short while at least, she'd had the consolation of the boy.

~

The cellar walls weep dampness, and the whisky barrels where he has stored the offal are cool to the touch. He opens one and shines his light down, the smell causing him to hold his breath. Empty, just as he thought. He confirms the same with the second barrel. The third is perhaps half-full. If he's to solve the problem of the food, if he's to keep the mink going until they can be culled, he must be clear-eyed about what he has left. To thrive, the mink require an abundance of fish, although chicken entrails will do, if he's left without a choice.

His gaze falls on an array of empty glass jars on a shelf and he picks one up and studies it. The label is still legible although it has darkened and curls away from the glass. It is written in Essie's hand. Strawberry Compote. It had been difficult to cope with it all after Essie died – the cooking, the washing of clothes. And giving care to Harry. The child's exuberance and his unquenchable need for affection battered Connor at first. He'd felt shocked, stunned by the relentlessness of it. There were nights when Harry had finally sobbed himself to sleep and Connor would ease himself down onto the dusty parlour rug, his gaze stuck to the ceiling. He'd give himself over to despair, sorrowful groans coming up from his depths, his thoughts spearing him with dark intent. *I could jump from the railway bridge into the Pine River,* or *I have a rifle in the shed.* Eventually, he'd collect himself off the floor, a stubbornness in him taking over. In time, the boy's needs changed, and his demands were fewer, and the two of them had managed to make a life.

He feels the stirring of guilt — *be truthful now,* he chastises himself – *that was Kat.* Katrina Ault. *It was Kat's care for them that made it possible for him and Harry.* He would never have managed to go on without Kat. He thinks of her now, the light that seemed to come out of her skin, the lunar pull of her still felt deep in his blood.

He blinks at the gritty half-filled shelves. His life accumulated in small bits, like tools and gadgets in a work shed, which when surveyed give no sense of their purpose or use. He hasn't always noticed changes, like Harry growing six inches in one year, and Essie's currant bushes, so overgrown they died for want of pruning. His mind turns on what the loss of Essie has meant to him. He can't remember sadness, not precisely, not in the pointed sense he felt about Kat, or after Harry left, although he had missed Essie at first – her dedication to the boy which was more than reassuring. It had also been a current of joy.

When Connor finally emerges from the cellar, he blinks into the languid blur of light. Above him a stream of crows fly like dark wraiths against a feathered sky. He trudges in the direction of the mink house, grimly calculating the number of weeks left for the kits.

He contemplates the choices left to him. One source of feed remains, and it is an unlikely one. His neighbour, Robert McNeil.

2

June 1913
Goderich Telegraph Office,
A Blank Slip

The first time Harry saw Flo she was sitting at a desk in front of her typewriter, a soft line to her shoulders and her fingers poised and ready over the keys. A lavish coil of brown hair was pinned at the nape of her neck and there were threads of grey at her temples.

Her face was slightly turned as she intently regarded the message, which just a moment before, she had taken from the print machine. Her telegraphy instrument sat demurely next to the typewriter. Unprepossessing, it put Harry in mind of a bug.

The office had a staleness about it, scuffed walls and dusty ledges but Flo's presence struck Harry as singularly vital and warm. Seeing Harry at the counter, she stepped up to help. "Good morning. You're off the boats," she observed, smiling. Lakemen were easy to spot by their reddened faces and he hadn't been to the lodging house for a clean-up yet.

Perhaps it was in that moment, in her arrow-straight approach that he began to love her. Although later, he would think of her as always having been there, a familiar landmark, commonplace, even plain from a distance until the gap between narrows. Up close, Flo utterly suffused him. She wore a coffee-coloured uniform, a telegrapher's apron tied at her waste, her sleeves rolled back to expose firm sun-touched skin. Her large brown eyes were softly hooded, and her gaze was steady.

Harry was nervous and he scrubbed his knuckles into his own unruly mass of hair. Once sent, a telegram seemed like a promise, and he didn't like the idea of making promises he couldn't keep.

"What is it you want to send?" Her voice was bright, the words direct.

"Hmmm," he said. The truth was he hadn't worked out what he wanted to say. "It's to someone in Kincardine. Nothing urgent at all. I just want to say hello to a friend."

"Well, that doesn't sound like a long message. And if it isn't urgent and it doesn't need to go by night, it won't be costly." She studied him for a long moment. "Think about what you want the recipient to take away after reading, what they should understand. That's always the best way to approach a message. Take a fresh form if you like. Sometimes a clean start's the thing."

Harry nodded and took the blank slip she offered. For a long while, he wrestled with the words. He intended to write to Macey, to tell him that he was still on the lake boats. That part was easy enough. He owed Macey a debt of gratitude and besides, seldom a day went by on the water when he didn't think of Macey at the helm of the *Grace.* Macey had been the first lakeman Harry had known. He imagined Macey peering at the telegram, savouring it, the questions forming in his mind as he read. *Which boats? Are you on freighters? Canadian or American? Are you working your way up the ladder, Harry? You don't want to be a crewman forever. Get your wheelsman ticket at least.* Harry warmed, thinking of Macey's steadfast interest.

Sometimes, during the last few seasons while sailing down the lake, he would stand at the deck rails facing Huron's eastern shore and look for Macey's tugboat. As far out in the lake as he was, he never saw it.

The real trouble with the telegram was that he didn't want Connor to have a fix on him. Harry had created a watery boundary around himself since he was on the lakes. Macey would want to bridge it, not to interfere but to try and make things right between his father and him, and Harry wasn't ready. He might not ever be.

Leaving Harry alone to work out his message, Flo slipped away to her desk, put on a pair of wire spectacles, and returned to the incoming message. She would read it in code, translate the dashes, dots and breaks into a meaningful sequence of words, and type them up on thin white paper. (Harry knew this but he had never paid much attention before now.) The result would be a telegram, meant for someone to hold in their hands, to read. Hoping she would look at him, he noisily dropped his pencil on the hard counter and then picked it up again. When her face lifted, she let out a soft sound, not quite a laugh, but not a sigh either. It was more like the sound someone makes when they are noticing. She carefully placed the coded message to the side of her desk and made her way over.

"It's so hard to know where to begin," she said. Her eyebrows raised in an expression of offering. "I could write it down for you."

"I do know *how* to write," he said, realizing that she probably saw many lakemen who didn't. He grinned hopelessly. "I'm brick- stupid when it comes to this." He pushed at the slip of paper with the dull end of his pencil. "I

start with something and then talk myself out of it. I just go around and around."

She looked briefly down at the form and then removed her round wire spectacles. When she smiled, faint lines spidered down from the corners of her eyes like thistledown.

"So, tell me, what is it you are having trouble putting in your message?" When she placed her hands onto the counter between them, her fingers softened into an arch. Her nails were uncoloured and trimmed very short. She wore no rings. The fingers were broad and strong.

"I'm not sure."

She nodded as if she completely understood. "Telegrams are short, and that makes them more difficult to write than a letter. You must get to the point quickly. Maybe you haven't decided what to say? That's the hardest part. You might have to work that out first. We can get the rest of it right after –"

She'd read him perfectly. "I'll take a day or two," he said, "and come in again."

"That's fine. I'll be here whenever you're ready."

He came back the next day, not to send the telegram to Macey, but to ask her if she would walk at the beach with him later when her day in the office was done. He hadn't worked out the message, but he would like to take in the beautiful June evening, he said, if she had the time. Flo told him not to worry too much about the telegram. She said he would probably know when he was ready to write something, that it would be a rush he felt inside, like a need, and then he would form the intention and the message would come from there.

They spent the rest of his shore leave together – five days in total. And he returned a month later for another full week, and then again for a few golden days in early September.

3

Thursday November 6th, 1913
Fort William Harbour,
Girl on a Bike

The breeze is freshening, breaking the surface of the water, and a skim of ruffled cloud streams across the pale sky from the north.

Harry straddles his duffle bag, gazing at the harbour through the slant of a golden autumn sun. Up and down the docks, storm warnings are flying. The red flags unfurl and salute atop their straight poles. The Meteorological Service is hedging its bets, he muses; as if tossing a coin, the weather in November is notoriously fickle.

A single hard gust sweeps upward from the dock, raking his eyes and throwing grit into his hair. He must look a site. Harry barely glances in a mirror to shave while he's on the boats. In years past, with the season over, he'd gone straight to a barber, but this fall is different. He'll wait for Flo to cut his hair — not long now before he sees her. He imagines her concentrated look as she stands behind him, her strong fingers working through his unruly curls, the decisive clip of the scissors. His old, jumbled self falling away, Flo assuredly sweeping up the wayward bits and pieces into the bin.

Sliding his gaze to the mouth of the river, he starts to count the lake boats. It's like trying to count a flock of birds in flight – the movement dizzying and no singular vessel distinct. Fort William's harbour, which sits tight inside the river's shoreline, is restless, almost feverish. And watching the scene from the distance of the dock, he's transfixed. Boats vie for a berth while others make their way out to Lake Superior. Lakers plough serenely through the choppy water and the fishing tugs, sloops and steamers zig-zag and turn in order to avoid them. Horns sound and make a wild kind of music, like the bone-dancing sort he's been hearing in music halls in Chicago, Detroit and Buffalo. Pianos and clarinets, trumpets and stringed bass. Music that pulls a person forward in a rush. Harry could listen to it for hours.

He blinks as if to restore his vision, passing his hand over his eyes, forcing himself to conjure an image of the water without the boats. The lake boats will disappear once the weather truly turns. He'd grown up close to Lake Huron and seen how, during some particularly frigid winters, the water is transformed into vast, forbidding plains of ice. The emptiness of the lakes in winter is staggering, the idea of summer defenseless against it.

A small boat slips away from the dock, the water closing resolutely behind her, only a thready swirl left behind in her wake. A wistfulness lingers over all harbours, thinks Harry, no matter the brightness of the day. His breathing slows as he traces the line of weather-blackened warehouses that flank the Kaminishiquia River, his eyes coming to rest on the silhouette of Thunder Mountain, the only visible bit of relief. Beyond it is an extravagance of water, a glittering stretch, seemingly endless. Although that is just illusion, the enormous lake imprisoned by its shores as all lakes are.

A band of men saunter toward the line of docked lake boats that sit in the water, nose to tail. Deckhands, Harry surmises by their oversized sweaters and ruddy skin. They shove and needle one another like oversized children, all except the one who calls his name, walking a few steps ahead of the others.

"Harry Darling!"

The men are close enough now that Harry recognizes the front man as Jake Spence, stalky, well-muscled, his expression at once guarded and flinty. When their eyes lock Jake's face opens in an unexpected grin.

"Thought you'd be on a train."

"That's what I aim to do," Harry scuffs his boot on a dock board. "Saying my farewells for now." Harry's train is to leave at four and his ticket is already bought, stored safely inside an oilskin wallet kept inside his pocket.

"Those would be long-winded farewells, with you still here on the docks," Jake says pointedly, spearing Harry with a look. Jake is almost simian. His nose is bent to starboard, and a heavy white scar snakes across his left cheekbone. His eyes are a coppery colour, the irises ringed with rust. He keeps his gaze pinned to Harry's. "Weather's still holding." He jabs his head toward the busy harbour.

"But it's a bugger season to be crewing," Harry says, thinking of the coming changes. First, the winds and the rain. By December, the temperature will drop, eventually freezing the water to a gulls-egg blue, and by the New Year, dark fissures will creep like veins through the ice.

"You'd make a good bonus if you took one more run," Jake says, spiking a shoulder upward, his head wrenching to one side before it finds its center. His past in the boxing ring has left him wracked with random twitches and grimaces, the movements sometimes ambushing his body, sending ripples through his muscles and over his skin. The ticks suggest the outer limits of tolerance, a scant containment of hidden affliction or pain. He's retained a professional's devotion to discipline, completing one-hundred push-ups on deck each morning, pummelling sacks of grain hung from loading hooks to keep up his boxing form. Harry doesn't know how or why Jake's career came to an end. They've made several trips together over the last couple of years, an undemanding friendship growing between them, but Harry doesn't ask the deeper questions, quietly content to be spared the same questions himself.

Beyond his vision, a tug's horn brazenly sounds and is soon answered by the deep commanding bass horn of a cargo freighter. A cockiness is often on display in these lake harbours, a show of nerve. Jake restlessly hurls a stone into the water and watches it land perfectly between a mooring post and the hull of a tug. "Heard of the *James Carruthers*?" he asks. Harry has. The huge laker is newly launched in May out of Collingwood. "She's my last ride of the season. Maybe she'll be the best ride of my career on these goddamn lakes. A beauty. Double-bottomed hull and extra steel framing."

Harry laughs. "Must be love, Jake." He thinks of Flo. "I'm tired of boats. Not sure I'll be back next season."

Shielding his eyes with his hand, Jake gazes with a fierce yearning down the length of the dock. "Signed onto the *Carruthers* yesterday." He turns and regards Harry with a loaded gaze. "You should come."

"No, not this time."

"Captain's a good man," Jake goes on as if he hasn't heard him. "You know Captain Wright?"

"Don't think I do." Harry doesn't have a high opinion of lake boat captains. After six weeks of sailing, the last captain he served with hadn't bothered to learn the men's names, although he'd not hesitated to order them to do longer shifts, all to raise his bonus.

Jake's mates have gone on, presumably to find their boats. Jake plants his flat gaze on their backs. His temple twitches, the movement scurrying the length of his cheek. The light bounces sharply off the steel hulls and Harry briefly closes his eyes against it.

A short, authoritative bray of a horn, the sound almost cheery, the harbour master's ferry chugging past, the small steamer on a schedule, modestly going about inspections. There is comfort in the purposefulness of the little boat, the way it seems to belong absolutely to these waters. Harry looks up at the pale blue sky, the clouds slightly thickening, streaming across it like banners.

Jake waits, frowning, his relentless energy fixed to a spot far out, in the lake.

"I'll think on it, Jake."

Inside the long silence between them, there is a vibration, and it perturbs him, as though he hears something in it that he can't understand. "It would be good if you joined," Jake says finally. "It would mean something to me, Harry, but do what you want."

Harry laughs. "Won't say yes."

"But you're not saying no. Not yet. At least go in and check the *Carruthers'* specifications." Jake jerks his head toward a row of buildings set back from the harbour's gritty

sprawl. "She's with the S.C.N. outfit, and if you change your mind, she sails in four hours."

~

The St. Lawrence & Chicago Steam and Navigation Office sits neatly between two of its competitors. It's a square wood frame building, flying a Canadian Ensign, and smart with white paint and blue shutters. Inside, there is a bustle of action – officials checking waybills, captains brusquely signing contracts. Harry wanders over to the bulletin board where he finds information about the company's active freighters. Running his finger down the short "outgoing" column he finds the details about the *James Carruthers'* size, her weight, her cargo. Her dimensions show her as an impressive five-hundred and fifty feet from bow to stern. He whistles through his teeth. A red stamp reading *Manifest Closed* appears next to her name. It's a relief to see it there. If he's been harbouring an unacknowledged itch to join her, the closure notice handily quashes it. Of course, it's doubtful that manifests and crew rosters are worth the paper they are written on. Last minute alterations and additions are commonplace, especially in November.

Once outside, he reaches into his coat and pulls out a cigarette but doesn't light it. Instead, he taps the blunted tip lightly on the back of his hand, settling the tobacco, dropping it unused into his pocket. He still has an hour before he should make his way to the train station, and the *Carruthers'* expected time for sailing is, as Jake said, late afternoon. More than enough time to have a look, collect a final impression of this last word in lakers, like a postcard he'll tuck away as he turns away from the boats.

He takes the direction that Jake took earlier, past the assortment of docked freighters and tugs and ferries, and then he finds her. It is her size – more precisely her length – that stuns him. Sliding his gaze along her lines, he's barely able to take-in the whole of her. Bloody workhorse, he thinks. She is fresh looking with new paint – ugly in the way that new straight-deckers are. Pugnacious, something proud and haughty in the jutting bow, and remarkably square – all steel and stiff lines and awkwardness.

Her design, though outsized, is familiar. The boxy deckhouse rises at her bow and contains the pilothouse as well as quarters for the captain, senior mates, wheelsman and some of the crew. At the far aft sits a marooned structure, the stern deckhouse – galley, dining room, additional cabins – the engine room hidden there, deep in the boat's belly. In between the two superstructures and placed at intervals along the deck are the boat's gaping hatches.

He is a long while, contemplating the enormous boat, affection and admiration already taking hold. Scores of men teem over her, hoisting cables and cranking the loading winches and all the while she stays firm to her air of forbearance. It is this, her unexpected grace that captivates him.

Later, Harry won't remember the precise moment he decided to join her. A girl on a bicycle is riding past, her messenger bag slung heavily across her slight torso. Her face is pinked with effort, and she seems in a hurry. Putting out his hand, Harry stops her. "Can you take a message back to the telegraph office for me? "

Breathless, she eyes him. "Not supposed to do that. These are outgoing messages headed for the harbour master. You should go in yourself and send it."

The telegraph office is a long walk and there is likely a queue at the counter. Yesterday, while there, he'd had to wait for a half-hour to have his message taken. He'd felt no hesitation when he sent Flo the message: *Docked and on my way by train tomorrow without delay. Love. Harry.* He'd been satisfied after writing it down, certain that Flo would appreciate the sureness, the brevity of it. But now that he would be delayed, the message isn't quite right, off by at least two or three days.

"I know I should take it myself," he pleads, "but I haven't got the time and it's really important. Will you do it for me?"

The girl looks uncertain but then, as if on impulse, she nods her head. "Won't go right away. I've got a lot of deliveries."

"That will be fine," Harry beams at her, knowing full well what effect his smile will have. "You are an angel," he says. "I knew it as soon as I set eyes on you."

She stares, her pink colour deepening.

"They'll be waiting on me." She looks over her shoulder and then back at Harry. "You'll have to write it quickly."

Harry nods and slips his notebook and pencil from his bag. Despite the girl's impatience, and the hurried activity around the laker, he takes his time with his words, wanting Flo to understand from the message that she should expect him, that he is on his way. *An unplanned outbound job working the James Carruthers. Will catch train once I get to Midland. With you very soon. Can't wait. Unceasing love. Always. Harry.*

"There," he says with a sigh, folding the note and then handing it to the girl. "And this, to pay for the message. There's extra in it for you. "

She lights up when he gives her the money, quickly tucking it and the note into her pocket before wheeling away, her coat open and flapping, her braid bouncing at her back. A beautiful little bird in flight, he muses. He's filled with bright confidence, watching her.

After the time spent with Flo, Harry knows roughly how telegraphy works but still, he imagines the girl swooping in, dropping the message straight into Flo's waiting hand. *From me to you*, he thinks.

4

Friday
Goderich, Telegraph Office,
The Current Between

Flo isn't surprised by the traffic going in and out of the office today. The men queueing at the counter are red-eyed from too much end-of-season celebration, unshaven, their clothes dishevelled. Despite their rough condition, they're in good spirits. The messages they send concern arrival times and train numbers and transfers in Toronto or Detroit. "NOT COMING HOME" one telegram states in a merciless and perfunctory manner that makes her smile. At least he'd made his intentions known; some of the lakemen will simply drift away without a word to anyone, fading into the bush or into cities where there are no claims on them. She has come to think of these transient men as ghosts, not inhabiting any single place.

The large railway clock on the wall shows that the time is half-past noon, but she doesn't have to look to know this because the east-bound train for Guelph has recently jugged away from the platform. Its departure, which she registered without much thought, is scheduled for twelve-twenty, every second day. At first, when she came to Goderich, the sound of the incoming and outgoing trains had created longing in her, a wish that she might step on-board and return to her city life where there were sidewalks and people, coffee shops and music halls. But over the last years, resignation to the quiet town, perched on the edge of the faceless lake, has stolen in, and the comings and goings of the trains are no more emotion-laden than the predictable chimes of the clock.

Although the office is housed in the railway station, Flo works for the Great West Northern Telegraph Company, while a second telegrapher named Ruby is employed by Canadian Pacific Rail. In the past they've pitched in to help one another if there is a pile-up of messages, and they've enjoyed sharing tea breaks or lunch. Soon after she'd first arrived, Flo reclaimed two old chairs from the station's shed, painted them red and put them under the eaves at the back of the long station house. They often sit together in the late afternoon, sometimes under a rug if the weather is damp, Ruby talking excitedly about planning her family. Flo isn't terribly interested in cradles and quilts, but she loves Ruby's tireless industry, her obvious sense of purpose. It has been two and half months since Ruby left her post to have her first baby and although Ruby hasn't said so, Flo doesn't expect she'll come back.

Having a family of her own has never been a distraction for Flo and besides, the chance is long past now. Flo answered an urge to leave home when she was barely eighteen, curiosity as much as anything leading her, and then she'd fallen into her work, and it has carried her.

Telegraphy is a system of communication that can unlock the world, one of her instructors at the training institute in Toronto had said. It seemed a pretentious comment to Flo, implying that somehow, without the telegram, a person was barred from a *real* life, or at least a life that counted. Coming as she did from Saskatchewan, a rural place where people endured a great deal to remain in touch, she dismissed the

claim as high-flown. Each week, her mother and her aunt had walked several miles just to meet and to hug, always exchanging something – a jar of pickled beets, a hand-stitched pillowcase, a particularly warm pair of woollen stockings. The walk had seemed a small price to pay for the chance to greet one another.

But Flo's head had been turned by telegraphy when she took up a junior position at the G.W.N.T. A solemn-looking building with sternly arched windows and squat columns, the central office located at 347 Bay Street in Toronto gave no hint of the hive of activity inside. Very quickly, Flo was swept up by it. Each day, after pulling open the heavy double doors, she eschewed the elevator, instead trotting up the marble stairs to where she joined a small army of telegraphers on the tenth floor.

The room was cavernous, jammed with furniture, machines, aides, and operators. Telegraphy, she soon learned, was not a tidy business. There were overflowing bins of wastepaper, dirty ashtrays, litter strewn over the tired wood floors. Darkened wainscotting hemmed the high, scuffed walls and on bright days, shards of sun came through the streaky windows and struck the metal shells of the operators' typewriters, the glare flooding their eyes until someone thought to pull the shades.

Except for the manager's desk, which was sequestered, they worked with no partitions. She remembers the familiar taste of dust, disturbed by the pounding typewriters and the footsteps of running aides. They drank gallons of tea to wash it down, the tea brewed in a huge kettle three stories below.

The operators sat close together at long narrow tables, heels knocking shins, elbows brushing one another. Flo would often smell the perfume of the woman next to her, or hair pomade if it was a man. They'd bathed in the frenetic atmosphere of 347 Bay; telegraphy printers spitting out messages, the rip and tear of paper, the more subtle tapping sounds of the telegraph instruments which were, after all, the pulse of the place. Managers hollered urgent instruction to aides. Newspaper men, not feeling obliged to stop downstairs at reception, flew in demanding their press's overseas communiques, practically breathing down the necks of the operators. The vigor and speed of operator-typists was catching, like the spreading fires she'd seen as child on the prairies, each burning blade of grass quickly igniting the next.

Many of them came from far-flung places, and all of them at Central Office aimed to be part of something bigger than what they'd come from. They were a sort of family, bound by invisible currents, the lifeblood of a great looping circuitry.

What Flo often recalls, in the relative quiet of the small Goderich office, is the sound of forty typewriters hammering all at once. This was something felt rather than heard, the rhythm vital but transient, and hard to conjure now. Like a flock of geese lifting from a pond, the air vibrating with the beating of wings. The typing was inevitably followed by a descent into code, the world silenced beneath her headphones, everything vanishing except the *tap, tap, tap.* She relished this feeling of diving in, finding the singularity of each sound, and the spaces between, meaning emerging, a shadow filling in. Flo wouldn't have wanted to remain there, just with the code, like holding a breath for too long, her lungs threatening to burst. Sooner or later, she had to return to buoyancy, to the clamour and to the mess of people. It was the back and forth she really loved about the work in Central Office, like the great sweep of a pendulum: inside and outside, and then inside again.

She'd felt her life tamp down, coming here, the line between the inside and the outside flattening, becoming obscured in a sort of dullness. The Goderich office, situated at the north end of the station, is small, with two separated desks and a long wide counter. A portrait of King Eddie has been hung above a jam cupboard which, until recently, held Ruby's baked offerings, but now holds only a few mugs, a tin of dry tea biscuits, a linen towel and an old throw rug left there by the former operator for reasons unknown. A heavy walnut cabinet, housing paper and supplies, has been pushed between the two desks. A single square table sits in the middle of the room and on it is the mechanical printer from which all receiving messages come. It's a noisy thing, old, and as it spews out streams of paper, the table beneath it dances and jostles. Flo regularly writes to the head office requesting a replacement and although she receives reassurances, nothing ever comes.

Goderich is a working harbour and she sends many commercial messages – the weight of a load of iron ore, the approximate volume of a load of grain. Often there are bits of information attached, a series of dates and times and numbers. She does these efficiently, precisely but they strike her as lifeless.

And then of course there are the personal telegrams. After they've trained, all operators begin with these, but Flo had risen well beyond that level of transmission by the time she left Central Office. The personal communiqués she took on in Goderich seemed like a demotion at first. But looking back, she sees that she had been raw when she left Toronto, hurt to her marrow by what happened there and the emphatic, sometimes bluntly painful tenor of intimate messages left her feeling bludgeoned by someone else's pain. She had deadened herself with exactitude and remove and rarely allowed herself to think of telegrams for longer than it took her to transcribe them.

And then, in her first early spring in Goderich, a woman came to the counter, her features frozen, her mouth a stiff, anguished line. She said nothing to Flo while she filled out the message form. Her hand didn't shake as she wrote. The scant containment of the woman's pain was a fragile but determined thing.

After the woman paid, she leaned for a moment against the counter, sighed a heavy, exhausted sigh, and drawing herself up again, she squared her posture and left. Flo took the message to her desk and read it. *He fell from the roof and broke his neck. He was loved. He was all I had.* Flo sat for a long while, blinking down at the words. It was as though the woman had stripped herself bare before her. She felt her heart thud in her chest, something coming alive, the part of her that, for the months since leaving Toronto, she had exiled.

It was after that telegram that each private message seemed to create a hum in Flo. Like putting her hand on a struck bell. Sometimes the residue was sad, sometimes joyful or triumphant, sometimes defeated; a one-legged woman, receiving her long-awaited prosthesis only to end up with two right feet. The birth of triplets. Deaths, greetings from afar. It was as though, against the still backdrop of her world in Goderich, the details of these *other* worlds, beneath the dots and dashes, had become even more distinct. Guilt, pride, pained reluctance, love. Naked and startling feelings. To convey such intimacy in so few words, now seems to Flo, miraculous.

~

Flo hasn't fought terribly hard against solitude. Perhaps she has been resigned to it. She is thirty-five, and years ago stopped imagining a shared life. After the mess that happened in Toronto – the stew of emotion she endured throughout her involvement with Terry Eldridge – she'd turned away from any prospect of giving herself over again. The business with Terry had cost her too dearly.

A Class One telegrapher and highly skilled, Terry was educated in England, a quiet gentle man who liked poetry and talked a great deal about star constellations and telescopes. The company trusted him with the coveted London-Toronto news circuit, perhaps because he had lived abroad for many years. The general opinion among the female operators was that he was a fuddy-duddy, too old-fashioned to be of any real interest, but Flo had no trouble talking to him. She usually didn't have difficulty talking to people, and her straightforward manner brought out a kind of shine in him.

He'd shyly asked her to lunch and before long, they spent two or three evenings a week together. He was handsome in a befuddled sort of way, a beautiful chin, fine grey eyes. A ruin of a face, she thinks now, although she hadn't seen it then.

He told her about living in London, his trips to Italy and Germany. He spoke beautifully, elegantly, and Flo, barely off the prairie, began to gather up pieces from him, feeling the need to complete the neglected places in herself. There had certainly been a tenderness between them, she doesn't doubt that, even now, but there were illusions too. She didn't know him, really.

One August night, in her small room, after they'd gone to bed together, Flo said it was hot and that they should take some air. "Yes," he said, kissing her head. "The park? I can walk home from there." They lay side-by-side on their backs, the tree frogs loud in their ears. "It puts your life into perspective, looking up," he said. "All the grey bits of everyday life go away or, at least, they don't matter so much." She'd laughed. "Your life isn't so bad, is it?" After all, she thought to herself, they'd found one another, and what was the likelihood of that, amidst all the people everywhere? The time they shared, the world they inhabited seemed uniquely lovely and probably rare.

For a few moments he hadn't said anything. "No, I suppose it isn't."

He'd put an arm behind his head, his pale eyes fixed like dried flowers inside the pages of a book. "Soon we'll all be traversing the skies, and information will move even faster than it does now." Terry often liked to sink into lecture; Flo listened, always erring on the side of patience. "Humans want to close the gap with religion, poetry, science." His tone was wistful. He was sad, she'd imagined, because it was a sad idea, shot through with disappointment and separation. Although later, seeing him more clearly, she would decide that she was wrong, and that he was simply self-indulgent.

"I've made a mess." His voice suddenly broke. Bewildered, he blinked up at the flinty stars. "I'm sorry, Flo. You probably expect much more from me." He'd awkwardly squeezed her arm, which now, thinking back, might have been meant as an apology.

At the time, she'd been surprised by what he said. What *had* she expected, exactly? Of course, Terry, a bachelor, was

hesitant about settling down, and she enjoyed her work, her life in the city, the friends she'd made. There were years ahead to consider children, if they wanted them, and Flo wasn't certain that she did.

~

A year after she and Terry began seeing one another, the office manager slipped a note beside Flo's typewriter, asking for a private word. Flo had been excited. She showed the note to Lucy, the operator stationed closest to her and a good friend. "Oooh," said Lucy, her hand covering her mouth. "You'll be a Class One now." Flo dared to believe it might be true. After all, she had her mandatory five years by then, and her precision with code was remarkable. She had also achieved exceptional speed as a typist while maintaining very decent accuracy. Her abilities had not gone unnoticed and just six months before, she'd received a letter of commendation from the company.

There would be a pay raise involved if she was promoted. She would have the responsibility of training new recruits, assuring efficiencies in the system. But what was more appealing to Flo was the nature of the transmissions she would be sending – the Toronto office did a lot of government work and only the Class Ones were entrusted with it. These were important communications and far-reaching. She knew because Terry told her what he could – flare-ups of tensions in foreign countries, coal worker strikes, political intrigues. He couldn't tell her everything, of course. Much of the work the Class Ones did was kept in the strictest confidence and Terry would never have stepped over the line. But he told her enough that she understood the significance of conveying facts, their importance in bringing about a speedy and appropriate response, the sensitivity of time in vital matters.

The manager, a young man with a narrow, sallow face, looked nervous when Flo came in. "Have a seat," he'd motioned vaguely. There was little privacy and the noise in the office made conversation almost impossible.

"How are you, Florence?" He said, his voice reedy over the din.

"Fine." She smiled widely at him. Some of her fellow operators thought he was a poor choice for management. Lucy maintained he was afraid of women. Flo felt sorry for him, as if he was a little out of his depth, as though he might be happier if he'd remained an operator, without the responsibilities of managing people. But the male operators, being in the minority among the telegraphers, were quick to rise through the ranks. "I hope you are too," she said loudly.

"Well, I won't keep you long, I'm sure you have a lot to do. I'd rather not have to talk to you about it but here we are." He placed his hands on his desk. "You know that Mr. Eldridge is married, Florence."

She'd sat very still, frowning, trying to comprehend what he'd said.

"I don't understand -"

"There isn't any question. His employment record is clear. Dependents, too. Children. They must be almost grown now," he added pointedly.

Flo remembers the feeling of the floor dropping away. Her mind quickly went over the last two years and ferreted out the gaps, the rigidity of schedule, the insistence on not going out to public places. Terry had never woken up in the morning in her bed. She was suddenly bludgeoned by recognition.

"If that's true - "

The manager was waiting, giving her a furtive look, a man caught at a peephole. And then he capped and uncapped his pen. "Anyway, we can't have a side show here, it won't wash. The work we do is too important. You see the problem?" He'd taken a sip of water from a smudged glass, put it down, looked out the window. "I'm surprised he's been able to hide his situation for this long." She thought about how Terry was very good at keeping the cogent bits of stories veiled, all the while providing the grand outline of things. His head in the stars. She didn't have experience with liars, and she saw quite clearly that she'd been stupid.

"In any case, my job is to keep things working here. Terry's a Class One. He's very productive."

She felt a terrible, spreading heat. "I am too," she said tersely. "Productive, I mean. A word speed of forty-seven words a minute in code."

"Yes, you *are* excellent. We are well aware. Topnotch, and likely to get better. But right now, you have a choice. You can take a transfer to a more remote office, or you can leave us and find something else. Maybe the railway, or a secretary somewhere? You have excellent typing skills, and those can be applied broadly."

She thought about what he was suggesting. The railway would take her to a bush town, at least to start. And secretarial work? "I trained for *this* work, for code," she said, "and not for something else."

He scrupulously studied the papers in his tray, frowning as he sorted.

"I'll give you until tomorrow to think about it."

After leaving the manager, she stopped at her desk and slipped the cover over the typewriter. It belonged to the office and was standard issue. She wouldn't give it a second thought. The New Haven, her telegraphy instrument, was another matter. She had carefully bought it from her savings years before. The wood base was a simple rectangle, narrow in profile, the metal apparatus on top a straight bar and key paddle. A modest instrument but true, reliable, and it was hers. With great care, she freed it from the circuit box.

After carefully placing the New Haven in her carryall, she snatched her coat and handbag from beside her chair. She had tears in her eyes by then and Lucy, seeing them, was horrified. "What?" she mouthed, arching her eyebrows. Flo could only shake her head.

As she left the office, she glanced at Terry, who was slouched at his desk. He seemed stricken, his face ashen, his eyes sunken and aged. There was no question that what she had just heard was true. No one could look that sorry unless they had something to answer for.

In the end, she accepted the position in Goderich, and she adjusted to the change, although there were still periods of loneliness. Two summers before, she'd met a medical doctor, a widower holidaying at the hotel and they'd taken a short sail and had dinner together. He'd gone back to Chicago, and she never thought much about him after. There were always lakemen but they were rough around the edges and Flo could not muster the interest. She had crossed an invisible bridge into middle age without even noticing she'd done so.

~

Since coming here, she sees the lake every day. In summer, it's a spectacle: the water is an impossible blue, and the passenger boats are adorned like wedding cakes, the pretty sailboats with their crisp flags. She loves the deposits of colour along the beach, the blues and reds of sunshades, and at the park on the bluffs, the pavilion often strung with bunting. But when the holiday visitors leave and the lake boats are gone, the colour disappears and the water and sky fuse in unending gray. Flo dreads the lack of light, so different from winter in Saskatchewan. When Harry comes, this year will be different.

At the start, she'd told herself she'd imagined the spark between them. After all, she is older than Harry by more than a decade. And Flo, who doesn't put much store in appearances, knows that she's not beautiful.

She was drawn to him that first time. Harry had a wide-open face, an unstoppable grin, a slight pinch of bewilderment at the corners of his eyes. His curly hair, long when she first saw him, gave an impression of softness. In his lakeman's clothes, he appeared oversized, shambling. But he was earnest, his effort so clear as he wrestled with his message, intent on making it true.

It wasn't until the next day, when they walked together at the beach, that her pulse raced and thinking herself ridiculous, she'd taken a deep breath and made sure to give no sign. There were no obstructions when she looked at him, no shadows. The brightness of the day seemed to slow their pace, as though they were pushing their way into a sort of fullness, although Harry laughed and said he was having a hard time keeping up with her. She liked his eagerness. He told her he'd come from a place barely forty miles up shore, but he hadn't been home in five years.

"Is that why you are having trouble with your message? Is it hard to imagine going back?"

He'd looked puzzled for a moment and then he closed his eyes and smiled. "Oh yes, that's it exactly." When he opened his eyes again, he'd seemed relieved to see her still standing there.

She argued with herself during that first leave, and she sternly told herself to not get too fond of him. This was no more than a lovely encounter, an unexpected reminder that she was living, and not yet old. And then one night, with the window open to a soft and steady rain, he told her he had a hard time being certain of many things, but he was certain about her. It occurred to her that Harry was the most believable person she had ever known.

He was back a month later for a week, and then for a stretch of days the month after, and lastly, in September. Sometimes, working in code, the *tap, tap, tap* comes to her as a knock on the door, and opening herself to it, Flo feels herself taken into the message's heart. This is where she meets Harry, she thinks, in that place inside the words.

5

Friday November 7, 1913
Lake Superior,
Circumnavigation

More and more, Harry has sensed the weight of his life shifting toward shore. Before he met Flo, he often asked himself: *Where will I go? What will I do when I done with boats?* In truth, he'd known for some time he wouldn't continue leading the oblique life of a lakeman.

For a few months each year the lakemen scatter, their lives turning from the water and toward railyards, sawmills, tanneries and factories. For Harry, over the past several winters it's been housebuilding. It suits him, and he has fallen under the spell of cheek cuts and fascia and dovetails. He loves seeing the bones of a house rise straight and true from raw ground. The work is always easy to find, the world having gone mad with new building. Many times, he's thought of pursuing year-round work as a carpenter.

In 1911, he worked a small provisions boat along the shores of Lake Superior, the boat delivering winter stores of food and supplies to far-flung lumber camps. The hard-eyed men who emerged from the woods were reliably eager for a drink and for conversation.

"These lake boats will only take you so far," one lumberjack, a former wheelsman, told Harry as they unloaded boxes of medical supplies. The lumbermen were known to regularly crush a foot or sever fingers. "Sooner or later, you end up where you're trying to get away from on the lakes," he'd declared. "The water runs out." When he told Harry he was working his way to a cousin in Alberta, Harry looked around, puzzled, at the morose scrub and swamp.

"Don't see how you're going to make your way out of this bush" he mused, feeling sorry for the man because of the forest that hemmed him in. "Can't see an end to it."

"There's an end," the man said flatly, "and once I get closer to it, I'm goin' to get on with the railroad. That's a straight ticket west. No trees to cut on the prairies. No 'round and 'round the same watery stretch of miles like you got on those bloody lakes. Just sky and grass wavin' you on."

The idea of leaving the lakes behind had appealed to Harry and occasionally, over the years, he imagined himself joining the wave of ragtag men on their westward migration, picking-up building work in towns along the way, but he's held in place to the lakes, as if they are a part of him or he of them.

~

From his vantage point next to the gangway, the *Carruthers* claims the whole of Harry's vision. He can see the rivets in her metal hull. The boat is new and already bears the mark of water, the paint slightly discoloured at the water line and in places where the deck-wash runs down her sides from her scuppers.

Gazing down at him from the deck, Jake's hands grip the rail, the sun an orb behind him. Harry can't make out Jake's face, only the tensed and ready tilt in his neck and shoulders.

"You coming then, Harry?" There is restrained surprise and excitement in the tone.

"Rocks for brains," Harry quips, dodging a river of dockworkers and crewmen as he trudges up the gangway. The *Carruthers* has been baking in the sun for hours. There is a tangy smell about her, and the more intimate smells of metal, coal dust, oil, and something slightly moggy, the density of stagnant water.

Jake walks with a deliberate nonchalance and when he stands next to Harry, he crosses his thick arms, his eyes darting to a mail boat that pushes into the wake of a larger vessel. A vein throbs at the side of his temple. "What made you decide to come?" For a small man, his voice is deep, as though it comes from the bottom of the world. He doesn't wait for Harry's answer. Instead, he looks away, toward the teaming harbour. "Loading is balled up," Jake goes on, "so we'll be later leaving than planned. Anyway," he gives Harry an obscure look, "glad to not have to make this last run alone."

It seems a strange thing for Jake to say, the *Carruthers* maintaining a crew of at least twenty people. Harry waits for an explanation, but Jake has shuttered himself, his coppery gaze flattened to the hull of a passing laker.

At the south side of the Empire elevator wharf, at the mouth of the river, a red light blinks forbiddingly. Harry recognizes it at once as the Fort William light, a lonely-looking structure affixed to an ugly metal pole. Beyond it, the cold lake spans, incurious and vacant.

He thinks longingly of the lighthouse in Goderich, its simple rectangular lines, the lovely French pane glass that encloses its lantern room, the brightly coloured ridge turret that sits atop like a hat. Seeing the staunch little fixture on the

Goderich bluff always lifts him up. He is brought back to an afternoon in early August with Flo. A crystal-clear day and the lighthouse gazing down as they dangled their feet from the pier. There were no shadows, the high sun bright, urgent, and the moment, with Flo, was wide open, everything around them exposed. Their arms touched but nothing else. Flo thoughtfully studied the lake. "How many boats are out there, do you think? More than one hundred?" Harry hadn't thought about it, not until she asked.

"Including the fishboats, the mailboats, all the rest? More, just on Huron alone." Harry pointed out the lake boats he recognized, Flo asking practical questions about his life on the lakes. "How do you bathe?" and "Is there an icebox on board?" She noticed small differences in boat design, "What about that one?" she asked, watching a passing laker. "Its bottom is rounded and its front end is quite wide." Harry nodded, his eyes following the laker. "That's an older boat. A Whale Back design, but things have changed now. They build the boats with straight decks, mostly because of the locks."

A warm breeze caught her hat and she moved to secure it, her hand brushing Harry's chest, setting his skin to tingling. He wanted the moment to go on and on, and he'd felt undone with the greatest kind of happiness. As he looked up and saw the lighthouse, he was grateful to it.

It was that afternoon that he talked with her about the pull he felt toward his father. "Like the needle on a compass dragging north," he said. "But I keep resisting and now I'm seeing things," he confessed, laughing at himself. "Going daft." Flo hoisted her bare feet and settled them on the surface of the pier, and then she wrapped her arms around her shins as if to plant herself there, next to him.

He told her how, earlier in the summer, sitting in a Collingwood hotel over a beer with a few of the lads, talking about the Boston Red Sox, the gobsmacking season they were having, he thought he'd seen Connor stroll in. A slight frame, a stiff, off-kilter gait. Arrogance in the forward set of the chin and the sharp face more creviced than when Harry had last seen him. The blue eyes looked tired and there was a creeping sadness around the mouth. Instead of the outrage of Harry's first years away, or even the disdain that later replaced it, he'd felt a confusing scratch of pity. But the figure wasn't Connor, only an old dockworker or a fisherman, and Harry wondered, even worried, why it was that he was seeing his father when Connor wasn't there.

He studies the water now, thinking that Flo is on the other side of it, about to go home, packing up her instrument, slipping the cover on her typewriter. She might take a walk along the harbour first before settling in for the evening, Flo always seeking open air and the chance to stretch her legs. His eye catches on the throbbing and remote point of light at the wharf, and it occurs to Harry that he can't escape the idea of Connor. Just the apparition of him has a hold; he would like to leave the sense of haunting behind after this trip, to sever it like a cable. And this is why he's come on this trip, he thinks. Minutes, hours, lengthen on a laker, memories and stories turning up in the spaces between landmarks and in the watery gaps. It's time he pays attention, that he stops the endless looping around and around. Taking in a deep breath he feels the start of a new resolve. He wants to see clearly the thing that drags on him. Bringing a tentative gaze to the open water, his eyes narrow and catch on the flashing, restive waves.

~

"Wright won't want us to be last out of the gate," Jake is saying. Harry blinks, then looks to where Jake points, to the dock below where captains and company men pace, anxious because of the boggle of delays. "His pride won't take the bruising,"

"Is Wright with that lot?" Harry nods toward the animated figures.

Jake shakes his head *no* and then gestures to the gangway and to a man making a lumbering ascent, a bear-like curl to his back, his red hair tumbling ecstatically from beneath his cap. "That's him now." Jake straightens. "I'll fix it so you'll get a berth." He pushes his way through crates and workers toward Wright, and then turns impatiently toward Harry. "Come on, Darling." Jake's eyes are screwed down against the sun, his expression unreadable. Harry studies him for a moment, and then readjusting the bag on his shoulder, he crosses the deck.

When they reach him, Wright is surveying the slow march of thickening cloud that has begun to darken what was, not long ago, a wistful shade of blue. His mouth is slightly open, and he has an oversized portfolio tucked firmly under his arm, likely full of load details and perhaps the manifest.

"Thought we might need another deckman, Captain." Jake torques a thumb in Harry's direction. "This is Harry Darling and as you can see, he's got a strong back. Sure you can use him, being that it's end of season."

Wright is relaxed and easy and Jake is dwarfed by his enormous stature. He turns toward Harry, fastening him with a curious gaze, his blue eyes friendly and sharp above the

luxurious red moustache. "Have experience on one of these, do you?"

"Five seasons and I've worked straight-deckers before, but none the size of this one."

Wright's eyes shift and travel the deck, stopping at the swarm of dockworkers around the open hatches. "No, you wouldn't have. We've barely got the feel of her and she's full of surprises, but we're getting to know her tricks. You'd have to bear with us, lad."

"Just to be clear, Captain Wright, you won't find me on the manifest, Sir. The lists are shut down."

Wright's expression breaks into an enormous grin, the moustache parting. He gives a dismissive wave. "Company men are twits, Harry." It's affecting to hear Wright use his first name and Harry feels himself instantly buoyed. "We'll claim an error at the other end, when you get your pay packet." Wright extends his hand. "Welcome aboard."

A crewman, evidently the cook, scurries past making for the aft house, his thin arms holding an enormous box of onions. He smiles almost childishly at the captain. Behind him, someone else approaches, a weary-seeming fellow, grey woven through black at the temples, his face heavy. He addresses Wright in a quiet, level tone. "We still set for today, Captain?"

Wright studies the loading dock and pulls out a pipe, which he puts between his teeth unlit. "Harry, this is our wheelsman, Burt Ross. Burt, you know Jake Spence. This is Harry Darling, only just joined on."

Ross gives a solemn nod and sets his eyes back on Wright. "Feels like a change."

Wright glances briefly in the direction of the harbour office and then looks away. "Just been to the dock offices.

There is some talk of weather, a bit of squawking but I'm not awfully bothered."

They all look at the frenetic activity along the docks. The day is getting away from them, and there is still so much to be loaded. "There *will* be a change." Wright levels his gaze on Ross. "But you know that, Burt, just by the cut in this air. You'll chart for it." He turns, addressing Harry and Jake, his eyes softening. "Wind will keep shifting 'round to the northwest," he explains patiently. "Could be an uncomfortable ride with the swell behind us." He frowns comically at Harry. "You don't tend toward upchucking when there's a roll, do you lad? Still time to change your mind."

Harry shrugs, grinning. "Mostly solid-gutted, Sir. Besides, looks like she can hold her own."

Wright's grin dazzles briefly and then he turns again to Burt Ross, his expression serious, the confidence of authority carefully loaded in his tone. "We'll put her through her paces. She's up to it, Burt. We'll leave soon as she's loaded."

~

Jake is leading Harry in the direction of the bow where the fore-cabin and wheelhouse are. "A quick tour," he says, glancing over his shoulder. "You should know what you've signed up for." Jake has been on the *James Carruthers* for just a few hours, but he already seems to have an intimate familiarity with her. They step inside a lower passage, dim-seeming after the expansive light topside. A short man pushes past, charts beneath his arm and a pencil tucked behind his ear.

To the left of the staircase is the crew's hall, its pocket doors left partially open, a large room, with three sizable portholes that give it brightness. Newspapers are stacked on a table. There are ashtrays, a checkerboard on gimbals, and screwed to the wall is a gated shelf holding beer glasses. The chairs are ample, each bolted to the hardwood floor. Peering out one of the portholes Harry watches the Fort William harbour as it gently rises and falls. It's as if the *James Carruthers* is breathing, so rhythmic and predictable is the motion.

Lakers like this one delight his burgeoning carpenter's eye, and he would like to take more time to appreciate the unexpected loveliness of the room, but Jake is waving him on from the passageway.

A wooden staircase rises to the next level – oak, Harry surmises, and gleaming with varnish. At the top of the stairs, they find the State dining room and Captain Wright's cabin, the doors securely closed now, a simple, green-framed bicycle cleated with rope to the panelling in the passageway outside.

"When he's ashore, Captain likes to sail 'round town on that. He brings it with him so he can get to wherever he wants to be. He rides it up and down the deck sometimes. For exercise, he claims. Quite a spectacle, seeing Wright balanced on top of that contraption. Like an elephant on a pony." They stand together in the passageway, Harry struck by the absurdity of a bicycle on a boat and the miraculous vision of Wright riding it. Beside him, Jake shifts and strains toward motion.

They take a second staircase, narrower than the first, to the wheelhouse above and find Burt Ross in the charts room hunched over a large, angled table, a mug of tea in hand. A reverential quiet governs here, the same that Harry felt stepping into St. James Cathedral in Toronto on a late November day. He'd been kicking around the city one Saturday with little else to do. Sitting on the polished pew, for a few moments the stillness of the place had taken hold and he felt himself anchored, but when he left to walk among the strangers in the city, the old ghosts of dispossession were with him again, and that vague sense of drift.

Harry peers into the communications room and sees the equipment intended for messages travelling between locations on the boat. Headphones rest nearby and a large marine clock is fixed to the wall above. The system, which is modern, has been built into the boat's structure rather than added as a retrofit, although it isn't the ship-to-shore that some of the new American freighters have. Canadian captains have eschewed the idea of a constant connection between themselves and the shore. No one wants harbour authorities or the company men breathing down their necks. Harry assumes that Wright is no exception.

They step into the larger wheel room where a brass pressure instrument sits insect-like inside a coffin-shaped glass box. A barograph. The captain's chair, solid and securely fixed with heavy fittings, is next to the wheel. Beside it and attached to the console is an enormous swivelling mariner's compass. A smoking pipe and a pouch of tobacco, carefully folded, sit on top of the console, the pipe's bowl polished with handling. Harry can imagine Wright here, in his wheelhouse, the pipe between his teeth, a man who appears to relish life. Unlike poor Ross, who seems burdened by an overabundance of caution.

"Everything all right, Burt?" Jake's tone is sharp as they move past Ross again. The stillness of the wheelhouse has unsettled him. "Not going to put us aground, are you?"

Burt turns his weighted gaze on Jake. "I certainly hope not," he says flatly. "Haven't yet."

Harry looks at the chart table and Burt Ross's instruments laid carefully there: a silver-cased pencil, a straight ruler, his sextant. Ross's world is one of making straight lines through what looks to Harry, studying the charts now, like infinite circles. The *Carruthers* would take a route Ross has charted dozens of times before. He knows every shoal, every sandbar on the lakes, but its the wind that would be his worry. Ross's eyes slide to the barograph where a pressure chart unspools, the barometric needles crawling downward, trailing lines of red.

~

They make a quick stop in the engine room where a team of men ready the piles of coal while others oil and clean the machinery. It's an airless place, eerie with echoes and the men whistle and sing, and wisecrack as if to cut the dead air.

They leave the engine room and make their way through the stern section, which despite its extreme remoteness from the rest of the boat, feels snug. Harry steps into the crew's dining room where light from the two tiers of portholes pool onto the floorboards. Pleasant galley smells have collected here – coffee, frying meat — and underlying those, the faintly sickening tang of new varnish. At the far end sits a compact coal stove. Three long wooden tables have been fastened to the floor, with heavy chairs pulled companionably tight around them.

The aft-cabins, marginally smaller than those found in the fore house, are situated off the hall and behind the galley. Even here, in a relatively unimportant area of the boat, the millwork is lovely. Harry thinks again that he'll look for full-time work as a carpenter in Goderich; Flo will have something to say about it, of course. She'd made no secret that Goderich was not where she'd expected to end up. Flo who years before made her way east for a larger life. They might try someplace else, a city perhaps, where she could find work in a central telegraphy office or try her hand with the telephone company.

"Head's just down the hall, portside." Jake is brusque, uncomfortable in the closed space. He opens a door and Harry peers in at the quarters they'll share for the next couple of days, a small cabin with tongue-and-groove panelling and a swivel lamp.

Jake's duffle bag sits unopened on one of the bunks. Ducking under the bulkhead, Harry steps in, tosses his bag onto the foot of the other mattress and surveys the cabin. There is a recessed closet with drawers, a pull-down basin with an accordion style mirror. Polished oak everywhere, the place tight yet perfectly made to purpose. He runs his fingers over the amber surfaces, fascinated by the fittings and finish, its evident ingenuity.

Jake, growing more impatient, shoots Harry a look. "Move your arse, Darling, we can't get away until she's loaded. We'll be needed in the hold." Harry pauses, not wanting to be torn away from what strikes him as so beautiful. He regards Jake, and although he hasn't thought it before, it occurs to him now that it is a selfish thing for Jake to be so restless.

~

Even divided by her traversing bulkheads, the hold on the *Carruthers* is apparently limitless. Working below decks, surrounded by small mountains of wheat, Harry doesn't feel like he is on a boat, but rather a great ocean-going ship, like the leviathans the deckhands from Halifax and New York wax on about. Still, the *Carruthers* is just a lake boat. When Harry was a boy, Macey, ever the lakeman, had schooled him to never call a laker a ship or risk the ridicule of every lakeman within earshot.

Valerie Mills-Milde

"*Boats* sail on lakes and *ships* sail on oceans, Harry," he'd said pointedly. "Makes no difference the size or the purpose of the vessel." Macey's tug the *Grace* had been the only boat Harry had ever been on. The *Grace* was snub-nosed and scarred and Harry sometimes helped Macey as he patiently repaired, varnished, oiled her, tenderly tucking her up each fall under a canvas tarp. A man unafraid of sentiment, Macey had been wet-eyed and sorry to be parted from her for the winter months.

When the work in the hold is finally finished, Harry, relieved, climbs the ladder to the topside. He's overheated from his labours, sweat lining his neck, the fabric of his shirt swampy under his arms. He breathes in the scrubbed air, the slicing cold refreshing him. The weather is changing, just as Wright said it would. The wind has picked up and not a single star lights the sky. He watches the last of the dockworkers shuffle down the gangway, so exhausted they don't speak to one another. Not one gives the *James Carruthers* a backward glance. With their backs to the toothy gusts, deckmen shift stiffly from hatch to hatch, sealing those that remain open. It seems a sparse, almost skeletal crew after the numbers that swarmed her decks earlier. As the minutes drag, the men smoke, the tips of their cigarettes solitary points of light against the surrounding black. First Mate Levine gives the *all-aboard* signal and the boat's horn bellows just as the engine of the *Carruthers* surges against the holdback.

As the deck vibrates and the steel cables begin to hum, an unexpected hammer drops into the moment of waiting. A peculiar sadness comes over Harry and there is the sensation of tearing away as the gangway is tugged off the hull by a team of heavy horses. The horses protest, the metal underpinnings of the ramp whine, and with the clamour of the ramp dropping to the dock, the moment for leaving is unceremoniously past. Without her ramps, the stationary boat sits orphaned. Her newly fired engine creates a white boil at her stern, and he watches the foam lengthen and then surrender to the silk black of the lake. Harry thinks of watching waves break onshore; not an uninterrupted disbandment, but a tug of war, the land pulling and then the water dragging against it. This is what he will feel, going to see Connor again, a horse balking at the fence, brought up short by Kat and the inescapable loss he feels.

Kat. He was barely more than a baby when his mother died, and he can't remember a time before Kat. Preoccupied with work, Connor hired Kat as Harry's caregiver. How old had she been then, he wonders? Still young, just past school age, maybe seventeen or eighteen. For him, she was ageless, neither young nor old, a phosphorescent presence that lit up all his days. In the early years, she'd watched him in her workshop; later, when he was too old to be looked after, he'd wander over to her after lessons, and at some point, Harry doesn't know when, Connor stopped paying her. She'd become permanently fixed to them, like mother, sister, or something else he is unable to explain.

~

Kat told Harry that when she and her family came to America, they came on a passenger ship. She was just a little girl, and the ship was tightly packed with people, most speaking languages she couldn't understand. She studied their clothes, she told Harry. The wear of the fabric, the cuts. She saw the roughness of their complexion, and the way they might move with a limp or an easy swing of their limbs. She could imagine then where they came from and how they had lived before. The ship landed in New York and she and her family made their way to Ontario, to Kincardine, to where Kat's father had a cousin.

Kat was fourteen when her family made the decision to go home. Kat stayed behind. She liked the freedoms that a Canadian life would give her. She would continue in school; she would learn her trade. He thinks now about how hard it must have been for her after her people left, how terrible for her parents, her brothers and sisters, who returned on the ship without her.

His first memories of Kat are of someone beautiful, all valleys and plains and height; a wide forehead, pale hair always worn in a simple braid. Her eyebrows were slightly arched, her expression one of surprise and attention. There was a slight accent to her words and sometimes, when she was very happy with Harry, the endearment *Liebschen* would slip from her, the word a mystery to Harry, who never learned what it meant.

~

The *Carruthers'* engine remains fired but still, she doesn't move. David Lee, a crewman Harry knows from pervious trips, points accusingly at a gaping hatch. "Damn pain in the arse, these are. Taking too long to close up. Captain told us to leave the rest of 'em open so we can get underway." Harry raises his eyebrows and looks questioningly at David Lee. "Not a regular order, leaving her unhinged to weather." Usually, hatches are quickly dealt with by a few strong crewmen, but Harry has never seen hatches like these, which are mechanized and worked by steam-powered winches. David shrugs, as if to say, who can make sense of a captain's orders? David isn't a man for conversation. He spends his spare time curled over a sketchpad, busily drawing cartoon figures: comic, leering faces, dogs wearing three-piece suits, elephants driving motor cars. "We're way behind schedule," he says.

It is past midnight and Harry feels fatigue dragging on him, the cold finally having climbed inside of his clothes. Someone, not David, hands him a heavy rope. "We're away," shouts Levine. The engine belches and the deck crew walk out the rope until the boat has cleared the dock.

For a plain-faced freighter, her movements are graceful, effortless. Harry watches as the Fort William lights grow smaller and the boat turns to take up her course, the land becoming only a dark line, more remembered than seen behind them.

~

In the dining hall, Harry devours his food, too exhausted to really taste it. Across from him Jake's eyes flit to the clock. "On night watch," he says, abruptly sliding back his chair. "Sweet dreams, *Darling*." Harry reflexively smiles at Jake, too tired to play off the quip of his last name. Many men have had fun with it over his years on the lakes and Harry is endlessly indulgent. But tonight, the name – his father's name – burrows, determined to find some repose like an animal over-wintering. *Connor Darling*, Harry thinks, puzzling through his fatigue, trying to capture a full-fledged rendering of the man but only a single, flat view emerges. Connor, the last time he saw him, obdurate and closed-mouthed as Harry's world fell away.

The men not taking a watch disappear into their cabins. Harry kicks off his boots and falls gratefully into his bunk, the great boat rocking and coasting on the swells beneath him, her engine vibrating through layer upon layer of metal bulkhead. The rhythm of the *Carruthers* makes him drift but not yet sleep.

The boat holds him close, her sounds soon weaving together and making a kind of song.

~

He is thinking of Kat's workshop. He had loved it as a child. As he often does before surrendering to sleep, he tries to remember every object, as if to pin himself into place. Efficient and spare in her tastes, Kat didn't cover the windows with lace or fabric, preferring to work with the frank and unsparing outside light. Along one wall of Kat's workroom were three matching heavy oak dressers, which had been set flush one next to the other. Brushes of all shapes and sizes, with soft or coarse bristles depending on their purpose, were laid perfectly aligned in the top drawers. In the second set of drawers, there were powders – rose-coloured, bronze, shell pink. Combs made from ivory were in the next, and then scissors which varied in size, neatly arranged from smallest to largest. There were ribbons and buttons and hairpins. Her laying-out bag, a soft-sided valise that held a sampling of all her tools, was set next to the door. It was the same bag she'd brought years before to prepare Harry's mother. The impression he has when he thinks of that room now, with Kat at its center, is of resolute and unstoppable kindness.

She'd taught Harry how to organize and sort. She'd made him want to be helpful. He'd stuffed pouches with lavender, and carefully poured rosewater into mason jars. There was beeswax to melt down and lengths of cotton to cut. He sat very close to her and watched the fine muscles around her eyes tighten with concentration. He could feel the rise and fall of her chest as she breathed. Sometimes, being near to Kat, in the intimacy of her workroom, he would feel a mysterious tingling in his body, and then a push of blood in his head that was both alarming and thrilling. He would want to touch her breast, but even then, as a boy the idea was shameful to him, dangerous although he couldn't have said why.

Kat provided him biscuits from a tin, the same tin each time, aged and ornate with deutsche Schrift lettering. It had been sent from her parents in Germany years before, she'd once explained, and although its original contents had been consumed long ago, she treasured it. "It's just a sentimental thing, I know" she said, musing, "but they sent it all this way, across an ocean and here it sits. It keeps them close." He loved the tin, how it was tied to Kat and to a life she'd had before him, an old-world place complete with parents. But he was jealous of it too because the tin claimed a part of Kat that had existed before him. The possessiveness was alien, filling him with strange heat, making his blood rush. He'd pushed it away, smiling. "I would like to go there one day, Kat," he said. "With you."

"Perhaps one day you will. But not until you have finished school. It's a very long way, Harry. Across an ocean on a ship." He would have liked that, to be on a ship for days with Kat.

Her skill was artistry, but it was more than that. She read things into her subjects. "How do you know how to *finish* the people?" Harry asked once, eyeing the assortment of pots and colours and dyes. He was about nine years old then, and he'd not known how else to put it.

Most of Kat's work was done in family homes – parlours, bedrooms, kitchens – but occasionally she would arrange the deceased in her workshop. When Harry arrived after school, his books under his arm, his appetite peaked for biscuits and some tea, he remembered her discretely covering her subject with a

Valerie Mills-Milde

clean linen sheet. Because she was natural and tender with the dead, he never felt a shred of fear in their company. "The body tells a lot," she said unfazed, "like an ink-stained hand, for instance, or knuckles swollen with overuse, and the death itself can point to how a life was lived. I always ask the family to tell me about their lost one. There are many stories, and these are important, Harry. The most important thing. And if I'm very lucky, there are photographs to work from."

Harry had thought about how it was that people could know one another. Kat, for instance; everything Kat did and said led him to trust her, to love her without reserve. "So, you gather up bits and pieces of the people from stories about their life, and those give you an idea of them."

Kat was thoughtful. "I try and see in them what their people saw, and what it is that's been taken."

~

There is an all-hands whistle at 3:00 and Harry opens his eyes. It's obvious from the way the boat yaws and pitches that the conditions have worsened. He rises and joins a stream of other sleepy-eyed crewmen who stumble along the passageway, pulling up collars and tugging on caps.

On deck a shock of cold slaps him awake. The wind has shifted resolutely to the northwest, and the lake is all black waves, cuffed with rolling white. Jake, still on watch, is grinning vacantly, like an idiot, spray accumulating on his tightly coiled hair. There is no smile in his eyes and Harry is uneasy watching him. He looks instead toward mid-ships, to where First Mate "Leaps" Levine stands, tall and gangly, his long arms wheeling like a windmill as he directs the men to close the hatches.

Apparently, Leaps' father, also a lakeman, is a close friend of Wright's and Leaps has sailed with Wright for the entirety of the *James Carruthers'* first season. Leaps turns, pointing first to Harry and then to Jake. "Get a line 'round those winches, you two, and make sure that second hatch is closed up tight." He doesn't wait to watch them, there are too many other hatches to check, and he lopes away, a stretch-legged man, more bird than human.

Together they drag the heavy line to the steam winch and release the valve. The winch begins to turn, the cover's overlapping sections gradually un-stacking, and then without warning, the mechanism makes a nauseating scream.

"Christ!" Jake grimaces, striking out at the winch with his foot. After a few moments, the screeching stops. They peer at the enormous hatch cover, its layering of panels reminding Harry of the scales of a fish. It appears firmly clinched to the middle and to the sides. Harry sweeps his eyes over it for signs of trouble, and then he carefully surveys the winch, but he doesn't know what he's looking at.

"Seems all right," says Harry doubtfully at first. Then, "Yes, I think it's fine."

Jake nods but doesn't answer. He is already on his feet, no longer interested in hatch 3, but rather regarding a gaggle of deckmen as they struggle with another release valve. When he moves to help, Harry follows, and when all the openings appear to be closed, Leaps addresses the deckmen, his face gaunt in the partial light.

"Get in, dry off a bit. Might need you again before long so don't get too snug. Makes it hard to come back out."

Not turning toward the fore house, Jake's eyes stray to the sheets of water that now regularly drench the deck. "I'd rather not go in."

Levine glares at him. "I'll tell you if you are needed, Spence."

Jake's face is wet and glistening. For a long moment, he doesn't move, his eyes remaining locked on Levine who is no longer looking back at him, but instead scowling at another pair of deckmen who linger at the rail, smoking. "Pitch those," he barks. Jake watches the men flick their cigarettes over the side, turn, and make their way to the fore house. And then, as if breaking from a trance, he shakes himself like a wet dog. "Come on, Jake," Harry says, leading the way, glancing back to make sure Jake follows.

They meet Wright coming from the companionway, pushing open the door. He wears his oilskin, and his head is uncovered. He's beaming, apparently relishing the weather. "Hello, lads. You've got the covers done up?"

"Right tight." Jake answers blankly. "But those new winches are a bitch."

"They are. Agreed." Wright regards them, nodding with satisfaction. "Go and take a nip, boys. Might as well. We're in for a ride."

~

Harry takes the afternoon watch on Friday, the laker rolling hypnotically as it pushes eastward down Lake Superior. After the many hours of heavy weather, he anticipates her movements, his muscles bracing as the laker sways and then slips down the backside of the waves.

The rain is now laced with sleet and snow, and streams of white eerily dance across the surface of the water. A proper blow, he thinks. How different the lake looks today, all coils and swells, when yesterday it was just a bit of chop.

He is thinking of Flo, how fascinated she was by the way the water changes. "A prairie is still a prairie, even when it's buried in snow," she told him soon after they met. Harry was sitting in her apartment, a towel draped around his neck. She'd never seen the Great Lakes before she'd trained in Toronto, she said. "Sad, or beautiful, depending on the season." She methodically combed a curl of his hair straight before cutting it. "Gray in winter. Who ever thought water would feel so empty? But in summer, it's heaven."

Flo lived on the top floor of a solid brick house close to the square, and a few blocks back from the water. "What's it like on the prairie?" he asked her.

She tilted her head, seeming to consider the question. "Well, you can see a very long way."

She was precise and careful, cutting his hair, stepping back frequently and measuring her work. "You've done this before." His words hung for a moment while Flo snipped another lock.

"I always cut my brothers' hair when I was at home. If I didn't do a decent job, I would never hear the end of it. They were without mercy."

Harry chuckled. "Were they hard on you?"

"No harder than they were on one another."

She didn't seem like a person who'd had special treatment of any kind. He imagined that she carved out her own way, prizing her independence.

"Toronto must have felt a long way from home." Even for Harry, who grew up in Ontario, Toronto had seemed like another country.

"It was the only place where I could get the telegraphy training I wanted." She stepped back for a moment, and then began to cut again. "I was ready for the adventure when I left, and my parents weren't against it. The years just went by, you know how they do, and the time was never right to go back. Now, my parents are gone, and the boys, my brothers, have families of their own. We all make our way and it's fine. And we write, and of course, I send messages." She laughed. "They probably get more telegraph messages than any of their neighbours because of me. I would be happy to see them if they came this way, but I don't think they will." She'd hesitated. "It was a good decision to explore, and I loved my life in Toronto, at least until near the end. There were friends, and there was music. I love music. I wish I could play an instrument, the piano maybe. All those notes going off in different directions. My telegraphy machine is the closest I'll ever come."

"I love music too," he said. "It helps with the loneliness." Harry had thought of this often while sitting in music halls. The new sort of music he'd heard in Chicago and Detroit was especially wonderful. The clarinet answering the piano, which answered the bass, the whole thing beginning all over again. It was a kind of conversation.

After she was finished cutting his hair, she brought him a hand mirror to look in. She bent down beside him, her face close to his. "That's an improvement." She frowned deeply, her eyes searching the mirror while she scrutinized her efforts. "But a barber would have done a better job."

Harry tilted his head and took in his image. He appeared young, his face fresh, despite the colour he'd gained from the previous weeks on the water. His eyes looked back, unexpected shyness beneath the usual good humour. He was suddenly self-conscious, and intensely aware of Flo, so close to him. He caught her scent – scrubbed and clean, with a hint of citrus. He put the mirror down on the table and smiled at her. "I don't think a barber could have done any better than this. Anyway, thank you. I needed that."

"Well, it looked to me like you hadn't seen a barber in a while." She took the towel from his neck, shaking it lightly. After she swept the hair from the floor, she stood at the basin and cleaned the scissors with soap and water, drying them and then opening the top drawer of a small white chest and placing them inside. Her back was straight, her hips curved and full beneath her skirt, the outline of her body sturdy and sure.

"Kat used to cut it for me," Harry wasn't sure why, at that moment, he should want to tell Flo this. It was the soft heat in the room, perhaps, or just that he felt relaxed. Flo was slicing lemons and then squeezing them, her fingers strong around the yellow rinds, and watching her, he was put in mind of an aproned Kat rubbing pomade through his hair, a pair of scissors next to her on small, wheeled table. Kat wouldn't cut his curls because she loved them, she said. "You are a heavenly creature, Harry." She turned a curl around her index finger and then released it, lightly trimming here and there, particularly around his eyes and ears. Connor complained that Harry looked like a girl, with his hair hanging down. "Like a bloody halo. He's got ringlets." Harry remembers hardness in the words. "He ought to have a razor put to those. He's old enough." Kat ran her hands through Harry's curls, her fingers lightly caressing his

scalp. "I won't do it. You'll have to find someone else, Con." When Harry was close to ten, she cut it shorter, razoring the temples and Connor retorted, "Thank Christ."

Flo had her back to Harry while she prepared the jug of lemonade.

"Kat. She was the person at the centre of your falling-out," she said.

He hesitated. "She looked after me, when I was a boy."

Flo said nothing, pouring out the lemonade for them, setting the glasses down on the table, pulling out a chair. She seemed to be waiting for him to go on, opening a space for him to speak.

"Your mother?"

Harry shrugged. "I don't remember her. She died."

"I'm sorry, Harry."

"My father and I had some trouble about Kat. It went badly and I haven't seen or spoken to him in five years."

Flo set her gaze on him, her look concentrated, curious. "And Kat?"

Inexplicably, tears came into Harry's eyes then. He shrugged. "I don't know."

~

The laker pitches and yaws and each time she comes back to levels. His watch is done. As Harry sits on the floor of the games room, he can feel the lake's drumming, the vibrations travelling through his sodden boots and along the vertebrae of his back.

Three of the crewmen play a game of carpet-bowling, with no carpet of course, and no pins, just a wide-mouthed bucket turned on its side. The bucket rolls ridiculously, the target always moving. A man pitches the painted wooden ball, the ball careening, then bouncing off the leg of a chair before burying itself in a heap of newspapers. "Superior's a bitch in November", he says grudgingly while the other men whoop with laughter.

David Lee is hunched over a table, drawing and Harry moves closer to peer over his shoulder. For such an ungainly man, David's hands are quick, his fingers agile. He is deftly shading an image of the *James Carruthers,* the lake boat riding the back of a giant wave, striations of deepening black around it. An outsized Captain Wright has wrapped his stout legs around her mid-decks, one hand tenaciously holding her wheel, while the other rests on her aft as though he is riding a bucking horse. The ends of his moustache come almost down to his knee, and his belly threatens to bust the straining coat. His expression is excited, flinty, with a hint of avarice in it.

It's a surprising image. "I don't see Wright that way" Harry puzzles, pointing to the page. "Does look a bit like some other bugger-captains I've crewed for, though."

David doesn't stop his shading, his eyebrows tightening in consternation. "Because I drew him fat?"

Harry grunts, shaking his head. "Not that. It's what you've done to his eyes. He looks like a greedy bastard."

Taking his left hand from where it rests on the page, David scratches absently behind his ear. "Not all the captains went out," he says. "Some stayed back. The flags were up."

Harry laughs. "Flags are always up this time of year. Anyway, she's come through all right."

David gives a non-committal shrug, his shoulders thin looking in his big coat. He furiously smudges some of the pencil lines that comprise the water, and Harry shifts his position, taking another view of David's work. He's captured a quality of obstinacy in the captain. Or determination, depending on how he looks at it.

"Wright didn't want to go for pay-out." David studies the drawing and then deepens the line around Wright's mouth, emphasizing the characteristic smile, and instantly Wright's charisma comes through. "He doesn't care so much as other lake captains about that. He's set to retire anyway."

Harry waits for a moment. Talking to Lee is a bit of a cat and mouse game. "Well? Why did he?"

"He wanted to, that's all. To *have* her." He tilts his head, the thread of the conversation trailing off, David's enthusiasm for talk nearing an end.

Harry peers at the picture, appreciating that the drawing is at once comic and revealing, although how true it is, Harry can't be sure. "Wish I had the talent to do something like that."

David Lee sits on his haunches, his back bent over the picture. Without looking at Harry he tears the page from the sketchpad and hands it to him. "You can keep it if you want. It can be your souvenir – a remembrance of your trip."

"Well," says Harry, blinking down at the picture in his hand. "I'll be glad to look at it this winter. It will be a good reminder of why I'm happy that the season comes to an end."

For a short while, a dull grey fills the portholes and then gives way to black. Harry sits quietly, watching David and listening to the sound of sleet assaulting the glass portholes. When the ship's bell rings for supper, the men rise and put on soggy jackets and leave the fug of the games room behind. They laugh together, lurching like drunkards toward the stern section, their legs unsteady after the hours of sitting. The snow comes at them out of the darkness, a startling fury of white.

"Merry Christmas," jokes one of the men, leering, as he pulls open the door.

74

6

*Saturday
Huron Shore,
Yellow Curtains*

Connor's feet are stiff on the bare floorboards. Going to the window, he tugs apart the yellowed curtains. Essie had made the curtains soon after they arrived here, the pattern a deep cream with small sweetheart roses on green stems that crawled left and right, up and down, as if to make a dense hedge. Since Essie's death, the curtains have remained hanging in their room, a neglected presence, loyalty keeping him from tearing them down. Or, more specifically, ambivalence and a strange sense of powerlessness, as if he isn't capable of getting the step stool from the back of the woodshed, climbing to the second step, and taking the dispirited curtains from their hooks.

In a strange way, it was Essie who first brought Kat to him. Kat stood on their stoop, tall, her face strongly formed, her sky-grey eyes set wide. She was young and strangely grave, and she carried herself like a woman rather than a girl. "I don't usually like anyone with me while I work," Kat said, stepping in, unpacking her equipment from a neatly arranged bag, which she'd set on the kitchen worktop. She hadn't said "I'm sorry for your loss," or any of the usual expressions of sympathy. Instead, she asked a question.

"Do you need help bringing your wife down to the kitchen?"

"I'll be all right," he said. Essie's body had been as light as an armful of kindling. He carried her from the upstairs room and laid her out on the table, which Kat had covered with oil cloth. Crouched nearby was Harry, a finger jammed into his mouth, the other hand clasping a rag doll. His eyes were huge, but he wasn't crying. He continually looked up at Connor, Connor absently ruffling the child's mass of curls.

Later, he would think that Harry must have thought Essie was sleeping. In her last weeks, despite the awful physical alteration in her body, Essie remained essentially herself. She didn't seem to know that she was dying. It was Harry who had anchored her to life, even Connor could see it. The boy was content in her bed, his arm around a toy as he pressed himself into her. Connor had to wrestle Harry away when it was time for him to eat or wash, Harry crying inconsolably, his fists clenched around the quilt. The anguish of those weeks and the child's howls were like a voracious beast that clawed at Connor's neck. By the time she died, he was numb.

Kat wanted to be alone with Essie. "Why don't you take your boy out, go for a walk." It was springtime, a flush of green over the fields. He might have taken Harry to the stream to look for minnows or perhaps down to McNeil's beach. There would be ducklings on the water to watch, stones to toss.

"I'd like to stay." She'd looked at him steadily, as though she saw the whole of him, the absence of his love for Essie, the threadbare bond with his son. "Put the boy in the parlour then", she said, "and close the door until we're done here."

"He won't want that. He doesn't like to be apart from her, he's barely left her side."

Valerie Mills-Milde

Kat looked around. "Have you got flour?" she asked. "Give me a couple of bowls and some spoons." Connor gathered these up and Kat took Harry's hand, leading him to the parlour. She sat with him on the braided rug, emptied flour from the sack into the bowl, showed him how to stir and pour the flour from one bowl to the other. Harry was delighted. He took to the game, transferring the flour from one bowl to the other, his fingers sifting and stirring, each time looking to Kat who radiated back a smile. Once he was completely absorbed, they left him to it and Kat gently closed the door.

"Now," she said, "bring me some of her dresses." Essie's death came after a fast-progressing illness, her rounded body rapidly shrinking, her eyes sunken and a yellowish tinge blossoming over her skin. None of the dresses he brought would fit. "Never mind that," Kat said. "I can pin it." She chose a light blue dress, simple in cut, no sashes or bows. It was the kind of dress a grown woman would wear. A mother.

Kat had taken a great deal of time with Essie, first washing and towelling her. Every so often, Connor would check on Harry. He brought him his supper and then finally put him to bed.

It was late in the evening when the dress was fitted properly. Kat began applying flesh-toned powders to Essie's hands and face, rouging her cheeks, tinting the lips. She brought lustre back to the dark brows with the smallest application of mineral oil and she filed Essie's nails before she coloured them with a blush-toned lacquer. Her hand lingered on Essie's arm as she worked, a carefulness in her movements, a gentleness. She fixed Essie's dark hair in a simple long braid that she placed over one shoulder, the end tied with a blue satin ribbon. Finally, she slipped a pair of dove-coloured shoes on her feet. Connor had been transfixed by Kat's every movement, as if she held the answer to the riddle of his life, his impetuous flights, his aggravations.

"Fred will bring the casket in the morning," she told him when she was done. She was a long while at the sink, using the carbolic soap she'd brought with her, and then drying her hands on her own towel. Her bag sat packed and ready. "Why did you want to watch me with her?" she asked, turning toward him, her face open and curious. "Is it hard to let her go?"

He gazed down at his wife, puzzled and ashamed that he felt so little.

"I'm not much good at partings."

She'd considered this for a moment. "Take care of your little boy," she said. "He'll miss his mother, even if he doesn't show it."

~

Connor's head aches. He touches the yellow curtains. Essie's imprint, so close on the heels of his thoughts of Kat, makes him miserable. He'd hated the curtains but hadn't told Essie so. He showed Essie very little about what he thought or felt, but it didn't seem to matter. She'd been preoccupied with making a home for them in those first months of their being here, sewing and pressing, whitewashing the kitchen, scrubbing the pantry with a wide bristled brush. She'd laid up conserves, put vegetables in the root cellar, mended old blankets that had been her mother's. He'd thought her ridiculous. "You must think that Harry is the Second Coming," he joked one day seeing her straining to lift a carpet to the line, mercilessly beating it. He'd meant it as a tease, he told himself, but there had been a cut in the words. Essie's face was flushed with effort, glowing with purpose. She'd looked back at him, her joy an impenetrable fortress.

Through the parted curtains, Connor sees that the golden-coloured light of the previous day has bled into flannel gray. Late autumn has stolen in overnight; he is irritated by the change, the shift in the weather signalling the approach of culling. He pulls on his trousers and puts on his shirt. He should make his way out to the animals right away, but he doesn't, choosing instead to sit, slouched at his kitchen table, lingering over his cooling tea.

Not long after Essie died, the intimacies between he and Kat had come on with breathless urgency. One day, soon after Kat began watching the boy, Connor came to Folly's to collect him, and not finding either of them in Kat's workshop he'd gone around back. Kat was in the driveway, reaching up into the wagon for her bag. She stood on her toes, like a heron on a rock.

"Hello," Connor said, his voice hoarse with the strain of the day. "Come for Harry. He here with you?"

Kat looked over her shoulder, surprised, a hint of a smile around her mouth. Her hands strayed to her skirt. "I had to call in at a place near Ripley," she said, "and so I asked Mrs. Folly to watch him for the afternoon. We can get him now, together, if you like."

"That's fine," he said, not taking his eyes from her.

She took the harness off the horse, her fingers working at the buckles and straps. Connor shook himself from the stupor and stepped in to help, and they brought the rig into the carriage house. The place was in semi-darkness, light filtering through the gaps in the plank walls, dust falling through the still air. Folly was labouring in his workshop, and the sound of the hammering drove Connor's feelings ever deeper, ever sharper. It seemed inevitable that he should take her face in his hands and trace the outline of bone with his thumbs. A spare and utterly beautiful face. There was no coyness about her, no expectation. Just that strange stillness, a kind of readiness. He kissed her and she slid her hands beneath his shirt, her palms pressed to his skin. Cool hands despite the heat. Neither of them made a show of objection.

7

Saturday
Goderich Telegraph Office,
Missing Pieces

On Saturday morning, Flo spends much of her time at the counter, collecting hand-printed forms, typing them before giving a final word count and then having the men sign off. With so many lakemen leaving, there are more outgoing messages than there are incoming ones. Every so often, she props the *Please Wait* sign next to the silver service bell, and resolutely sits down at the New Haven, the telegraphy instrument always settling her. She puts on her earphones and picking up the first outgoing message, she begins the light *tap, tap, tap* on the key.

There are still many outgoing forms in her tray. She is fast with code, and precise, and the telegrapher on the other end rarely asks her to repeat. Still, for all Flo's efficiency, she could use an extra hand. She should implore head office to send an operator or ask Ruby to press CP to send one, at least for the duration of her leave. Really, they need a permanent third. The traffic on the lakes in recent years has multiplied, and shoreline towns and cities have ballooned. Their small office will have to keep pace with the changes.

Flo should have asked for relief before now, but each time she decides to contact head office, she hesitates. When an office grows, they send a man to manage. Whoever he is, he'll want the classifications system resurrected – they always do – and he'll take the first-class messages for himself. She feels a part of herself shrink, thinking of giving up the variety in the work.

She picks out a form and places it next to her typewriter. She'll carry on as is, wait and see what happens when Harry comes back. She thinks of the telegram she received from him yesterday, sent from Fort William. He was onshore, making his way back by train. Perhaps he'll be here by tomorrow, she thinks. Monday at the latest.

The last time she saw him, Harry talked enthusiastically about the building going on in Goderich. "But if you don't want to be stuck here, Flo," he'd said, "I mean, if you want a bigger place, that would be fine. We'll be together, so it won't matter." Seeing his face taken up in a grin, she'd thought, with a surge of joy, that he looked like someone who'd found home again.

A fidgety man wearing spectacles approaches and drums his fingers on the polished wood counter. She rises, smiles and then points to the box of blank forms. Before he begins to write, he tells her that he's glad to be off the boats. "It's starting to blow on Superior," he says, "and that's always where it starts." He has a narrow, bony face and a nervous twitch tugs at one eye. "Snow I heard, but we were ahead of it." Earlier, she opened a window, the office feeling stuffy with so many waiting customers. Now, there is a chilling breeze. She glances outside, taking in the altered view. The sky is darker than it was earlier, and the water is leeched of colour.

"What are you coming from? A freighter?" She likes that she knows the difference in the lake boats, the proper terms.

Valerie Mills-Milde

Her work here has taught her so much. And Harry too, of course.

The man doesn't look up from his form. "A laker, yes." Flo thinks about the enormous carriers that she has seen coming and going from the Goderich docks. Monumental things, the newer ones made from steel, the wheelhouses, from the vantage point of the dock, seemingly a mile high, standing like the grain elevators of her youth. Their rigid midsections were strangely narrow for their height, giving the impression of an object easily broken. "Good that you are off the boats, for this year anyway," she says. The man nods impatiently. He's eager to be done with his message, to settle into a train carriage and sleep away his hangover.

~

The foot traffic is lighter in the afternoon. Every so often, she pulls the incoming telegraphs off the machine, taking them down quickly in shorthand and then banging out each message in type before marshalling them into various piles. She sits back, sighing, looking at the growing stacks.

She straightens the messages for delivery, then sets them on the edge of her desk for Ted. He'll be along after his lessons are done. Thank goodness for the boy. He is her messenger, small for his age but fast. She never saw much of the messengers in the central office. The aides whisked the sorted telegrams to the main floor where an overseer distributed them. Sometimes, on her way in or out of the building, she'd see a messenger breathlessly jumping from a bicycle, or shifting a shoulder to redistribute the weight in their bag. Then they'd set off again.

Ted, who is her only messenger, has russet-coloured hair and a gap between his front teeth. His eyes have a bit of the devil in them, especially when he grins. He's trouble, Flo imagines, but she likes how joyful he looks on the bicycle, something in him like her brothers back home. Ruby had spoiled him. She frequently provided Ted with treats to take on his deliveries – a coconut square or a tea biscuit. Flo isn't much of a baker, but she gives him tea and a slice of bread and jam, and they sometimes sit together outside on warm afternoons, their chairs pulled into the sun. She enjoys listening to him chatter on about people in the town. Ted is a fount of information, but today there will be no time for that.

The service bell rings, bright and urgent. Another man, soggy-looking and a little forlorn, stands at the counter, and seeing him there Flo rises, smiles, and asks if she can help.

8

Saturday
Huron Shore,
Shadow Country

This morning, the shed is especially dark, and before Connor scoops the offal into the minks' troughs, he pulls the lantern from the wall. He holds back more from the minks' feed than he had the day before. The animals feed furiously, the offal disappearing in the blink of an eye. It's difficult to know when a mink is losing weight, their bodies naturally taught but these look spindly, the bones at their haunches angling out.

Yesterday, when he opened the gate to McNeil's yard, seeking out offal, he'd found himself hoping that McNeil wouldn't appear. One of McNeil's sons was in the yard and when he saw Connor, he nodded a friendly greeting. The boy was tall and blond with a fall of hair that swept heavily across his wide forehead.

"Looking to get some offal from your chickens off you."

"For the minks?"

"That's right." This son was named Donald, Connor reminded himself, and he was looking at Connor with stolid curiosity. "Dad's in the barn. He'll fix you up." With an untroubled self-assurance, the lad turned, and after a short time, he came back with his father.

McNeil hadn't paused to look at Connor. "Haven't got much," he said, leading him to the slaughtering shed. "But you can take what I got." He'd been tight-lipped as he shoveled the chicken entrails from the floor. "Heard from Harry?" He finally muttered.

Connor gave a vague shrug. "Don't expect to. Maybe he went west. So many of them do."

McNeil continued with his shovelling. "And Katrina. Do you hear from her?"

As he watched the older man work, Connor's face felt hot, his failure with Harry, his incomprehensible abandonment of Kat, fatally on display.

"No –"

Pausing, McNeil placed his shovel against the wall, the skin on his face ruddy with effort. "You wouldn't know if she ever came back, then."

"Katrina?" Connor gazed, chagrined, at the partly filled pails. "If she had, I wouldn't know about it."

When McNeil finished, he was panting and looking his age. Connor stared dumbly at the bloody floor, remembering that Kat had helped McNeil and his wife after they lost a little girl. "I'll bring payment when the pelts are sold."

Silenced by the mention of the mink, McNeil's lips pressed into a thin line, and he grunted softly.

"Strange animals for farming, Connor. I don't want money from them."

"Well, you'll have it, either way."

~

Connor steps from the mink shed into a strange light, the yard bathed in a purplish hue, like a bruise. The temperature is dropping. Autumn finally catching up with itself, Connor thinks, a palpable November setting in. The wind urgently stops and starts. Perhaps by nightfall a skiff of snow will come, although it isn't cold enough for a serious freeze-up. In winter, he must be sure to keep the animals' water reservoirs free of ice. But the kits will be gone by then, he reminds himself, and he'll have only the mating pairs to worry about. Unsure about what to do with the rest of the day, he decides to repair the glass in one of the two kitchen windows, the pane shattered last summer when a bird flew into it. At the time, he'd hammered a board over the opening to keep out the weather. Half the kitchen had fallen into a perpetual grey.

Suddenly, he wants the light to find its way in.

He'd put the glass on credit months ago, and now he retrieves it from where it is stored in the woodshed. After he walks to the boarded-up window, he begins to pry away the board from the frame. He's forgotten to bring the putty. Putting down his tools, he goes back to woodshed, discovering he has none.

~

Connor hates the gloom. When he was a boy, on sullen days, his mother, Sophie, as if in a frenzy, would light all the lamps. She was always chasing away the shadows. She'd set the place on fire if she could, just to make certain that the darkness didn't overwhelm them.

When Connor was young, Ethan, his father, would plant himself in the doorway, watching her the way a man might watch a dragonfly. Sophie seemed unaware of him as she moved from lamp to lamp, humming loudly as if to drown out any lingering ghosts. Looking up, seeing Ethan there, she'd startle, her expression quickly easing to relief.

Sophie was an effusive and enthusiastic mother, much like Essie would have been if she'd lived. Connor was the eldest, and three years older than Dorothy, or Dot. *Tough as a little penny*, Ethan liked to say about Dot who was dark-eyed and secretive. Dot had a coppery strength despite a cleft in the roof of her mouth that made her speech awkward. Two years after Dot came June, *bonny June*, Ethan called her in his muddied accent. June's hair sprung joyously in a perpetual bright tangle. (She especially adored Connor, following him to the barn or over the uneven fields. Occasionally, impatient with her, Connor drove her off. But in truth, June was his single greatest joy.)

The children grew differently, each taking his or her own direction, like saplings, each reaching for his or her private sun. Although his effort on the farm was doggedly given over to his sheep, in a strikingly unsentimental way, Ethan loved all three of them.

For her part, Sophie possessed feeling enough to lavish all her children with frank attention (even Dot who, in Connor's estimation, wasn't easy to love), but she reserved her keenest interest for Connor. Amid the crowded market or coming out of the church, she stood close to him, her hand placed lightly on his shoulder. Sometimes, she stepped into a room just to see if he was there. He often caught her holding him in a sideways look, her expression a mix of pride and worry and something else unrecognizable to him.

Whatever her consternation about Connor, she tucked it away, an ease coming over her as she watched him go to work

with Ethan, bringing in sheep from the taciturn fields or readying the fleece for market.

~

Connor was thirteen when a strange man lightly stepped from a green polished buggy and surveyed their farm, his gaze intently sweeping the house. It had rained hard earlier and now a mist rose from the fields. A sly sun darted in and out of the skirting clouds and the air was both close and cool.

Connor, cleaning stalls, the barn door open, leaned on his fork and studied the stranger. He was compact-looking, wiry, and he wore a long dark coat and tan-coloured boots. A city man, and perhaps a new buyer for the wool.

They were unaccustomed to people coming to the place, and Connor instinctively looked for Ethan, and then remembered that Ethan wasn't there. Wolves had been howling the last few nights and Ethan, concerned for the sheep, had taken the dog Brownie and the gun to the far pasture. Connor felt Ethan's absence keenly then, the strangeness of new responsibility pressing down on him. "You looking for my dad?" he asked, walking toward the man, adopting a kind of grown-up swagger, then stopping short, his thumbs hooked on his pockets. He'd felt himself stretch an inch or two, as if trying to meet the stranger eye-to-eye. "He's out in the field but I can get him."

The man looked him over, his eyes dancing with curiosity. "Would you be Connor?" It made Connor uneasy, hearing the man say *Connor*. It confused him, like hearing his name called from deep in the woods and not knowing the direction from where it came. The accent was strange, not like Ethan's – it was bright and bell-like and had an overly friendly tone. Connor nodded warily. "Do I know you?"

"Not really," he smiled, "but I've a notion about you, lad." He winked.

Connor felt himself close over when the stranger leaned in, the grinning mouth making his heart pound.

"Anyway, there's no need to worry. I've come to see your mother. I'm a cousin of hers."

Sophie always told them that her people were from further east, from a town down river. When talking of herself as a girl, she described a crowded house with too many children. "There are limits to how many people should be living under one roof," she said with a hint of disgust. Anyway, she lost touch with her family, she said vaguely, except for one brother and his wife with whom, once or twice a year, there had been an exchange of letters.

The stranger gave two light taps to his chest, just over his heart. "Carey's the name." He nodded his head as if to reassure. "If you run in and tell her Carey's here, I'm sure she'll come out to speak with me. We're great friends, Connie, your mother and me." Connor hesitated, while Carey, this unknown cousin, stood perfectly still, a hint of amusement on his face. "I won't bite, I promise you." He hadn't taken his eyes from Connor. "This is a remote place, isn't it? A *lonely* sort of place. You probably don't get much company dropping in. She'll be glad for the visit, believe me," he grinned again. "It will be a great distraction for her."

"I'll go and get Dad," Connor repeated, furtively glancing toward the outer boundary of the farm where Ethan was. He resisted the urge to go. He felt foolish, running to find his father, a boy his age, almost a man himself. Instead, he called out to Ethan in his thoughts, not to Ethan as he really was, but instead a father who was straight-backed and strong and fifteen years younger. A father who was an easy match for this cocksure man.

As if reading his mind, Carey volunteered brightly, "Ethan spends a lot of time away with the animals, does he? I understand he's a good sheepman." He nodded as if to convey understanding. "Best for a sheepman to keep a sharp eye, eh. I imagine you'll do the same when you take over this place. If you *want* to take it over, that is. It's early days for you to be knowing what you will do with your life."

Sensing a falseness in his interest, Connor remained silent while Carey held him in his razor-sharp gaze. "She's never mentioned me, I guess. No wonder I've surprised you. Well, good, you won't be spoiled with preconceptions." He seemed to think he'd made a joke, his eyes dancing, the sun catching on the mother-of-pearl buttons of his maroon-coloured vest. There was an iridescent gleam in his oiled hair that put Connor in mind of the blue-black feathers of a crow.

Connor was staring stupidly. "Dad'll be 'round soon anyway, but you could come back another time." It wasn't clear what Ethan might do, even if he did suddenly appear. Certainty had suddenly leached from the farm, Carey's presence strangely altering the place, turning it into a version of itself that was both familiar and not. Connor dug his heel into a rain-softened rut in the ground, crossing his arms, first shrugging one shoulder and then the other.

There was not a hint of impatience in Carey. He seemed to have all the time in the world. Nodding, he took some tobacco from a pouch in his breast pocket. He placed his neat hand on the broad shiny neck of his horse, now gnawing at a tuft of chickweed.

It was compelling, how Carey meted out each moment, his deliberateness somehow a torment. Connor felt himself to be imprisoned. "If you can't wait," he said in a rush, his face on fire, "I'll see if she'll come out."

"She'll come, you can be sure of it." Carey put out a lightning-quick laugh. "Like I said, tell her it's me who's out here in her yard."

Connor found Sophie in the upstairs hall at the small arched window, her face white, her eyes enormous. "Carey's here, waiting." He could see that she was perfectly aware, that she'd seen them talking.

She turned to him with a wild look. "What's he been saying, Connie?"

Connor shrugged. "Nothing. Just that he's your cousin, here to visit."

"Come," she commanded, sounding strangely angry. "Come here." She tugged him close, her grip pinching his skin. "Stay while I go speak to him."

"I'll go down," he said. "Maybe get dad."

"No, you'll not move from this spot," she said. "Do you understand?"

He watched her fly out of the house like a cat with its tail on fire. Carey's face lit up when he saw her. She didn't pause, not for a moment. She circled him, her long skirt twining around her legs, muck catching in the hem. She went around and around until Carey placed a hand on her arm as if to still her. They stood like that for a long time, Carey nodding up toward the house where Connor still stood at the window, and then in an easy way, as if out of habit, he reached out and placed a single fingertip to her lips.

It might have been the way that she paused, her face tilted, her hand softly unfurling like a leaf at his chest that made Connor unsure of what he was seeing. As a boy, he'd understood such gestures to speak of tenderness. They stood close, this man and his mother, Sophie not pulling away, but rather loosening, dissolving in the man's grasp. There was something awful about the two of them. Watching from the window, he'd felt bereft, as if he were alone in a falling darkness. Panic beat hard in his chest.

Suddenly, Sophie's hand was fisted. When she struck him, he looked surprised but then his eyes screwed down, as if to see her more clearly. Taking a half-turn around him, she raised her fist to him again, but this time Carey was ready. He snatched her by the wrist and her arm dropped like a bird shot from the sky. He dragged her closer and spoke into her ear, Sophie hanging off her own frame like something near dead.

The thought came to Connor that he should run down the stairs, go to the barn, take the shovel from where Ethan had left it. He would beat Carey with it until he let her go. But now, alongside Sophie's fury, there remained the awful image of a mother willing to let herself be taken, stollen, her fingers pliant as they came to rest on Carey's chest. A stone had formed deep inside, hard and sure, like a truth he couldn't speak of or even name. In the end, he didn't move from the landing, he couldn't, not until he heard her come back in.

Connor barely recognized her, she looked so stricken, as if she'd been whipped, her face white with shock. With a long backward glance, Carey had driven away, the wheels of his buggy spinning off mud from the lane.

She said nothing in way of explanation to Connor. Not a word, but in the months after Carey left, they were overtaken by an enormous shadow. Sophie was fitful, cranky, occasionally maudlin. She set her sights firmly on the girls, endlessly brushing out June's hair and pleading with Dot to sew a set of curtains with her. But she was different with Connor. More and more when he came into a room, she slid her eyes away.

The unfairness of her retreat, her fussing over the girls left a hot and flashing wound and he became sharp with his sisters, sending June away when she followed him to the barn. He mocked Dot mercilessly about her impediment, mimicking the curl of her mouth, the twist in her words. Dot, familiar with ridicule, remained indifferent, but Sophie was stirred to rage. "You are bully-boy," she said coldly, her face white, her eyes burning.

One winter afternoon, Ethan, witnessing one of Sophie's outbursts, put down his mug of tea and fixed her with a narrow look. "The boy's done nothing, Sophie."

"I can't bear it," she said miserably.

"You certainly can. You have done."

She gave Ethan a look full of pleading and fled from the house. When the door slammed behind her, June burst into tears and Dot got up and wordlessly cleared the table.

"Go after your mother, boy," Ethan said, levelling Connor with his gaze. But Connor felt himself frozen to the chair, an appalling fear crawling over his skin, stealing up into his throat. Sophie had become a mystery, a danger, and he was quite suddenly furious with his father for not going out to her himself.

"Am I supposed to apologize?" he asked Ethan, not caring that there was cheek in his tone.

Ethan shrugged. "I'm asking you to sit with her, take her a coat, bring her home."

In the end, he found Sophie sitting on the bench of the unhitched wagon, her head in her hands. When she saw him, his face lit by the lantern he carried, she'd stared, transfixed, her expression a storm of emotion – horror, love, regret.

"Oh, Connie," she said. Tearing her eyes away from him, she held out her hand. "Help me climb down."

9

Saturday
The James Carruthers,
Green is the Colour of Spring

When Harry takes his watch, the weather is no better than it was on Friday and by afternoon, Wright gives the order to put in at an anchorage. "We'll wait this out, boys. Not that she couldn't do it," he shouts enthusiastically through his bullhorn, "I'm sure that she can but this will give the engineers time to oil her up, make her smooth as silk for locking."

As the laker noses her way into a fog-shrouded Whitefish Bay, they can barely make out the other boats at anchorage, ghostly shapes hunkered down, lights burning feverishly from the fore and aft cabins, the midships sullen and dark. The *J.H Sheadle*, a large steamer carrying grain, is there, as are some of the other boats that left Fort William with them.

The men are fatigued from the pound and roll of the recent days, but celebratory too because the *Carruthers* has ridden the blow so well. Taking his rest before they lock down the river, Harry goes to the cabin and lies in his bunk while the boat gently strains and balks at her anchor. The porthole above him is awash with grey. A light flares, cast by a ship's lantern. It gleams against the polished walls, traversing the surface as if it were on its own little voyage.

The wood glows where the light caresses it, and he runs his fingers over its smooth grain. It's warm to the touch despite the cold outside, the texture like satin. Kat had laid a satin dress over her chair in her workroom, he recalls, the dress intended for a young woman she would lay out the next day. Here and there, the folds held a bit of shadow and in the play of light, the dress looked as though it might move. Harry asked if he could touch it. "Of course," she said. "It's meant to be touched." It was a pale green dress. The colour of spring, Kat said.

Spring is different on water. He's spent five springs on lake boats, and perhaps there won't be another, not if he leaves the lakers for good. As he falls into a light sleep, it is April again a clean light striking the lake as if it wants to wake something in it, the water still dark and winter-cold. There are no smells of earth, or living greens, no stench of thawing barnyards, not like there are on shore where life madly, greedily jumps up.

~

There had been a particular spring day, a memorable day, when he had been seven or eight, and Kat was in their kitchen preparing a picnic. She sliced the bread, then wrapped the ham and cheese in cloth, packed knives and cups, a bottle of milk, some coconut squares for dessert, and then she pulled the plaid blanket from the bed and laid it overtop the hamper.

"You put in a lot of food, Kat".

Tucking the edges of the blanket securely, she said, "Because your father is coming too. He'll be starved – he's been helping with calving over at the McNeils' since two this morning."

Harry blinked, hearing that Connor would be coming. It's true, Connor hadn't been sitting at the breakfast table. But Kat was. She must have come to the farm very early. Harry hadn't given Connor's absence much thought, he was often not around, and Kat more than made up for his absence.

"He said he would come?"

Kat laughed. "He did. He'll pick us up and we'll go together."

"He doesn't like picnics."

"He never has them," she said, "so he doesn't know."

Connor came back from McNeil's exhausted and wordless, and he hesitated when Kat handed him the hamper. "Come on," she said lightly. "We'll miss the warmth if we wait too long."

Connor and Kat sat on the driving bench with Harry between them, Connor silent while Kat talked about a woman she'd met who had bees. "She makes medicine, ointments, poultices from the honey," she said, admiration in her voice. "She's very enterprising."

The trees along the shoreline were fragile looking, their leaves still furled, and as they drove down the road he could see past them to the water. The water was big and shining, like a promise, and Harry had been excited when they arrived at the spot. He ran ahead to the beach where the sand was cool and damp. Kat and Connor walked together behind, and then Kat spread the blanket over the sand and began to put out the food. Connor strolled to the water's edge, his eyes on a fishing tug coming from the harbour.

Harry found the path that wound through a slip of forest behind the beach. He was beyond adult surveillance there, free to lose himself in the thick grove of cedars. Soon he discovered an eagle feather and the skull of a sheep. The ground was damp and bright green moss grew in mounds over rocks and logs. He burrowed his fingers into it, feeling its bristling softness, the sensation causing a strange stir in him. He could hear the waves, breaking and receding, and the repetition made the time slow. Scooping out a soft hollow in the earth where he could lie down, close to the moss, the unevenness of the ground cradling his spine, he closed his eyes. He might have fallen asleep, or he might have just been daydreaming. There was a quick and startling cry, or a laugh – or something in-between. Perhaps a gull. He made his way back along the trail, to where Kat and Connor were just visible through the tangle of brush. They lay together on the blanket, Connor on his side, his hand relaxed and resting on Kat's startling white and exposed breast. The sight created a rushing sensation, a nervousness, and Harry felt his face colour. It took courage to finally come away from the woods. Connor saw him first and with a jolting motion, he rolled onto his back, hoisting himself up. He didn't look at Kat but walked purposefully to a nearby log where he sat, his eyes pinned to the water, a tightness in his face. "Kat has food here for you, Harry."

Kat wrapped her shawl around herself, and she gazed at Harry with no hint of embarrassment. Her attention on Harry, in that moment, was absolute, her care undisturbed. "I thought we lost you to the woods, Harry. Come sit beside me and we'll eat. Then we'll walk the beach together."

It had been the beginning of knowing without seeing – like the presence of a shoal just beyond a visible point of land. The imagining is enough, and with it a tingling of horror, a thumping in his chest. There was a vague notion of Kat and Connor together, a separate thing from *Kat* or *father*, different from *Harry and Kat.* He'd felt somehow hurt by it, and scared, and he was happy that Connor didn't go to the beach with them again.

~

It is late in the afternoon, when the boats at anchorage make ready to sail, their captains eager to get through the locks by nightfall.

On the deck of the *Carruthers*, Harry and a few other crewmen stand ready in a knot beside the big winch while Leaps stares up at the wheelhouse, waiting for the captain's signal. The sounds of departure are all around them, firing engines and clattering chains. The sounds cut through the heavy air, reverberating off hulls, bouncing off the granite cliffs of Whitefish Bay. All just echo upon echo, and it isn't possible for Harry to locate the source.

10

Saturday
Lake Huron Shore,
A trip to Town

To break the weight of the day, Connor will go to Kincardine. The trip to town is long overdue. He's almost out of tea, oatmeal, tinned ham, in fact he's almost run out of everything. And he should get the putty to finish the window. He aims to bring back just the barest of essentials, enough to tide him over until he can market the pelts.

As he drives down the lane, he can hear the mink, chattering and screeching, chastising him for going. And then he is at the county road, and seeing it wind away, there is a quickening in him, a sort of reach. *An invitation*, he thinks, *but to what? To Kat. The road to town always makes him think of Kat.*

~

"Did your mother love her cousin?" She'd asked him, years before.

He and Kat were lying beneath the eaves in the room he and Essie had once shared. Their limbs were entwined, her hand soft on his belly. He told Kat what he'd seen as a boy in the yard at Darling Farm, how it changed everything.

He spoke of Sophie's strange torpor, and the violence in her after, the grip of Carey's hand, the terrible show of Sophie's feelings that followed, like something rabid. And his father, useless in the face of it all. He stopped there, not wanting her to see how incapable he was of altering the course of things. Turning to her, his finger traced the outline of her collar bone. The constancy of Kat, the certainty was at times almost unbearable. "I don't think any of it was love."

"So what was it, then?"

Connor didn't answer, sure if he did, she might see Carey's shadow in him. Instead, he rose from the bed and went out to the mink, allowing the anxiety they produced in him to spill from his mouth in a stream of whispered curses.

~

The horse's ears twitch under the deepening sleet and its chestnut coat quivers. Connor shifts uncomfortably on the bench and wonders at himself for turning from Kat that day while there was still so much to say. He supposes that a certain meanness of joy has dogged him for much of his life. He has never believed that joy can last.

Weeks after he spoke about Carey, Kat told him plainly about the pregnancy, her face lit up with unspoken happiness, her expression proud. Like a man taking a run before leaping over a creek, he convinced himself he would ask her to stay with them once the baby arrived. But in time, and in-step with the life that grew inside Kat, an ever-expanding worry took root. He'd remembered how he was with Essie, no better than a sleep-walker, and then after she died, Harry's cries, his needs so limitless that Connor had contemplated a lonely jump from a bridge.

He'd reminded himself that this time there was Kat, always Kat, and that she would coax out the best part of him, whatever that was. On a spring day, Kat's belly still small but round beneath her dress, they went down to the cool and inscrutable lake with Harry. Kat spread a green-checked blanket over the sand, and Connor set down the hamper of food. There was a tangle of thick cedar behind a gully and Harry, keen to explore, soon disappeared down the ragged path.

Curling himself around her, Connor buried his face into Kat's neck, awkwardly undoing buttons and resting his hand on the fullness of her breast. He'd found himself silently crying, although he wouldn't let her see. "I know it was hard for you with Essie." Her voice vibrated along her back and passed through his scull. "I didn't love Essie," he muttered, not adding *as I love you,* although that's where the torment was for him, in the power of that want of her. Moments later, she'd caught sight of Harry, standing at the place where the grass began in the sand, his eyes huge. "But you have Harry," she'd whispered, and it was true.

She lost the baby two weeks after and for a blinding moment he'd thought that perhaps he was cursed, that it was his telling her about Carey that made a baby impossible. He'd stared wide-eyed at himself, feeling weirdly culpable, but also feeling a sense of release.

For her part, Kat held her grief for the lost baby close, refusing to impose it on him. As he peers through the sleet, the village ahead emerging from the wash of wet, he thinks that she hadn't trusted him with her sadness, believing he wouldn't know what to do with it.

~

The dry goods store on the corner in the centre of the village is the only place for miles where he might still get credit. He climbs down from the wagon and then, at the threshold of the store, he knocks the wet from his boots. Behind the wooden counter is the grocer's wife, a woman in her fifties, three grey whiskers sprouting from her padded chin, her eyes small under the grip of her eyelids. Connor has dealt with her in the past and he prefers her husband.

"That's a day," he says, brushing off his coat, trying to make his voice friendly.

The grocer's wife regards him warily.

"I need oatmeal, canned goods, peas and peaches, maybe, and putty if you have it. I'd like to put the order on my chit." He clears his throat, wishing for water. "I'll pay my bill before Christmas."

She lifts the glass lid from a jar of hard candy and then mindlessly puts it down again, the sound dull and final in the crowded confines of the store. "My husband said we extended credit far as we could. I'm to tell you."

"Is he here?"

"He is. But he's lying down. The weather makes his head hurt."

"Well," says Connor. He looks around him, the place cluttered, dust on the higher shelves, some of the items not having been moved in months if not years. A place in need of resurrection. "I'd take some older stock. Anything. And I'll still pay full price later, when I can." The request chafes the inside of his throat, although recently, he's had to get used to asking for things.

"Please. It will only be a few weeks longer before I have some cash."

The woman regards him with a doubtful gaze. "We'll need payment before New Year's. Full payment or that will be the end. Without question. And we haven't got putty."

Connor nods, looking down at his hands. It's odd that there isn't putty. Earlier, along the back wall, he'd spotted mouse traps, scrub brushes, twine. The ordinary things on which people rely to repair and to clean.

She stares implacably at him. "Take the ladder and pick twelve cans from the top shelf. Then you can have a large bag of the oatmeal."

He loads his crate quickly while she stolidly watches. "Thank you."

"The weather will get worse," she says flatly. "You should get back to your place in case the road is closed."

Connor says nothing as he fills the crate. He nods at the woman on his way out. There is still time to go and see Macey. He's not in a hurry to get back to the animals, not eager for the lonely trip home. The sleet is hardening, more ice than water. He stands on the street, reedy streams of white taken up on gusts and then vanishing.

11

Saturday
Poe Lock,
Downbound

A gaggle of lake boats wait their turn at Poe Lock while the *Carruthers'* crew walks the deck, smoking, chatting in clusters of twos and threes, an ease in the men now, with Superior and the bad weather behind them. Harry and Jake lean against the aft house, Jake tensed, his gaze pinned to the shore, something in its stillness unsettling him. When he tosses his cigarette, it makes an orange spark that dies somewhere over the black water.

Nearby, a barge is packed tight with cattle, the animals tied together and chained to the deck. "That couldn't have come through what we did," Jake says suddenly, nodding vaguely in the barge's direction. "Must have just been loaded somewhere close to here."

Harry surveys the square, blunt-bowed barge sitting low in the water. It's more a shore runner than a cross-lake vessel. "No one would transport those animals like that in wild water," he says finally. "Probably going to a livestock market down river."

Jake grunts in agreement and then drifts away to another section of the deck where he joins a group of deckmen playing Euchre. A lantern has been fixed to a cable and it sways languorously over the players' lowered heads. There are hoots

and then gruff curses, and it's likely that a bit of money changes hands.

Harry shifts his eyes to the mulish barge nestled amongst the long freighters. He has never seen livestock shipped over waterways so late in the season and it seems a sad and reckless endeavour. From the barge's deck, a cow bawls, the sound like a foghorn in the still air. It's an abject call and Harry's chest feels heavy, hearing it.

He is brought back to the farm and to the constant frantic caterwaul that came from the shed, the mink constantly petitioning for care, protesting, scolding.

Connor had seemed deaf to them. "Let's put blankets over their pens," Harry suggested once, "and maybe they'll settle." Connor shook his head in what seemed to Harry as an unnecessary withholding. He sometimes wonders why Connor hadn't chosen different work – cash crops or housebuilding, anything but animal husbandry.

~

The timing around the cull struck Harry as erratic, although now he realizes it had everything to do with the animals' food running low even if Connor would never admit it. He made a show of the minks' readiness. Placing a forbidding stick between himself and an animal, Connor provoked it to stand on its hind legs, the stick held across the throat as the mink clawed the air. "To inspect the coat," he told Harry flatly. "There is no other way, and you, Harry, keep your hands away from those pens. Unless you've got your gloves on."

In truth, the mink were always half-starved by the time Connor harvested them, and he did the culling himself, stalking into the shed with grim determination, his head down, a deliberate shutting of the door behind him. There had been something perversely private about the whole thing, and Harry wonders who his father became inside that shed on culling day. But the larger question circles back and finds him. Who had his father ever been?

After, Connor would try to get market value for the pelts. They drove for miles to an auction, but because the furs lacked shine and the skins were cracked, they were seldom evaluated as first, or even second grade, and the mink brought in next to no money.

~

When Harry was about fifteen, a furrier came to the farm without notice. She arrived in a motorcar, a driver at the wheel wearing a red and green cap and driving gloves. Harry can still the see the pale blue scarf looped around the woman's throat. She climbed from the car wearing a long brown sable coat and shining boots. Her hair was set in rows of perfect waves.

Walking over the uneven yard, the scarf trailing behind, she seemed to float. Connor and Harry were stacking wood and when Connor caught site of her, he held his hand over his eyes, as if shielding them from a glare, although the day was sunless. They walked to meet her, Harry two or three feet behind his father. Earlier, Connor had been chopping wood and now sweat banded across his back, staining his shirt like a giant handprint. He wiped his palms on his trousers.

Close up, Harry could see that the woman's lips were darkly outlined and then filled in with vivid colour. He had watched Kat draw such lines around the lips of the dead, the women at least, but the effect hadn't been this alarming. The furrier gave a brief, tight smile for Harry and then turned her gaze to Connor, extending her hand, Connor reaching across and lightly taking hold. "Don't think you're special, Mr. Darling," she'd said smiling, a joke hidden in the loll of her words. Harry hadn't understood it. Her way of speaking seemed wide and flat – she must have been an American, only rich Americans drove motorcars, although Harry wouldn't have known that then. "I'm touring all of the fur farms in this part of the country. I thought I would swing by and have a look at what you have. The market for mink is turning favourably – you must have seen that it would, getting into this when you did. Granted, it's slow in this country. You're always a little behind." She'd smiled again, giving Connor a long look. "Still, clever you." She'd pulled out a silver cigarette case and then leaned in close to Connor, Connor lighting her cigarette, his hand cupping hers, his eyes bright above the lit match. She rested her fingers on his arm, the nails painted a crimson red, a gold bracelet sliding across white skin. "Let's take a look at those animals of yours, Mr. Darling." Connor was quick footed as he led the way to the shed, the woman behind him, her coat swinging languorously on her tall frame. The driver of the motorcar pulled out a newspaper and, with a look of indifference, glanced at Harry before taking up his reading.

It might have been that only a few minutes passed, or it might have been longer when the woman came out. She carried her coat balled, held close to her body almost like she cradled a live animal. Her long linen skirt was streaked with mud. The blue scarf was missing. She walked past Harry as though he wasn't there, a vacant expression on her face, and then she'd climbed up into the waiting car and was driven away.

There are moments of knowing which germinate, then expand, branches reaching and intersecting, blotting out the sky. This was such a moment for Harry. Connor emerged from the shed not long after, his face red, his chest heaving. He leaned against the roughened doorframe and lit another cigarette, his hands seeming to shake. Behind him, the mink shrieked, their sounds stabbing into the dullness of the day. Harry stared, an eerie sense of deja-vu coming over him, at least that is what he remembers now, although perhaps it is just in looking back that he finds an alarming familiarity.

"Did she buy the lot?" Harry asked later over the cold supper Kat had left for them.

"No," Connor answered heavily.

"Will she be back?" Harry had wished that Connor would say no, that she would never come back. But instead, he said, "we'll see."

~

The vision still burns inside of Harry. At the time, he couldn't have explained what he saw, but he had an idea. At fifteen, he had already felt that heady rush of heat in his body when dancing close to a girl. And once, he'd exchanged a long, soft kiss with Rebecca Robertson behind the stone livery building in town. The woman, Connor's eagerness with her, her strange and dishevelled appearance coming from the shed left Harry feeling both enthralled and sick. He went to Kat the next day, desperate to see her, yet feeling complicit because of what he had seen.

Harry found Kat in her workroom leaning over the body of a small boy. His face was grey, and his small fine lips were a pale violet. The eyes, left open, were empty and blue. Kat turned to Harry, surprised to see him standing there, her face streaked with tears, her hand gentle on the crown of the boy's head.

He'd never known Kat to be so overtaken by sorrow in her work. It disturbed him, seeing her changed, and it felt as though she'd slipped away to a place he couldn't follow. There had been a frantic need to reel her back, to know what unleashed the strange torrent of sadness, to stop it. It didn't take him long for his mind to settle on the source. The furrier's visit. The vision of the woman presented itself like an apple ready to be torn from a tree. In that moment, Kat's anguish and the woman furrier fused, the furrier and the child becoming bound up with one another; the greyness of the child's skin, the absence in the woman's eyes, the unstoppable wet on Kat's face. Harry stared, wide-eyed, his face burning, a terrible hardness in his throat.

She'd wept because of what Connor had done.

"Wait, Harry. I will cover him. I couldn't bear to close his eyes." She pulled up the sheet and turned to him, her long braid riding over her shoulder, her sleeves rolled up, exposing the firm, straight wrists. She'd lingered over the child and then came to Harry, holding him in her arms, and Harry knelt and pressed his head into her breasts, not knowing in that moment what he felt.

"I'm sorry, Harry." He has not remembered this until now – the urgency of his own body when he was close to her. He burns again, as if it is new – the shame and the terrible longing.

He'd told Kat he loved her again and again, as if that might save her. As if his love for her alone would be enough.

~

Harry gazes down the river into the waiting blackness.

"Lovely to see, isn't it?" Captain Wright has slipped beside him, his hand on the rail as he regards the other boats in anchorage. The two men look out at the long narrow freighters, pressed together like butter knives lined up in a drawer. The heavy air carries the voices of men as they talk across the bound-together hulls. "It's something, how such big boats can organize themselves like that."

Wright grunts in agreement. "Signals and lights," he says. "It's all about getting those right and getting them on time."

Harry glances over at Captain Wright, the silhouette of the man, a mountain rising from the horizontal deck. Wright leans back and studies the sky, his mouth slackening as he does. He squints at the darkness. "The snow's stopped. We'll have an easy run now." He lifts his finger and points out various lakers, commenting on aspects of performance and capacity, the individual quirks of each. When his shoulder leans into Harry's, Harry feels a press of warmth through the serge wool of his coat. Wright takes out his pipe from his pocket and lights it, taking a deep and satisfying draw. "Where are you headed after, lad?"

Harry considers the question. "Back to Goderich. I have a friend there. Then, I'm not sure."

Wright nods, takes his sleeve to his nose, then runs his fingers through his moustache as if to comb it. "You have family someplace, Harry? A special girl?"

Harry laughs because Flo is hardly a girl. "There is someone."

"Well, that's good. This can be a lonely business."

"You've been at it a long time," Harry ventures. "You must have found a way to manage the months away."

Wright nods. "I have loved these boats, but I'm happy when November comes, and I can go home. All the years I worked on lake boats, I had something to look forward to. Not everyone working the lakes has that." With a sigh, Wright passes his hand across his face and peers out at the water again. "The day comes when you don't want to leave home anymore. I started to feel like that last year and knew it was time to finish." His eyes narrow and he smiles at Harry, mischief and stealth in the expression. He looks like a man sneaking a second piece of cake. "But then I was offered the *Carruthers* and here I am, until after this run anyway. We'll take her back to Collingwood, make repairs and alterations over winter, any that's needed, and then next spring some other lucky fellow can have a go."

"What will you do, if you're not on the boats in the summers?"

Wright answers easily, his future already well thought through. "Work in the dock office, help with inspections."

Wright has allowed the railing to take his weight and he leans over the water, his one foot easily hooked behind the other. The lights from the boats, amassed as they are in the small mouth of Poe's Lock, are a pretty sight. "I've a son about your age, Harry. He could have followed me onto the boats, but instead, he became a metal worker. Works in the shipyard not far from the house, and he's home every night. He had a baby girl last year. I think it's a good life."

~

It's another few hours before they can lock. The *Carruthers* is finally in position and as she slips through the gates, a deckman is hoisted in a boson's chair, his hunched figure swinging crazily as he's lowered to the dock. Once down, he jumps from the seat and helps the lock crew to hold the guideline. Behind them, the lights from the waiting boats blink and bob in the dark like a hundred pairs of eyes. The emptying valve opens, and water pours out, and for a time the rushing sound is everything.

It takes a long while for the level to drop and for the down bound gate to open. The *Carruthers'* engine fires, and she slips almost effortlessly into the river. Harry, alone at the rail, can make out wide swaths of trees at the riverbank, dark spreading stains, the water alive with light from the boat's lamps.

They pass several up bound freighters, figures stalking decks and peering over railings into the dark, their eyes fixed to the glittering running lights of other boats just as Harry's are. An old-style steamer passes very close, distinctive with its affably slanted chimney, its determined little bow. Someone behind Harry on the *Carruthers* calls out to it: "That you, Styles?" Instantly, an imprint of arm waves in answer.

"Thought you'd be there. I'll put my head in at your old man's place in Midland. Hear he's doing poorly."

"Much obliged," comes the hollered reply.

They round the lazy bend in the river, and there are no boats to be seen, either ahead of them or behind.

12

*Saturday
Huron Shore,
Ice*

Driving down to the small harbour, Connor hears the lake before he glimpses it. When the water finally comes into view, he sees that close to shore, the water is stacked with white caps, and not far out the lake has vanished.

He finds Macey at the harbour kneeling by the *Grace*, tying off docking lines. He's wearing a thick slicker and his gumboots, and a mantle of white has come to rest on his shoulders.

"Starting to blow good," Connor says, crouching next to him. He takes hold of the line, and then helps to pull it taut.

Macey winds the line securely over the bollard and neatly secures it. "Jesus," he grumbles. "Bloody sleet, hard enough to scrape the skin from your eyes. Had to turn the tug in early."

The Kincardine harbour is jammed with fishing boats, all doubled-down and tied snuggly. The tugs should have been hauled ashore in winds like this, but the change had been sudden, leaving the captains to scramble to make their boats ready. "Looks like you're not the only one that packed it in," Connor observes.

Macey motions to Connor for help with the rigging. "We'll take this lot into the fish hut so it don't get torn away."

Connor steps aboard and helps him to loosen the deck bolts and the two men carry the rigging to the hut. "We'll take the netting too," says Macey, glancing back at the boat again and grimacing up at the sky. They lay the netting on the dock and then roll it, Macey lifting one end and Connor taking the other. When the netting is stowed, they bring out large tarps and stretch them over the wheelhouse and cabin, using the blocks and tackle on deck to lash them taught. With his shoulders humped against the wind, Macey tests the doubled spring lines for strength and surveys the battened-down boat. As he looks toward the lake, an unusual tension comes into his face, a worry that makes his eyes water.

"Hope there aren't no poor buggers left out in this. A miserable mess it is." Macey can be a sentimental man and his abundance of feeling embarrasses Connor. He wants to smile ludicrously, to abstract from the hard place where his own feeling should be, but he speaks instead.

"All of them in?"

"All the fishing tugs at least, as far as Harbour Master knows." Macey's eyes are roving, searching the water. "This truly is the end of the season." With an abrupt shudder, he shakes off the melancholy tone. His smile takes up the entirety of his face. "For your help today, I'll be forgivin' a portion of debt."

"That was hardly an effort," Connor scoffs, knowing that Macey looks for opportunities to grant him grace, no matter how little he does to deserve it. Macey's memory is long, and he's dogged about his loyalties. Years before, Connor and Macey were young men and working the winter months in the mill. They were moving logs with a steam-powered winch, a chain, and a team of heavy horses. It had been snowing and the logs were lightly iced. Macey was on top of the pile, wrestling with the chain when his foot slipped. He became wedged between the logs and steam engine, the horses startling and pulling ahead with the partly fastened load. Later, Macey told Connor that he was sure he would die that day. Connor, acting quickly, bullied the big horses, forcing them back and easing the tension on the chain. Wrapping his arms under Macey's shoulders, he hoisted him up until he was free. Macey had a broken leg and a cracked collarbone, but he mended. It had been a straightforward act on Connor's part, thoughtless. The two men have never spoken about it but he knows Macey has never forgotten.

"Like I said", Connor says, "I'll bring cash once the mink are culled."

Macey lets out an enormous laugh. "Christ, the mink again. Well, don't skin them on my account, little buggers. Not worth the effort." There is a pause. "You got a buyer?" Macey takes a deep and meaningful breath and waits for Connor to reply.

"Likely I'll do the same as last time. Don't have that nailed down."

Macey studies him for a moment and then turns toward the shack. "Come inside and I'll brew us some tea. Throw a good plug of rum in with it. You look cold, Con."

Connor grunts "This isn't cold. Not a bit. Just a little damp."

"Ha!" Macey claps his hands together as if to raise the blood in them. He turns, his feet shuffling as he leads them into the hut. After he's lit the small stove, he takes down two tin mugs from a single shelf and doses them each with a generous shot of rum. They sit, their fingers curled around the steaming mugs, the wind rattling the metal roof over their heads. The heat, the proximity to Macey's affable bulk, the sound of the other man's breathing softens something in Connor.

Macey blinks heavily and sighs. "Fair weather don't last forever," he says. "This is due."

Connor nods, remembering the Darling Farm, how cleanly brutal the winter could be. "Thinking of the place where I come from, how cold could kill a man."

Macey studies him for a long moment and then his face breaks into a smile. "Not a mink farm, was it?"

Connor gives him a pained look. "Sheep."

Macey snorts. "Bloody sheep."

His chin jabs toward the bunk he keeps for the days when the yields are high and he's out on the water by four in the morning "Sleep here tonight, Connie. Weather's a bitch and you've had a finger or two. I'll walk up home, leave you to it. It's comfortable enough if you can take the stink." Tonight, the hut smells of fish and rum and mildew, and beneath this is a tangy smell – Macey's smell, the smell of his years of effort.

"Got the mink to think of."

Macey grimaces. "Few hours of hunger won't hurt'em. Might make them grateful to see you."

A wave of exhaustion passes over him. He's tired of fretting about the animals, worn down to his marrow.

He rests his eyes on Macey. "Won't say no, I guess. And I appreciate you forgiving some of my debt, Mace. I do."

Macey shrugs. "Why don't you sell the goddam mink off and come and work for me next spring? Every season, I end up gettin' occasional crew who are either drunk or stupid, and what's more, a goddamn nuisance."

Valerie Mills-Milde

Connor stares into his half-empty mug, his head swimming in the rum. "Not much good on water."

"You'd learn, Con. You'd be fine. And you could keep the bloody mink too, if you had a mind."

Connor nods dully. "I'll think on it, Mace. Once the mink are culled and the pelts are sold."

~

After Macey leaves for home, Connor lies in the dark and thinks of Ethan, how he died on a day when Connor had been helping with the ice. The event altered everything, stripping out the points of light that had lit the way before. His sister June, and a young, tamed fox with tufted ears; the wooden raft they built for the pond which left them with slivers. On summer evenings, Ethan playing the fiddle, Connor dancing with his mother, his feet bare on the cool grass, Sophie with her head thrown back and laughing freely like a girl.

He and his father had gone to the frozen pond early, Connor already aching with cold. He had stupidly worn wool mittens instead of his sheepskin ones and his hands were freezing. Sliding off the mitts, he held his fingers to his face, coaxing them to warmth, stretching and curling them as if they were in conversation.

Watching Connor, Ethan let out a chuckle. "Whirl your arms 'round, Con. Like a windmill." Connor felt foolish doing it, but the windmill movement was effective, the action pushing a scorching heat into his fingers. Soon his hands throbbed with feeling, and Ethan smiled with satisfaction.

Later, he would look back and realize that his father frequently provided small prompts toward perseverance. *If you lost the sheep at night Con, and you fear she's gone to the bog, take the dog with you. The dog will show you the safe way. And a lamp, Con. Always a lamp.* Connor had felt he was being schooled, a sure sign that Ethan intended him to have the same life that he had, that his flat and dry wisdom would be encouragement when the days ahead were particularly bleak. Connor would think of other lives then, lives he might want, but a loyalty to Ethan, a love, had kept him from ever saying it.

Ethan went to the pond's edge to check for thickness, the ice an opaque blue-gray. "Good to nine feet down," Ethan proclaimed. "We'll do well by it, Con." The ice would stay good for months if it was packed in sawdust. In springtime, they'd go up the line with horse and cart, selling door to door, the blocks packed in crates. Their profits from the ice business were small and in Connor's mind, hardly worth the effort.

"A lot of work for not much pay out," he grumbled.

Ethan held him in a steady gaze, a wry look of amusement playing at the corners of his mouth. "We might as well get rid of the sheep and sit on our arses, eh Con? The damn sheep are work. Let's burn the house down too, while we're at it." Connor smiled grudgingly. Ethan lived by a baffling faith in the farm and a belief in labouring for it.

They chopped the ice at the rim with their axes and slowly a wedge, two feet thick, was revealed. Seeing it, Ethan nodded in satisfaction and went back to the wagon to retrieve the two-handled saw, the two of them working in tandem. Connor was at the pond's edge, Ethan further out on the ice, the enormous saw kicking up a frozen spray between them. Once or twice, Ethan stopped to catch his breath, nodding to Connor to go on, and then he dropped his head down, drew his arm across his mouth and started again.

It took hours to cut the blocks. The light was starting to drain from the sky when they headed back to the house, the wagon loaded, the blocks secured with rope. Connor remembers how, as they trudged along, the frozen trees creaked and popped, the horse's breath streaming in twinned plumes of white. A day immersed in crystalline stillness.

A single sound dropped into the frozen quiet: from deep in the bush came the cry of something wild – a large bird or a fox. Suddenly, with his hand on the horse's halter, Ethan stopped. At first, it was as if he was just listening, his eyes fixed and red with cold, a slight parting of his narrow lips. And then he slowly sank to his knees, staying upright for a few moments before toppling sideways into the snow.

~

Ethan left the farm to Connor, the will stipulating that Connor, now eighteen, take care of his mother and sisters.

Both the girls left school, which was a shame, because Dot, in particular, was good with figures. She'd mostly abandoned any habit of speech by then, her cleft pallet making her speech too difficult for her, or any of them, to endure. She swept through the rooms of the farmhouse, a dark little bird, her blue-black hair pulled high off her forehead, her eyes pinned to objects – the table that needed clearing, the basket of laundry on the step. Dot, at fifteen was brittle, efficient and austere.

June was already taller and stronger than Dot, her thighs dense with muscle, her face round and freckled. She was eager to muck out the pens, to help him with the shearing, the skirting, or to walk with Connor over the rugged fields. They did almost everything together. But when it came time to take the wool to the mill, he didn't take June with him, instead driving the fleece alone, fearing the sight of him with his sister would make him appear child-like. He could almost feel Ethan there beside him; *negotiate as good a price as you can muster, lad.* He'd looked over once, expecting to see the old man's lean profile, the stoic features, the bright gaze, but there was only the shadow of the horse and wagon.

Connor pulled into the woollen mill's yard which was cluttered with rigs and loads. The manager took a long time coming out of the office. He stopped at another wagon before he made his way to Connor's. "Ethan's boy," he said dully. He took only a minute or two with the fleece skirts. "They're chaffy and full of burrs. You're not cleaning the fleece proper," he said with a sigh, "and the quality's run down. Not like when your dad had the place."

Heat came into Connor's face then. "It's exactly the same. I did this work with my dad for years. I know the right way."

The manager looked up at the sky and feigned sadness. "Either Ethan wasn't a good teacher, or you weren't a good student." He took the fleece but under-paid for it, Connor seething while he pocketed the money, careful not to show himself, not wanting the manager to think he'd got the better of him.

Not long after, Dot declared she would hire herself out as a domestic. They needed the income, she said. There were people in town wanting housekeepers, laundresses, cooks and she was proficient at all of those things. Connor studied his strange sister, a fury at his own inability to keep them afloat taking hold. "You shouldn't leave the house. You're not fit. People won't want someone like you creeping around."

Dot glared darkly at him. When they came, her words were muddy, squished, so unlike the sharp cut of her. What he understood was that she would only work for other people during night hours.

He laughed openly. "You'll scare them half to death."

Dot said nothing. His cruelty had no sway over her, perhaps because there was a falsity to it, a sense in them both, deep down, that she was doing more to meet the widening crisis than he was. She found work in town, just as she intended, and each morning, when Connor watched as she walked to the end of the lane, her back straight, her eyes fixed on the road, a secret and shameful envy came over him.

~

On a day in July, Connor drove the fleece to town as usual. The manager strode out from his office, this time throwing Connor a smile, his teeth small and slanted in his narrow face. He held out his hand. "Step down a minute, Mr. Darling, and let's have a talk."

He'd never been inside the woollen mill before. He hardened his gaze on the man's back and then followed him to the glowering stone building, and into an office that was sparse and tight and damp. Far below, the river swept past, the sound urgent and indifferent.

"Take a seat." The manager waved amiably toward a wooden chair on the other side of the desk. "Seems to me you're having a time with that farm of yours. Barely able to make ends meet is what I hear. Now, far from me to tell you how to run your farm but as a favour to you, and in memory of your father, I feel I should ask. Have you ever thought of selling, freeing up your cash, Mr. Darling?"

Connor shifted uncomfortably in the hard chair. He had dreamt of leaving the farm. He had longed for it. "I haven't considered it," he lied.

The manager's eyebrows shot up and held in a look of feigned surprise. "It might be the prudent thing to do rather than grind the operation into the ground. Won't be worth a wooden nickel if you do that, will it?"

"I'm keeping the place up good enough."

"I'm an experienced sheepman, boy. How long do you think you can go on for?" He leaned back in his chair and studied Connor, his eyes hard with appraisal. "With only your sisters for help, and one with something missing." He tapped disparagingly at his temple with a bent finger. "Turns out I am in a position to make you an offer. Cash up front. You'd be able to walk away from the entire operation." He gave a terse nod. "I'm not going to make the offer again. I've my eye on another place that would do just as nicely for me but I thought I'd do you the favour."

Driving back, Connor turned over the manager's proposition, imagining himself away from the farm, cut loose from the paucity of the place and its hovering obligation.

It was already half-light when the Darling farm came into view, the land purplish with eruptions of rock, bristling as though it sensed a nearing betrayal, and his mind had wheeled around what it would mean to let the place go.

13

Sunday
Lake Huron,
Phantoms

After midnight, the *Carruthers* leaves Great Duck Island to the north and sets course on a rhumb line to Cove Island, and then on into Georgian Bay. Now, only the lake stretches before them, without markers or shore or light.

Though the wind is unsettled, the big laker's movements are steady and the men move freely over the deck without need of their safety lines. Harry is tasked with coiling a hemp line that had been messily stowed during yesterday's blow. Jake hovers at the laker's stern. He shrugs up his coat, turns, walks toward Harry, his stride still powerful despite the hours he's been awake. A man strangely at home in the cold emptiness, as though it has given his energy focus.

Finishing with the line, Harry tilts his head and sweeps the sky for a single star or a hint of moon. Jake is at his elbow, his face lifting too. "Don't think we'll get any help from up there," he says with an amused grunt. "Well, we've got Ross, and he'll do."

Harry makes a murmur of agreement.

"I don't want this trip to be over." Jake says suddenly.

"Why? What will you work at this winter, Jake? Will you box?"

Jake draws on his cigarette and then exhales. "I've taken a few too many blows. Happens to fighters." He holds up his right hand, the tips of his fingers shivering, a twitch coming across his cheek. Evidence of damage done to him over the years in the ring. "There's a fight club in Cleveland that needs a manager. I've been asked, but I'm not sure. I don't want to get too close to that business again."

"Managing would be different from fighting."

Jake shakes his head. "It's a small world, the fighting circuit. I've kept my name out of it for a while."

Harry has no idea of the boxing world or the life that Jake leads on shore, or the winter lives of most of the lakemen, for that matter.

"It's as dark as the inside of a sack out there. Makes steering her a bitch, I would think." Harry looks up at the wheelhouse, thinking of the charts he'd seen, the starred rocks, the blue markings for shoals and sandbars, the concentric black lines that flowed over the white flat paper. Beautiful and mysterious.

"Wright won't run us aground. He can smell his way if it comes to it." Jake rakes the cuff of his coat across his nose and then sniffs. "Bloody chill out here. Makes you feel every breath." An unexpected brightness blazes in Jake's eyes, and patches of red spread over his cheeks. There is a shine about him, a sort of relish.

"You didn't really mind about the storm on Superior earlier, did you? You would have come anyway, even if you'd known it would get bad."

Shifting, Jake glances briefly at Harry. He pauses, as if weighing his words. "I had an idea we'd be in for something. The morning on the day we sailed, I heard a company man talking to Wright, something about a telegram. It came from head office, Toronto, he said. Someone there had a friend in the American weather bureau who'd forecasted a big blow, although there was disagreement in the bureau about what *big* was."

Harry says nothing, this new bit of information slowly stacking meaning upon meaning. "And so the Service didn't up the warning?" He says finally.

Jake shrugs. "*Carruthers* is Canadian-owned. The report came out of the American bureau and it wasn't official. The fellow in Toronto should probably never have passed that forecast on."

"But still, Jake –"

"The telegram likely got left on someone's desk."

Harry frowns. "Some of the boats stayed back."

Jake narrows his eyes, as if considering why other captains made the choices they did. "They likely got their own information, or they took those useless flags more serious than they deserve. Maybe they read the weather for themselves."

"But Wright?"

"Wright never said a word. Probably thought it was fuss about nothing, that this boat would do fine anyway. And it has. This time of year, there's always a good chance of weather turning." He pulls back, stretching his arms, tilting his head from side to side as if to relieve a spasm. "You know that, Harry."

~

Only a few men remain on deck. The trip over the top of Huron is not unlike dozens Harry has made before, except for the darkness. Harry can't remember a crossing as black as this one.

Nothing changes on the water. He is lulled by the thrum of the engine, the movements of the boat. The cold numbs and to keep himself from falling asleep, he paces. Looking northwest he traces the direction from where they have come, hoping to see the lights of another laker, but finds none. Mid-ships, Craig Levine stands perfectly still, his head slightly cocked as if he hears something no one else can. He looks like a phantom, standing in the eerie shadows, the deck lights shivering above his head.

Harry, feeling weary, finds a quiet place to sit in the lee of a stack and wraps his arms around his shins. He was wrong about this trip mostly being like others he's taken, and it isn't just the darkness. The hours are without margins, time stretching on and arching back on itself. He is looping between past and present, drifting, and to anchor himself he composes a telegram to Flo in his head. *I want to be there with you, I want to be home.* It isn't the sort of message a person sends over the wires, and he's happy he doesn't need to write it down. He knows Flo already understands.

~

Thinking of Flo has brought new calm. Perhaps he briefly falls asleep. When Harry opens his eyes, his gaze catches on a startling movement. It is Levine, his head snapping to starboard. Levine appears puzzled as he peers into the darkness and lifting his palm he feels the air, as if he pushes against an invisible pain of glass.

A few seconds later the first blast comes, sweeping over the laker, assaulting the men with a scattershot of ice. A slanted fall of snow begins. Astonished, Harry looks up and finds that there are no demarcations between boat and water and sky. He braces himself against the stack just as the *Carruthers* sways grossly to port.

"Safeties," shouts Leaps, pointing at the men. There is warning in his tone, something left unsaid. "Only night watch out here with me – that means Bowerman and Morris – the rest of you, go in to get some rest."

It is stunning how this new storm swallows them. Snow is rapidly mixing with the remnants of coal dust, and a black film covers every surface. The long plain deck of the *Carruthers* is ugly-looking, little better than a roughly used barge. Leaps roars over the newly revived wind, apparently addressing the boat. "You're a working laker. Not a fancy boat for cruises or ladies taking tea. You'll come through good enough, and you'll clean up when we make harbour."

Crewmen stumble on the slick deck, the gusting wind pinning them as they struggle to rise from their knees. Jake stares out at the white oblivion that moments before, was the lake. "A bloody rebound, Harry," he says, his voice incredulous. "The blow's on our tail, dogging us, and it's as rough as it was on Superior."

As Harry stares at Jake, realization crawls over his skin. The warning, the flags – all the signs he didn't see – they dance in his head like apparitions. *This* is the blow they warned of.

He practically drags Jake in from the deck, Jake transfixed by the ambush of weather, reluctant to separate himself from its pummelling.

~

Harry lies on his back in the cabin, his eyes wide open, his mind fixed to every jarring movement of the laker. Next to him, Jake is silent. He'd said nothing more about the information he heard on the docks. Harry is filled with a maddening and familiar sense that he has a partial understanding, but is denied the whole, like seeing a fragment of shoreline through dense fog, his mind trying to conjure what's missing.

Jake should have told him what he knew long before now. Before Harry boarded. He feels a barb, lodged deep, almost like a memory. He settles on it: the certainty that something vital to him has been erased, withheld, ushered off beneath his nose.

But he should have seen for himself. There are always signals and changes that point to what comes next, and he's often missed them. Not long before he last saw Kat, there had been an exchange between Kat and Connor. Kat seldom came to the farm after. The three of them were perched around the table, Connor querulous, his face drawn. Earlier, while doling out the evening feed, a mink had bitten Connor, tearing flesh, leaving deep holes where its teeth bore down. Kat cradled Connor's hand in hers, and as she cleaned the wound with antiseptic, she began to talk.

"I'm surprised you can stand their misery," she said, her tone darker than Harry was used to. "Maybe you don't see it."

Connor looked up, anger sharpening the angles in his face. "Their *misery*?" There was the usual hard-pressed panic in the tone. "The bastard bit me, and when I was feeding it."

She studied him, her eyes searching his face. "Giving them *just enough* so they don't starve?"

Connor kept his mouth tight, his eyes shifting from Kat to a blank place on the wall behind her. Then he slammed his good hand down on the table, causing the spoons on the table to jump and the tea in Kat's cup to spill across her blouse.

Valerie Mills-Milde

"*Christ*," he roared, "I give them what I can." He'd looked at Kat like he hated her.

At first, she didn't move, the tea stain slowly consuming more and more of the creamy linen, her head tilted as if considering what she might say. Then, with great gentleness, she took his injured hand from her own and placed it on the table between them.

When Kat stood, she was beautifully erect, her long fingers coming to rest on the back of Harry's chair.

"You'd best take care of that wound, Connor, or else it will fester."

A signal had passed between the two of them, a profound warning, like two boats sounding horns when their passage threatens a collision. Kat hadn't hesitated as she closed the door behind her. Her stride was purposeful as she walked to the Folly cart, the horse nuzzling her hand before she swung herself up. As he watched her drive down the lane and disappear onto the county road, some part of him understood that he would lose her.

In the darkness of the cabin, he feels like there is a gauze behind his eyes. His fingers grip the edges of the thin mattress to keep from being tossed. He wants to settle himself, to clear his mind, and so he lets his thoughts rove around Kat's workshop. A length of robin egg blue ribbon, an ivory handled brush. A white ironstone pitcher and washbasin. A clutch of dried lavender tied with twine. Kat's tin. Her gift to him. Over the many years since he's acquired it, he has kept it close, coddling the image of Kat picking the box from the table and placing it in his hand. He's re-imagined the singularity of the moment over and over, the gravity of it.

Reaching under his bunk, he rummages in his duffle bag until he finds its slightly convex smoothness. He doesn't need to lift the box, he knows it by touch. He closes his eyes, his fingers resting on it, elation and guilt flooding him. A week or two after the incident with Connor, he'd gone to Folly's. He was bursting with lacrosse, excited to tell Kat that after his last game, a man from the National League had taken him aside. He was interested in him, impressed, and he'd encouraged Harry to attend tryouts in Toronto the next year. If the League wanted him, he'd be set to travel around the country, to get an education, but he would always come back, he told Kat. This was his home.

Kat was interested, attentive, but there was a new sadness in her movements and in the way she folded her hands. Harry talked faster, smiled wider. He re-enacted some of the best plays, the fastest passes of the game and she listened, her lips soft but not smiling. She was both preoccupied and oddly pained. It was as though they stood on either side of a precipice, Harry flooded with an old dread that Kat would fall away, and he would be unable to stop her.

Mr. Folly came to the door. He needed a few minutes of her time, "to speak about terms," he said, eying Harry. Folly was old, his skin callow and hanging, his eyelids flaking. Harry remembers thinking that he already looked like a corpse. Kat gave a small sigh and told Folly yes, she'd come, and then she went out, shutting the door behind her. Even straining, Connor couldn't make out everything they said, but fragments of their talk dropped like heavy raindrops into the room. *I'll take my bag and leave the rest*, Kat said, and then later, *it won't be right away.*

It was terrible, trying to understand what they said. The wait for her to return felt long. Earlier, he'd been too distracted to eat, ignoring the tea and biscuits Kat produced for him, but now his eye fell on the German tin, the ornate lettering odd, foreign, strangely beguiling. He picked it up, his thumb running over its dimples and notches. It was coloured in pale blues and greens and yellows, which here and there had been scratched away to expose tiny slivers of grey. He held it in his hands, this piece of Kat that was like an unknown continent, an archive, which spoke about the belonging she felt to another place, the love she kept inside of her always.

Harry wasn't in the habit of lies or secrecy, but he remembers this plainly enough. Kat didn't *give* him the tin, he took it. After, he wouldn't recall a thought, just the terrible press of need. The act had been at once thrilling and awful, and when she came back to the room, he sat, wide-eyed, the hidden tin quickly warming against his skin, knowing but not knowing that what Folly had said would change everything.

14

Sunday
Lake Huron Shore,
Electrification

The morning is very dark and the gusts push hard at Connor's back. He feels as if he is being hurled toward something, propelled by an invisible boot in the arse.

He'd slept poorly on Macey's bunk, the metal roof of the shed humming and banging in the wind. The day before, he left the cart and horse beneath a lean-to, the horse comfortable enough with some hay and a pail of water. Now, when he approaches, he sees that its head is down, its chestnut coat white with sleet. The creature is plainly miserable, the water Connor put down for it frozen over. Jabbing at the icy crust, he puts the pail to the horse's muzzle and watches it drink.

When the horse is done, he harnesses it to the cart and drives up the hill, past the centre of town. He is near the corner of the street where Folly's place was, or "Ault's" as it was properly called. He has an urge to turn, to drive down Kat's street, visions of their past drawing him. As he slows the cart, he thinks of her in the early years, with Harry, Harry as a round wee boy, his fingers clutching at Kat's skirt and his thumb jammed into his mouth. How beautiful the boy was, his head heavy with lustrous curls, his eyes a summery blue. It pained Connor, that beauty. It tugged at him, and Connor couldn't abide the pull. He'd told Kat she ought to cut the boy's hair, but she wouldn't. Kat was dedicated to Harry's childhood, steadfast in protecting it.

He thinks of his last trip to town to see Kat on a day early in December. It had been a day a little like this one, he thinks, though less of a tumult, and there had been a change between him and Kat, a terrible misstep that he hadn't recognized until it was too late.

~

"Ault's" had at one time been the Ault family home, Kat's home, a large yellow brick structure, with Kurt Ault's casket workshop connected by a breezeway at the back. When Fred Folly bought the business, he'd kept the name "Ault" on the signage. Kat, who was Kurt Ault's daughter, had grown up in the business. When her people returned to their home in Germany, she chose to stay, to work with Folly while occupying the small apartment upstairs. For years, Fred Folly and his family lived on the main floor just as the Aults before them had done, but after his children were gone, Folly and his wife moved to a small house a few blocks away.

With its various add-ons, the house was ungainly, and on that afternoon the front windows were too brightly lit, the cavernous rooms in the place mercilessly on display. Folly must be playing at his electrification again, Connor had thought, seeing the bare bulbs hanging from the high ceilings, the bluish light illuminating the cracks in the plaster and the soot in the corners. Long sinister shadows stretched across the walls. Fred Folly intended to use the rooms for viewings and receptions, just as Kat once predicted. In cities and towns, the business of laying-out was changing. People wouldn't like how unsparing the electric light was, she pronounced. The unnatural light would further deaden what was already dead. Her work would be more difficult, the artistry less convincing. "We are making a show of our dead," she said, disappointed. "They're little better than a spectacle."

There were setbacks and unexpected costs to the whole procedure of electrification and Kat thought that Folly would bankrupt himself before he was done. The electrification hadn't progressed to the back of the building, or to her workshop, and Kat was glad it hadn't. Connor went around and saw that her lamp was lit. He rapped twice on the door and waited for her to answer. When she appeared in the doorway, her expression was concentrated, her large grey eyes swept clean of distraction. He could see right away that she had recently been at work. She looked at him for a moment, and then her long fingers reached for the sleeve of his coat, her gaze fixed intensely on him.

"Why would you come on such an awful day? Is Harry alone at the farm?"

He stood with his hands jammed into his pockets. He was often wordless, seeing her. She was dressed in a long brown skirt, an apron tied at her waist, her pale hair braided and coiled neatly at the back of her head. Her hands were speckled with light pink powder, the colour of roses. Seeing him stare, she wiped them once on her apron.

"I'm in town for offal. I'm going to cull soon, early in the new year, it looks like."

She'd waited for him to finish speaking. Nothing about her moved, not a raise of an eyebrow or the flick of a lip. Kat was capable of an unearthly stillness and sometimes he felt he might drown in it. Without a word she pulled him further into

the room and undid his coat, her fingers deft with his buttons. She led him by the hand to a frayed chair by the stove.

"I have to finish," she said, pointing behind her at a worktable on which the body of an old woman had been laid. The woman's fine grey hair hung down from the end of the table, soft-looking with recent brushing. A smaller table had been set close by with a pallet of powders and creams, a large washbasin and a stack of towels. The woman was covered to her neck in a crisp white sheet. In profile, her features were sharp and piercing, the mouth an unconcerned line.

Kat picked up a small sable brush from the table and dipped it in a jar of reddish cream, then leaned over the woman, gently sweeping the bristles over her lips. Connor stood from his chair and moved closer. He liked to see Kat's artistry, the care she took, the precision in each stroke. As he watched, the bloodless face, that a few moments before was without warmth or life, transformed into a semblance of the living person.

~

When Kat finished her work with the corpse, darkness was firmly closing in.

"There. She'll be ready for Folly tomorrow." She turned down the work lamp, the woman on the table receding into shadow. "Would you like to stay, Con? I can fix us something upstairs." He watched her, eating her up with his eyes. Kat had barely aged over the years, although there were a few lines now, and a whisper of grey at her temple.

"And Folly?"

"Fred's gone home."

"All right, Kat."

She put a hand on his arm "Let's walk first. I feel the need of some air."

She put on her long blue woollen coat and a wound a thick scarf around her throat. He was reminded of how tall she was, as tall as he, her shoulders wide for a woman. Now, in the semi-darkness, shadows fell like fingerprints in the contours of her face.

"Where do you want to go?"

She looked at him. "It doesn't matter." She often walked alone at night when her work was done, rambling along the modest main street, past the hotel where men sat drinking. She wasn't afraid, she'd told him. No one would bother her, because of the services she provided. People were strangely awed by her, even frightened.

He didn't touch her. It was enough to hear the soft crush of her coat as she moved. It was enough to see the vapour of her breath. The town was quiet. The yellow brick houses sat squarely on their narrow lots, lights glowing in the windows. The anticipation of what was to come, their togetherness, made him slightly winded.

"The water's quiet," she finally said.

He glanced in the direction of the lake, which was a stretch of ink-coloured satin. He felt as though they were suspended, barely feeling the ground beneath him and he wondered what it would be like to fall with her, to sink beneath the water, to not return to the hardscrabble world in which he had never quite found his place.

Cedar wreaths hung on some of the doors they passed. Christmas wasn't far off. "You'll have Christmas dinner with Folly and his family, Kat?" he asked, thinking he'd like her to come have dinner with him and Harry but not saying so. She didn't answer.

The air seemed colder than it had in the afternoon, numbing their lips, their fingers, their toes growing wooden. Ault House received them dispassionately, without a single burning light. Folly must have left for the day.

"Come up, Connie. I'll get us something to eat." She'd led the way, her hand sure on the doorknob, her stride strong with intention.

They didn't make it up the stairs, other appetites catching them, stealing away their limbs. They devoured one another on the faded Turkish rug in the parlour, Kat everywhere, in every inch of him, her body at once lithe and buoyant. He felt wildly, stubbornly free. If it could just be like that always, no before, no after, no meeting his miserable self on the other side.

But they did finish, and the sadness descended, the strange loneliness, the seclusion. Kat's hair was loose and one long strand curled at the base of her throat. He took it between his fingers and studied it. Sometimes he thought that Kat had been spun from pale gold like a woman in a child's storybook.

Placing her hand at the base of his skull she kissed him on the mouth. He closed his eyes, lingering in that kiss, savouring it, pushing back the old restiveness, but it ascended his limbs, lodging in his chest like a rock.

"I'll have to go." He stood and reached for his trousers, which lay in a heap. "The mink will need tending."

"Harry will feed them."

"Harry will need the offal I have in the wagon to do that."

"I'll come with you, then."

"Not necessary."

"I want to. I want to come with you."

Her eyes followed him, the concentration of her, the stillness threatening to pin him. "Why do you always have to go?" He paused, struck by the question, the insistence in it unsettling. She stood, the quilt pooling at her feet, the fabric sewn in maroon, rose, and sage-coloured squares like stepping-stones – a path to the top of a mountain.

"You know what the animals are like," he said flatly. "They never change."

She nodded vaguely and then reached out to touch his arm. "I have to tell you something before you go." She lit a lamp and then pulled back her hair, her face now fully exposed. "Folly sold the place, Con. He's lost too much money on the renovations, and he says he wants to retire. The new man is having the work completed by his own people. They want it ready in one month's time."

Connor turned and looked at her. "Well, it won't change the job for you, Kat," he said. "Folly's sometimes been difficult anyway."

She shook her head. "The new man will do all the laying out himself. He'll have a casket maker for the carpentry. They don't have need of me. And they want the upstairs apartment for his mother. I'll have to be out in a month."

Connor tried dumbly to take in what she was saying. "So what will you do?"

She held his gaze, unblinking. "My father is doing poorly in Germany. Some kind of chest trouble, and I've thought about going there, to help."

He stared stonily at the unlit fireplace, completely at a loss. His mind was reeling. His mouth was dry. He neither knew how to hold on to her, nor how to let her go. When he found the words, he almost spat them out. "That's daft. Find work here.

Move to another town if you have to – there are undertakers in every place between here and Toronto."

A flush came into her face then, almost as though she'd been stung. "So that's your solution - "

"I don't know, Kat."

She took his face in her hands. "It would be different if I was with you and Harry, Connor, all of us together, if I had people of my own."

Kat had never gone that far, to name her wish, and he felt himself bear down against her, as if she had caught him out and roused him from deep hibernation. He was disoriented with doubts and longing and ancient disappointment. New frustration flooded his eyes.

What he said then came from the thing cornered and alone inside him.

"You're being selfish, Kat." He knew it made no sense.

Her eyes didn't move from his face. She wanted to tether him to her, despite his dark shadows. "It wouldn't just be because I love of you, but because I love Harry too."

At the mention of Harry something in him contracted and instantly ached, and he was filled with shame. He shook his head hopelessly and slid on his coat.

15

*Sunday Morning
The James Carruthers,
Listen to My Voice*

His sleep is shallow and doesn't last.

The vibrations assault him first: pound after pound, hammering through his ribcage. What Harry feels next is motion – a reluctant ascent followed by a terrible falling away.

His mind registers the change. The boat is labouring hard, that much is clear. A ship's bell is ringing. He looks over at the bunk across and sees that Jake is already gone.

Tugging on his clothes, he lurches down the passageway, to the dining room which is lit-up, the lamps swinging madly. When he glances at the clock, he sees that it is just past four.

Cook is in the galley stowing away the pots, and with each pitch of the *Carruthers*, he grasps hold of the worktop to steady himself. The air is close, steam from the kettle making the glass in the portholes sweat. Harry catches a whiff of something antiseptic. It is the smell of hooch, Cook apparently treating himself for seasickness. "Blowing awful," Cook, says not looking Harry in the eye. His face is white and greasy and there are purple-coloured smudges beneath his eyes. "Captain Wright's ordered to secure everything. This new wind came up quick." Cook looks suddenly stricken. "Some of the crew are saying we should have stayed back. The flags were up."

Harry says nothing about the warnings. He can see them now, in his mind's eye, as clear as day. "No one likely thought it would stay bad for long," he says gently. "The captain believed she'd do fine, and she will."

Cook is sick-faced and miserable. "I would have passed on this trip if I knew this blow would happen."

Harry smiles. "Most of us would have, except for a few crazy buggers."

He makes his way on deck, where the spray and water crash high over the railings, and enormous waves, higher than he has ever seen, engulf the fantail. The swaying lights make the ice shimmer on the decks and hatches, and the *Carruthers* glistens as if she is encrusted in diamonds. Leaps stands straight and tall at mid-ships, his fist around a cargo cable, his hair plastered over his forehead. "Secure what's loose," he shouts.

One man falls, slithering across the deck to starboard, miraculously grabbing hold of a great winch to keep from being washed over. "Jesus Christ," Leaps growls watching him. "Clip yourselves to the bloody railings. You don't move around in this unless you're fastened on!"

With each moment the scene changes as the great boat heaves and curtains of lake water fall across the mid-ships, the men invisible to one another for seconds, vanishing in a wash of black. Men fumble with safety cables, the clips failing to close over the accreted ice. If they do fasten, they don't slide. Leaps' mouth is twisted in a grimace. "Never mind. Leave it."

Gripping the icy railing, Harry pulls himself toward the fore cabins and wheelhouse, now buried behind the ever-thickening snow. His gloves have little purchase and every few steps, he stops, frees a hand from the rail and, struggling for balance, he flaps like a one-winged bird. The wind steals away his breath, and he grapples with the weight of his coat. A crewman is at the door, holding it open, encouraging Harry to step in, thumping him amiably on the back.

Inside is a different world, and he is met with light, and friendly smells: cigarettes, kerosene, wet wool, and coal. He stands, dripping in the games room, melting into the warmth, the immediate illusion of safety making him feel as though he is drunk. Perhaps the blow isn't so bad, he thinks. We'll stay snug and battened-down and be in Midland in a few hours.

Some of the men have taken the chairs while others trust the floor, their backs pressed firmly against hard surfaces. Four men play Euchre, the Kittie sliding on the floorboards between them as the boat mounts and falls. Jake is there, crouching with a few others, his thighs straining under his sodden trousers. He fixes his gaze intently on Harry and gestures for him to join. Harry would rather sit with David Lee, who huddles in a corner alone, his sketchbook propped up on his knees. His head is bowed, and his sandy-coloured hair hangs in desolate strings that half-cover his face. It's unnerving and impressive to see how he manages to draw in these seas as though he is deep below the wildness that moves across the lake's surface, given over entirely to his art.

Jake gestures to Harry again, his face set in a scowl, and Harry, realizing that David prefers his own company, weaves his way over to the card players. One of the men slides over, making a place for him next to Jake, who now glowers at the opaque porthole, his face a symmetry of hard, determined lines.

Sitting beside Jake is like being at the mouth of a cave and Harry feels the recent surge of warmth and camaraderie drain.

"I'd like to take a watch on deck," Jake declares. Another of the card players laughs and with a derisive gesture, he throws down a queen of spades. "Don't be an ass, Spence. No one wants to be out in this."

"We'd be better off than here."

We'd be better off. Harry feels himself tighten against Jake, vehemently resisting what feels like Jake's dark draw. "Now, you are thinking about how we could be better off, but you weren't thinking of that before, when we were milling about at the harbour, making ready to board. What was it you heard on the docks again, Jake? About now bad it might get?" He closes his mouth, feeling the other men's eyes on him.

"What are you talking about?" One of the card players asks, his eyes sliding from Harry to Jake.

"Just that there was word going around the Fort William docks of a big blow, and some of us might not have joined if we'd heard, that's all," Harry keeps his voice smooth, not wanting to start anything.

"Hearsay," says Jake tersely. "Not much more than tittle-tattle. Not a real prediction. And anyway, it wasn't picked up by the Canadian side."

Harry stares at him, thinking how easy it is for Jake to sidestep responsibility. Feeling Harry's scrutiny, Jake looks down at his hands, spread wide against the floorboards, the flesh turning white under his weight.

"Why *did* you come, Harry?" he asks suddenly.

The question sets off a new wave of frustration and confusion. Harry tries to recall making the choice to come — something to do with Connor, a pull to see him again, but also the sly wish to push the time off, to go around it. Just for a few days anyway, until he could sort himself out. And then wistful

Jake, on the Fort William dock, deliberately reeling him in, making his silent appeal.

"Christ, Jake. You pressed me, even if you didn't say"

"Don't be stupid. I said *I* was joining, that's all."

"It was more than that."   He spears Jake with a look, certain Jake's just lying.

Jake's eyebrows twitch upward, his eyes alive with a question, but before he can ask Wright strides into the room. Leaps Levine lopes behind him, dripping and wind-whipped. Men who had been speaking, are suddenly silent. Wright wears a thick navy sweater, and he stands squarely, bracing himself against the bulkhead.

"Now, boys – we've got new weather to deal with. You might have noticed." The men laugh and Wright grins. "We've made some small changes and you won't be in Midland tonight, sorry to say to those of you who've got sweethearts – *or whatever* – waiting for you there." More laughter.

Many of the men watch Wright with fervent admiration but to Harry, Wright seems off, his words too bright, too shiny. He feels himself strain to catch hold of the deeper currents in Wright, to really see the darker ebb and flow. He looks over at David whose head is cocked as he nonchalantly draws. He thinks of how David has drawn the captain, the picture still folded and in his coat. Dave had aptly captured Wright's puffed-up conceit about the *Carruthers* and his capabilities as Captain.

Wright beams at each exhausted man in turn.

"Wheelsman Ross has laid in a course that'll take us straight down the lake and away from the bay. We'll let the blow push us along the big water, safe from rocks, and find a snug port along the eastern shore. In no time, we'll put into harbour, and tomorrow, when all this nonsense is done, we'll make for Midland and drop the damn load. Think winter's trying to tell us something, eh? Time to change up our oars for our skates. Well, this boat," he claps the bulkhead lovingly, "will get the job done even if it means a bit of a delay. And we've got the best damn crew on the lakes to do it." The men cheer and those sitting on the floor thump the floorboards with their hands. Wright holds them all in a long and generous smile. As Harry looks around the room, he sees that the men, like him, need *this* Wright.

"All right then. Here's what we're going to do. Some of you will take a turn with engine room duties, relieving the stokers, coal passers and oilers. Those boys down there will be *awful* tired." Smiling, he looks over meaningfully at Leaps and Leaps silently points his long finger toward Harry and Jake and then two or three of the others – probably the largest or strongest of the deckhands. Harry nods his head, silently dreading going below deck in these seas. "Now, you others will keep the decks clear of debris and check for places where the water is boarding. We'll take whatever measures we must to keep her dry. Stay lively and listen to First Mate Levine here for any instruction, boys. This should all be finished quite soon. Maybe by mid-morning. In the meantime, you lads headed to the engine room, take a quick breakfast before you go. Cook will have something for you. Take care out there, boys. Use your safeties when you move around the decks."

David Lee suddenly and surprisingly speaks. His tone is level, unaffected. "The new safeties don't work with the ice, Captain."

Scowling, Leaps interjects, "You'll have to tie-off, using a hitch, big enough that your line still slides as you go." Someone moans in dissent.

"I know, boys," Wright raises his enormous palm. "You don't want to be fiddling with knots and ropes," he stares implacably down at his boots for a long moment, "as if this is a wooden schooner we're on."

Lifting his face, nodding encouragingly, Wright continues. "We'll get these new safeties improved when she's put up in dry dock. You tell Levine here when you come upon a bit of equipment that's not performing. Everything on the *James Carruthers* is modern but that doesn't mean all of it's better. I'm starting a list. But for now, we'll make do as we must."

Leaps is glaring, as if daring David, or any of the men to argue, but David doesn't lift his eyes from his page.

"Sunday morning service will commence now," the captain goes on, playfully formal, slightly irreverent, "even for those descending immediately to the fires of the engine room." Chortling and snorts from the men. Wright slips a worn black Bible from under his sweater. "We'll keep it short, mind. Just a couple of verses. I think the Lord will forgive us. And then to breakfast, the engine room lads first." The boat suddenly bucks and rolls and Wright is knocked hard against the bulkhead, but he doesn't go down. "She knows how to take those big ones, eh boys? Feel how she corrects?" His grin is complicit, infinitely affectionate.

Harry looks around him at the crew. It dawns on him how hard Wright works to keep them from being afraid. *That* is the false note. They should be worried. The storm is bigger, more voracious than they'd dreamed of, maybe worse than anything any of them had ever endured before. He wills himself to

imagine a harbour, and when he does, it's Goderich that comes to his mind. The movement of the boat will quiet as the great laker slips into the lee of the Goderich bluff, the heavy docking lines securing her to the waiting dock. They must simply hope for shore, he decides. They must pin themselves to it.

"We're in this together, lads," Wright says finally, his tone at once ceremonious and cheering. He nods at them in encouragement. "Now listen up."

Clearing his throat, he slides out a pair of spectacles from his jacket and positions the Bible at a comfortable distance. "Let's start with Genesis 1:9-10.

'Then God said, "Let the waters below the heavens be gathered into one place, and let the dry land appear"; and it was so. God called the dry land earth, and the gathering of the waters. He called seas; and God saw that it was good.'"

Wright makes a small grunting sound and the men strain, necks stretched, heads cocked like dogs, listening. "And there's this one. Jeremiah 5:22, is it?" He silently frowns down at the page, at first reading, only his lips moving. "Yes, so it is."

"Do you not fear Me?' declares the Lord 'Do you not tremble in My presence? For I have placed the sand as a boundary for the sea, An eternal decree, so it cannot cross over it. Though the waves toss, yet they cannot prevail; Though they roar, yet they cannot cross over it.'"

Wright is perplexed-looking, as though he isn't sure why he chose such a gloomy passage. One of the men calls out *amen* and others shift their weight. The moment passes and Wright moves on with a flourish.

"Psalm 95:5 – all right lads, we are almost done." He readjusts the Bible, his great fingers running over the page as if to further decipher the meaning of the words. 'The sea is His, for it was He who made it, and His hands formed the dry land.'"

Another of the men calls out a solemn *yes.*

"Well, and here's the kicker, lads. This all you need to know: Psalm 107:29. How many times have your father and I read this during a blow, eh Levine? And we always make port soon after."

"'He caused the storm to be still, So that the waves of the sea were hushed.'"

There is a moment of silence before the men struggle to rise, pull on wet coats, tug soggy caps over their heads.

"Your mothers will be pleased you lads attended service this morning," Wright says, winking brightly. "They'll want to *thank* me. You can tell them what a devout man I am."

"Thanks, Captain," one of the men says affably, doing up his coat as he files past. Others mumble their assent and one by one they all go out the companionway door and are swallowed by falling snow.

~

Over the days Harry spent with Flo, he'd felt himself emerge, as though he were stepping from a fog into a clear strong sun. The evening before he was to join the provisions boat, they sat next to one another at the top of the bluff, the ravine tumbling green and verdant, and beyond it, an apparently endless stretch of blue. They weren't touching but he felt her through his skin, an unequivocal presence.

Flo leaned back on her arms, squinting at the blazing lake while he told her about Connor and about Kat. "He treated her like she wasn't really there," he said. "She might as well have been a broom in the corner." He hadn't felt the need to explain a great deal to Flo. She was quiet as he spoke, making small escalations to show understanding, giving a measured and encouraging nod here and there.

"He was careless with Kat," she said finally, hooking one ankle over the other. "And with you, Harry. He made a lot of mistakes. Men like that do."

Harry shook his head stubbornly, not wanting to alter his view of his father. "He's probably still a bastard."

Flo looked over at him, her gaze steady, her body solid, relaxed in the warmth of the day. "Do you think he meant to hurt you, or her, like that?"

Harry shrugged. "How much work does it take to think of people?"

She bit her lip, frowning, one hand brushing a fly from her nose. "It shouldn't be work. It should be a back-and-forth."

That was precisely what he'd missed with Connor, Harry saw then, the back-and-forth, the assurance of a ball caught in the net or the feel of a weighted touch on his shoulder. "Not everyone's good at it," Flo went on. "I cared for someone once who was a complete failure." She reclined further, her elbows supporting her weight.

"Are you angry about it?" He asks.

"I was," she said, squinting at the water again. "If you go see him, you do that because it mends something in you, so it doesn't get in your way or hold you back, but you can't try and make people into what you want. It's pointless."

Flo had thrown open a door even if he'd yet to step through it. It occurred to him then that perhaps it would be possible to see Connor plainly, squarely, without the fog that seeped in from their past. He rolled to his side, his head propped in his hand and studied her profile. In the brightness of the day, and with the light pouring over them, he could see every line, every downy hair on her face. How beautiful she was, up close. He touched her neck, gently, where the skin was smooth and lightly tanned above her collar. Flo loved the sun, eschewing hats, often opening the top buttons of her blouse to the air. "I'm happy here with you, Flo. For the first time in a long while."

She turned and looked at him. "I am too, Harry. I'm very happy."

Harry took Flo's face between his hands, an astonishing face, and he kissed her. And she kissed him frankly, wholly, in return.

~

Thinking of Flo has not saved him from the hell that is the engine room.

After several hours of stoking so close to the boiler, Harry's thoughts swim as if his mind is boiled in a soup, and every muscle in his body aches and burns. The place is foul with coal dust, the air choking, and the men, like ghouls, wear cloth around their mouths and noses. Harry's sensibility slackens and dims.

Next to him, Jake vigorously digs a mound of coal, his shirtsleeves rolled back, his thick forearms levering up the load. His assault on the coal is punishing; nerves scurry up his neck and pull at the corner of his mouth. Harry is too strangled, too woolly-minded to see clearly but the impression he has, watching Jake, who remains welded to his shovel, is of Connor; Connor on the day that Kat left, heedless to anything or anyone around him, hearing nothing but the pulse of his own blood.

"Don't kill yourself with that, Jake," he mumbles through the maddening scarf. "The coal won't thank you."

"What?" Jake looks up, frowning, his eyes burning, perplexed as if he has only just realized that Harry is there, sweating and near-sick beside him. "You don't like engine work, do you, Darling? "

Harry stares back, gobsmacked at Jake's apathy. "The air down here's made you loopy," Harry says, laughing sourly, "if you think any of us *like* this." Jake shrugs and goes back to his digging, Harry slipping off his scarf for a moment, trying to grab hold of some air.

The heat has bent something in him, tugging him into a woozy swirl of grievance, dismay, his thoughts no longer his own but some dark thing that lurks much deeper. The helplessness he feels makes him pant.

One of the coal passers, a man named Donaldson, is on the brink of collapse. He drops his load, bends over double and surrenders to an agonizing coughing fit. Brown, a beefy-looking stoker, sets down his shovel and watches. "Not fit to breathe down here," he mutters through gritted teeth, stepping over to thump the man's back.

Chief Engineer Farley levels Brown with a piercing stare. "Cowlings", he snaps. Farley's irritation is palpable; it has fused with the terrible exertion of the *Carruthers'* moving parts, woven itself into the engine's whine.

"Listen to me." Farley peers at each man in turn, the men slick, filthy, and almost unrecognizable. "I'll explain this *only once*, boys. We've got two cowlings, yes? One of 'em has been twisted 'round by the wind and it's facing the wrong direction, so it's not letting in good air. It's a bad situation but you'll have to make do."

Brown stares dully at his shovel and then looks up at the stacks. "Another bloody design flaw," he pronounces. "How many of those does that make?"

Gordon Farley's patience has apparently run out. "Well *I* didn't bloody well design it, did I? Not supposed to have sustained winds like this on a goddamn lake, no matter how big the water is. But this is what we've got, so, get on with it." He turns his back on Brown who grunts and picks up his shovel.

Farley looks over at Donaldson, who still struggles to breathe. "Go aft and man that door at the fantail," he says, his tone slightly more encouraging. "Open it up for fresh air but when you spot a wave over the rail, you slam it shut right quick. You understand? Darling, you've been shovelling so long your arm's gonna fall off. You pass for a wee bit. And Spence, leave off the shovel and take up an oil can."

Jake leans on his shovel and studies Farley. Oiling is generally considered a lower-rung position in the engine room, just one up from the wiper, although oiling can be one of the most dangerous jobs on the lakes if the winds are high. Earlier, one of the oilers had almost gotten himself mangled in the engine, losing his footing when the boat had lurched sideways.

Harry expects Jake to be annoyed with the task, humiliated by it, but instead, he shrugs, his expression unreadable despite an explosion of ticks and shivers, the expression of a protest he won't acknowledge. Picking up the grease gun, Jake fills it with oil from the can, and squarely sets himself against the violent movements of the boat.

~

They are to push the engine to full speed so the *James Carruthers* might keep ahead of the swells. "Captain Wright's

Valerie Mills-Milde

ordered seventy-five revolutions per minute when her stern's down," Chief Engineer Farley grimaces "and then when her fanny's showing we throttle back, on his orders only."

He's been communicating with Wright over the on-ship telephone, constantly making adjustments to the throttle. The sounds of the engine have begun to change, the whine higher pitched and with it, there is a deafening rattle. Farley listens closely, his neck stretched, his eyes focused upward on the frantically vibrating bulkheads.

Wiping the corner of his eyes with his thumbs, he sniffs and leans over the wireless box, his shoulders humped while he taps in his message. With his headphones on, and his face and clothes blackened, he resembles a beetle. He pauses, frowning down into the box. "Christ." He taps in a message again. This time, after a minute of waiting, he throws down the headphones and curses again. "Not worth a damn. Wires are dead." Brown glances up for a brief moment, but looks away, saying nothing. They are all likely thinking, *add it to the list of ball-ups and failures.* Farley makes his way over to the communication tube on the engine room wall – an old-fashioned system that will carry his voice up to the wheelhouse through a series of metal pipes.

"Hello, Sir," he calls in. "Trying to raise you now, Captain."

Wright's disembodied voice is thin and tinny when it finds the engine room, as though Wright has been somehow diminished to the size of mouse. "Onboard electrical is done. Communications with it. We'll make do with the pipe works, Farley – it's tried and true, eh? Hasn't let us down yet." There is muffled muttering, as if Wright might have his hand over the tube, giving a direction to Wheelsman Ross.

Farley nods his head tersely. "Can't we slow her, Sir?"

"Seas are up again," says Wright meaningfully. "The troughs are deepening, the climb more strenuous and the drop sharper. Having the propeller turn too high with her backside up is going to have us losing a blade, or worse."

"She's straining, Sir."

"*New engine*, Farley. Let's keep her as happy as we can, and she'll do the rest. This has got to settle soon."

"Is there a break in the sky, Captain Wright? "

Wright doesn't answer immediately. "Everything blows itself out. Eventually, anyway. Keep a man on this tube and convey orders, minute to minute."

Farley turns to Harry. "Come over here and give your ear to the Captain, Darling. Call out orders good and loud." He leaves Harry with his ear pressed to the horn while he weaves his way over to the throttle and waits. Taking in a breath, Harry puts his mouth to the metal tube. "It's me, Captain Wright. Harry Darling."

"Darling! Good lad. Now listen carefully – make sure you pass on what I'm telling you exactly." Wright's words, directed as they are straight into his ear, pierce his centre, his chest heaving with a wish for direction. But there is also obstinate refusal. He's torn between wanting to cling to Wright's words, and the urge to wail at the man for leading them out in this.

The great boat's stern lifts, the engine room floor now put at a terrible angle, and Harry can hear the tell-tale scream of the propeller as it spins uselessly in the air.

"Stay with me, Darling. Listen to my voice. Throttle back, Darling. Tell Farley – throttle back."

16

Sunday
Huron Shore,
A Boy and a Broken Wheel.

A glittering telltale of ice forms on the road. The fog hasn't lifted, and a heavy dampness penetrates the wool of his trousers and coat. Connor eyes the musty sheepskin that lies roughly folded on the floor and tugs it over his legs. It is decades old, the fleece yellowed and flecked with black, the skin gouged; the dead weight of it sitting on him is repellent but he has nothing else with him. His sisters and he had worn sheepskins when they were children, the coats oppressively heavy, the three of them lumbering around the farm, awkward as toy soldiers. "Nothing will keep you warmer," Ethan had pronounced. Ethan was right of course. "A bit of discomfort's a small price to pay to keep yourself from freezing to death." What would Ethan make of mink coats and stoles, the garments light but dense, the fur tips discouraging of water. Ethan would likely not approve of the luxury, and ever faithful to his sheep, he wouldn't throw them over for a more profitable animal. The man was as unmovable as a bloody fieldstone; Connor smiles inwardly in the wake of unaccustomed affection. He'd felt the loss of Ethan, but it wasn't without bitterness. There were times after Ethan's departure when Connor felt his father had slipped away like a thief in the night, having foisted on him Darling farm, Sophie, the girls – all of his shabby burdens, in fact.

As Ethan's wagon clatters over the hardening surface, the icy slush bounces from the road up and over the wagon's rough wooden sides. He is barely able to see ten feet in front of him, the fields and woods paling away in the fog. He drives on, navigating by feel for the most part, reluctantly having to trust the horse. Trees emerge out of the murk like long-armed monsters, and seagulls cry. He can smell the water and the cold that comes off it.

~

He's been on the road for an hour when he hears the crack and splintering of wood, the wagon jumping violently and then shimmying off on an angle to the left before jolting to a stop. The horse starts and tries to break but the entrenched wagon acts as an anchor.

He knows even before he gets down to inspect it that one of the wheels has given way. Connor sits for a moment, swearing softly. *Christ!* Perhaps he's hit a rock or a bit of debris. A useless wagon, the same one he'd driven from Darling Farm all those years before, the same wagon that Ethan, and then he, had used to transport fleece to market.

Although he'd changed them out a few seasons back, the wheels have grown brittle. Crouching down, he finds that one has broken right through, and it hangs in two jagged pieces. There will be no fixing it. He rubs his hands together to raise the heat to his fingers. Standing, he pulls the tarp from the back of the wagon. Fixed to the wagon floor is a green-painted box, and inside of it is a spare wheel and a few scant tools, Ethan's tools, ancient-looking, the handles stained with black. He eyes them, taking in their simple practicality. Ethan had placed them there, knowing that someday they'd be needed. Connor blinks at the toolbox as though it might talk, wishing it might, wishing he might hear his father again, and he lifts it to the snowy ground. Grunting softly, he undoes the fastenings that hold the unused wheel.

He opens the hinged box and then, straightening, he stares into a world transformed by weather, remembering the shock of cold on the day Ethan died. He imagines the secret frailties in the old man's heart, which had simply forced it to stop. Ethan would not have chosen to go. Such dereliction wouldn't have been in his nature.

Endings come when they come, Kat would say, and Connor can forgive Ethan dying. But some obturate part of Connor holds Ethan to one particular failure, even while knowing it was unintended, even while recognizing that his own expectations of Ethan had been altogether unfair; Carey was that failure. For all Ethan's prosaic wisdom, and his steadfastness, he'd been utterly unable to keep the proverbial wolf from the door.

~

The day after the manager made his offer to Connor, Carey came back to Darling Farm.

Coming from the field and seeing the green-polished buggy gleaming in the lane, a shock ran through Connor. He found Sophie, calmly unpegging clothes from the line. She didn't wait for him to speak. "Carey heard about Ethan's passing," she said stonily, her back to him as clothes fell stiffly into the basket at her feet.

"Wasted no time, then, did he? It's only been a few months."

Sophie armoured herself with a frown, her hands not stopping, her eyes clamped down on her work. After a long silence, she dropped a peg into her wide front pocket and then took down a sheet, snapping it smooth before folding it. "As I said, he'd heard about Ethan."

"Well, news of a death travels."

She bent down, arranging the shirts and linens in the basket, her face angled away. "You might wonder why he came."

Seeing her crouched down, deliberately not looking at him, Connor thought back to when he'd last seen them together, Carey's finger pressed to her lips, Sophie quietened and limp as a doll in Carey's arms. It had been the start of an unravelling, only made worse later, with Ethan's passing. Connor felt a spark of anger in his chest. "I don't care why he's here, but if I had to guess, you have something to do with it. I'd say he came to see you." Feeling slightly sick, he'd begun to walk away.

"He's staying," Sophie's voice followed him, detached, and hovering like smoke. "Because he won't leave. Because I have no sway with him. He wants to buy the place, Connor."

When Connor turned, her face was blank.

"He's not welcome, that's all. Send him on his way or I will."

"If it was that simple, I would."

Connor stood, dumbfounded. The man didn't belong here, he had no place with them, and if it came to it, if Sophie was too weak to do it, he would run him off. Ethan's shotgun was stored in the tack shed. He imagined Ethan with the gun

resting on his shoulder as he trudged, bowlegged and wordless over the field, determined to guard his sheep. Ethan never hesitated to shoot, and it was strange that he hadn't thought to teach his son the skill.

The day after Ethan died, Connor had sat weeping on a hay bale, cleaning and oiling the gun, his grief for the old man catching him. In a childish and fanciful way, which could never be spoken of, he'd believed that the wolves had observed Ethan's departure, that they watched the farm with their narrowed yellow eyes, that they conspired against him, their furry jaws moving up and down, tactical in their deliberations. Now, thinking of Carey on the land, he'd thought of the gun and how he might use it.

"We don't want trouble," Sophie said darkly, as if reading Connor's thoughts. "We'll have to make the best of things. Besides, it might turn out all right. Carey won't stay here all the time. His work is in Montreal, and he hates the country. But he can help," she said obliquely, "with paying for things."

His eyes narrowed, regarding her. "Good you've worked it all out. That must have been quite a talk you had with him."

Sophie frowned down at the thin ground, as if gathering up what else she might say. "Your father would have wanted us to hang on here as best we could."

With the mention of *father,* the jagged thing he'd held inside stirred and then slashed its way out. His face felt as though it was on fire.

"Is that man really your cousin?"

He required no answer.

She watched him, suddenly wary. "You don't understand."

Tipping his head back, he looked away from her, his eyes pasted obstinately to the sky. "No."

"His people, in Ireland", she pressed on, her voice deadened, "are distant relations of ours. He came here looking for work and lived with us. He slept in the room with my brothers."

"A room close enough to your own." He still wouldn't look at her.

"You think I was that girl with her eye on the handsome young man, that I was flattered by his interest? It wasn't like that. It wasn't a *choice* to be with him. Carey gets what he wants, you have to understand that about him. He doesn't really care about other people."

At last, something in her seemed to give way and she sat down heavily on the ground, her head in hands. He took a step closer, awkwardly standing over her, strangely unable to help her or to leave. "He only watched me at first", she went on, "and then, one day he followed when I went on an errand for my mother. On my way home he took me by the arm to an empty storeroom. It's not what I wanted." Connor looked at the fields then, where the sheep were stupidly grazing, round lumps against a jagged line of trees. He recently lost a lamb and he imagined in the nights to come he would lose more. Brownie was a help, but no match for predators. His mind rambled away from Sophie, from the story she told, and he thought, *I'll have to use the gun.* "It happened twice more," she went on, not looking at him, her eyes screwed down in memory, "but after the first time, I didn't fight him."

They were silent for a long time and then she dragged herself up, cleaning her hands on her skirt. She picked up the basket of linens and looked squarely at him, willing him to hear. "I started to wear my sister's clothes to hide the size of my belly, but I couldn't conceal it forever. My mother was suspicious. She confronted me one day and I told her. What else could I do?" Her tone hardened and levelled. "I thought my father would kill Carey at first, and then I was worried that Carey might kill him. The best would have been if Carey left, went back to Ireland or to another place but he wouldn't do that. He's not one for giving up what he thinks is his."

She folded her arms across her chest as if to keep some unwanted emotion pinned there. "My parents were scandalized but I wasn't the first girl to get pregnant before a marriage. It was easily fixed. They decided we would marry in the church, either that or I would have to give the child up." She sighed, pulling a loose strand of hair from her face.

"I left Carey when you were just over a year old. I couldn't manage him. The rough treatment, but more than that the way he made me feel. One day when Carey was away, I packed a bag and I left. The train took us as far as Cornwall and I managed to find a job there, in a shipping office. It's where I met Ethan. He'd come in to arrange for a livestock shipment. He didn't ask me about why I was there, alone with my child. He didn't ask anything. You know how he was, content to watch over."

They were quiet then, with the mention of Ethan. "You remember the day Carey first came here, Connor. It wasn't hard for him to find me. He worked as a law clerk in Montreal after I left him, and then later, he trained as a lawyer – I suppose he knew where and how to look." She sighed. "But you must understand, I didn't *want* to be found. I cared deeply for Ethan."

Connor blinked, a numbness creeping over him, his earlier rage gone. There was no anger, no pity, just a blank nothingness, mistrust hanging on him like a set of outsized clothes.

"You see, there was no divorce between Carey and me." She'd looked at him, still willing him to comprehend. "He feels he is owed – *entitled* – to me."

They could hear Dot rattling a pot inside the house, and Carey's voice, his laugh, as he talked to her. He envied Dot then, and June, because Carey had no claim on them. He could remain as nothing to them if they chose.

"So that's what I am. I am Carey's," he said, his voice hollow.

"No. You are much more."

"But that's what you see sometimes, when you look at me."

She didn't deny it.

He could think of nothing to do then but to go back to the field. He took Brownie with him and sat on a large outcrop of rock near where the sheep were grazing. He imagined a life on the farm, Carey as an overlord, Sophie a shell of a person, someone he barely knew.

Early the next morning, Carey stood on the porch in his shirtsleeves, watching Connor and June as they brushed out the fleece. His demeanor was both attentive and relaxed, and he was smoking. He smiled over at them.

"Con," he said, "you know, you could go to school. The military college in Kingston, or any place really. This is backbreaking work. You won't want to do this forever, trust me." It was as if Carey had read his thoughts, seen that what he wanted was escape. But he also heard in Carey's words a nudge toward the road, an intention to supplant and Connor felt a twist inside.

June looked up, her bright face clouding over. "We work the place together," she said. "We don't mind that it's hard."

Carey studied Connor then. "Is that so? You like it well enough, then, Con? I could make it possible for you to go, to never have to come back again to this shitty place."

He stared at Carey, who was still smiling, one shiny patent boot hooked over the other. Behind him, on the other side of the door, Sophie and Dot were laying out breakfast in the kitchen, the sound familiar, haunting and bringing on a terrible and sudden sadness.

This was helplessness and it was a noose around his neck. He'd almost choked, looking at June, who so boldly faced this stranger.

"I have to take these fleeces to town today," he said, knowing there was only one thing he could do, short of killing the man.

~

It's heavy work, levering up the wagon, the jack resisting, then jamming. He takes a swing to loosen it and the skin of one hand strikes rusted metal, his hand tearing. It is a moment before the blood rises to the surface of his skin, beads and then begins to snake its way into his sleeve. He has nothing to wrap it with. Kat would have gauze and cotton and carbolic soap, but Kat isn't here with him. He thinks of the afternoon he drove with her to a farm where a man lay in a field, crushed by his thresher. The man's sons had been unable to move him to the house, the body pinned by a mash of bloody clothing. Kat had leaned over the shattered body, tenderly but determinedly cutting away the fabric, binding the man with sheets into a single piece so that they could lift him. He had felt awed and yet diminished watching her, and later, it came to him why. She showed no hesitation. She withheld nothing.

He remembers her now like a river. Kat never metered her love. It circulated effortlessly through her, and she didn't tug it back, as he had, like you would something dangerous.

The blood has begun a slow and steady drip onto the ground, staining the snow in vivid bursts of colour. He takes the tail of his shirt between his teeth and tries to rip it but the cloth won't give way. Breathless, light-headed, he closes his eyes, the cold feel of snow on his face strangely comforting.

Grunting, he turns back to the wagon. Using his one good hand, and with his weight against the wrench, he begins to loosen the old wheel. It takes a long time because the bolts are badly rusted. Part way through, he pauses to peer at his throbbing hand, the blood now pooled at the site of the wound. He thinks of Rob McNeil and his big-boned sons, how they do the ploughing with McNeil, the planting and the harvesting. He's watched them load timber onto McNeil's flatbed wagon, the lumbering horses pulling the load, the bright-haired boys easy and light-footed. In that moment, it isn't envy he feels but an impenetrable solitude. He is taken-up by it. Strangely, his pain is the only bit of light in the grey, his mind sharpening to it, the pain pulsing through him like the drumming of his heart.

By the time he has the wheel off, the fog is lifting. The lake emerges, slate-grey, and then vanishes again behind a thick fall of sleet. With some difficulty, he attaches the new wheel, secures it, and in the course of tightening the bolts, the aged wrench gives way. The gash on his palm opens anew, the blood streaming down his fingers. He wipes them roughly on his

trousers. He'll make do with another smaller fiddly wrench. There is an impressive selection of wrenches in Ethan's old box.

When he is finally done, he straightens stiffly and scowls up at the sky. The light has begun to change, and a bulbous cloud marches from the west. He shivers, damp through now to his bones. The cold is even more biting, and the wind is rising.

Connor sets his back against the horse, giving him his weight, the horse warming him through his coat. His loneliness is like a crow that scrutinizes him from one of the naked tree limbs, the world around him reduced to black and white, all colour gone. Perhaps it has been that way for a long time. He is brought back suddenly to the blue of Harry's eyes, the heightened red in his cheeks when he was excited.

There were pieces of Harry's childhood that Connor had missed, observations blotted out like sun behind cloud, moments of almost utter blindness. He hadn't always recognized Harry, at least not the *child* Harry.

When Harry was nine, he and the McNeil boys built a little bridge across the stream. They worked for two full days, cutting lumber, shoring up the posts, and nailing the planks together. McNeil supervised from a distance, advising the boys but letting them do the work. Once they were done, Harry came bounding like a puppy into the yard where Connor was splitting wood.

"We can cross, now," he said, breathless and bright with the spring cold. "Mr. McNeil says the bridge is a solid as could be."

"That's good work, Harry."

"Well, you could come see for yourself." He opened his arms wide in an inviting gesture.

There had been a moment of reluctance on Connor's part, Connor leaning on the axe handle, his gaze screwed down. "Rain's coming," he said in way of explanation. "Wood won't split itself." The smile dropped from Harry's face and something of the light in the boy faded. "But I can spare some time," Connor said, the meagreness of him on display, the insufficiency.

The boy had taken his hand, all forgiveness, all shared excitement. Now, as he thinks of Harry half-dragging him toward the stream, his cheeks vermillion, the round blue eyes eager, Connor flushes. Why has he imagined that expressions of delight, of affection are too dearly bought? Why has he felt he has to swallow his love for the boy as though he were swallowing a bag of stones? If the boy were to show up now and make such an invitation, he hopes to God he'd jump at it.

~

Connor slowly drives the wagon beside the line of bent and ragged cedars that separate the road from the beach. The lake is buried in grey-white clouds of spray that move upward through horizontal lashings of snow. It is the sound of the water, the thunder and hammer of the waves exploding on shore that make the lake impossible to ignore. Every so often, the horse shimmies with fear, then races forward before it veers away.

On the other side of the road is a wooded ravine, beyond which is the river. Already, new snow is building, clinging to the swaying limbs of trees, some still wearing the unfallen leaves of summer.

He traverses the river by way of the wooden bridge, the horse not liking the sound of the wooden planks beneath his hooves, his head pulling, his feet prancing. "Get on," Connor barks. "Steady."

Connor drives in a kind of trance with the drum of the lake in his ears, the snow swirling almost seductively in front of him. For the moment, there is only the illusion of road. It is too much of an effort to move his eyes from the tips of the horse's ears. He resists looking either left or right, preferring to rest his gaze in a narrow band of horse, and snow and more snow.

They crawl along through an ashen, unchanging light. He has no idea how long he's been on the road now. Beside him, to the east, is a fence, snow drifting high over the posts, the wind making twisters, and on the periphery of his gaze is an object: a dense caramel-coloured shape, stalky and stiff and pinned to a green motorized truck. He pulls up close, peering, his cuff to his eyes to clear away the wet.

It is an animal, a steer or a bull judging by the size, stiffened and leaning into the truck, its legs brittle and branch-like, its tongue lolling and covered in white. The small open eyes are filmy. The wire fence between the bull and the truck is buried deep in the animal's chest. The vehicle, an unusual sight in the county, looks utterly vacant, the driver's side door partly opened. It must have skidded off of the road and hit the unlucky bull. But now, the snow and the plunging temperature give the illusion that the animal has met its death by freezing.

He studies the frozen cattle beast as he drives past; he has no idea who owns it or the truck that killed it. The freshening storm and blowing snow have rendered the farms he passes unrecognizable. He wonders if it is McNeil's beast and tries to measure the distance he's come. Can he be as far as McNeil's place? No, he reasons, he can't be that close to his own home and not know it. Besides, McNeil won't have left any of his cattle out in this, not an attentive and observant man like him.

The mounting wind has recently brought down the limb of a tree and it sprawls across the road, the tips quivering in the gusts. It is obviously a part of a dead tree, sodden with rot by the look of it. He can either lead the horse around it or use the rope he carries in the back to drag it.

Ahead, perched on the limb is a smudge of dark, a bent figure, its back to the wind. "Damn," mutters Connor swinging himself down from the wagon. He stands for a moment. Who would be out walking in this? And then he thinks of the motorized truck, the dead bull. So, someone else was on this road with him. The horse stomps impatiently, its head tossing in the brutish wind and Connor grips the heavy strap of harness to keep himself from toppling.

"Who's there?" he calls, the gusts snatching up his voice. "You all right?"

There is no answer. He steps away from the horse and moves closer. A face peers up at him, a young face, round, congealing blood over the eye and down into the crevice of the nose.

Connor squints down and sees a boy who is no more than fourteen. The shape of him, the slump of his shoulders, the softness in his outline, seems strangely familiar. A thrust of recognition comes. This is the Murray boy from the farm on the other side of Rob McNeil's.

There is a lift in the wind, and with it a wall of snow screams in from the lake. The road and everything vanishes; the boy, the fallen limb, the horse and wagon. When the wind slackens, the Murray boy reappears from out of the slurry. He hasn't moved and his eyes have remained fixed to Connor, his expression unguarded and intent.

17

Sunday Morning
The James Carruthers,
Fighting Blind

A stoker, an Englishmen out of Bristol named Todd slumps over his shovel. He has never felt a ship's effort so much as he does the *James Carruthers'*, he says, not on all the Atlantic crossings he's made. "Long-hulled boats have no business in seas like this. She might buckle like a bit of scrap." His tone it too bright, his eyes feverish. Chief Engineer Farley snaps at him. "Keep your prognostications to yourself, Todd. Pull yourself together and put your back into it." Todd blinks at the glistening mound of coal. He grunts and stabs ferociously at it with his shovel. The air is electric, painful, and it contains the men's unspoken thoughts like a thousand stinging bees. Finally, at ten A.M. a fresh crew is sent down but Farley, whose face is racoon-like, his eyes ringed with black, his hair coarsened with coal dust, doesn't leave his post for relief. They all know that Wright won't trust anyone else with her engine.

They move on deck, lashed to the rails, while the hull of the *Carruthers* shudders, her metal bones screaming and groaning. Pushed by an indescribable wind, the snow is horizontal, the spray ascending so high it disappears into cloud. Towering triads of waves break over the laker, each wave larger than the one before, the third a monstrous wall of water

descending, smashing down on them like a huge fist. For a few seconds, the boat's stern is entirely buried in water and then miraculously, as if the lake inhales, the water clears, the boat levels.

A few feet away, Jake grips a cable, his stance wide and planted, his eyes fixed hungrily on the water. The lake gives the impression of paralyzing cold. Nothing in Harry's memory has ever looked so frigid. On their trough sides, the waves are a dense black, smooth as slate. The crests froth and crackle, and the backs shiver with a thousand ripples.

The deck of the *Carruthers* is tilting horribly to starboard. There, in a trick of the light, in the small movement of Jake's leg, the forward lean of his body, his hand loosening its grip on the cable, Harry thinks he sees Jake ready himself for a launch into the heaving lake. He reaches out, grabs hold of the fabric of Jake's coat. "We should get in," he says, pointing to the fore house where the others have apparently gone.

It's a long moment before Jake turns and looks at him, his eyes strangely blank. Harry awkwardly loops and then reefs his safety around a cable, taking it in both hands while Jake hitches his above Harry's. Together they walk, stopping with each new assault of water, and then the most immense wave of all is on top of them. Harry lifts his head just as the aft-structure is entirely swallowed.

In the pause that follows, he catches his breath and stares. The aft house is a ruin, its portholes and doors torn away, and the structure now open to the seas, the loneliness of it more terrible than the storm. It occurs to him that Cook would be in the galley and there might be others besides him, crewmen hunkered down in their bunks. He hovers over his choices, his body rigidly bracing for the next sweep of water. He can turn, move toward relative safety of the fore house, leave whoever is back there to their own luck, but he's instantly horrified by this shadowy ruthlessness in himself. *Go back*, a clear, still voice says inside him. Since sailing out of Fort William, he's felt something reach for him, a sort of reckoning although he's kept himself at arms length from it, battened down in memories. *All this mess must be accounted for, squared,* he thinks, gazing now at the gutted superstructure. *There won't be any turning away.*

Pointing aft, he gestures to Jake, his expression set in a question. Nodding, Jake turns, his shoulders humped into the wind, his back to Harry. They pass a crewman on the starboard side, hooked on with his safety and moving in the other direction. He lifts his hands to his mouth, hollering over the roar. "Just Cook left back there. Captain ordered everyone out, but he won't leave."

Time presses on them. Ahead, Jake is a small dark figure, bullying his way through the dark plumes of spray before improbably re-emerging. The iced deck stretches between them, each man moving, deaf and blind, as though he is utterly on his own.

~

Cook appears stunned, when they find him, his hands shaking as he haphazardly gathers cans, dropping them into a flour sack. Under one of his thin arms, he clutches a large slab of wrapped cheese. "Here, take the sack," he says to Jake, his eyes glazed and huge. He points at the communication horn on the wall. "Captain wants supplies brought forward."

Jake grunts and then throws the sack over his shoulder. "We haven't time for more."

Cook stares at him and doesn't move. His teeth are chattering, and his colour is bad. "I feel safer in here. I'll wait it out. Take the food with you."

"You can't stay here." Jake jerks his head toward the broken portholes, the water streaming in.

Cook stares at Jake with surprising obstinacy.

"I'll bloody well carry you out if I have to."

Pressing himself against the worktop, Cook inches his hand behind his back and then remarkably he produces a long-bladed knife. The blade trembles in his hand as he holds it before him, his lips pulling back like a terrified dog. "I won't go."

Seeing the knife, Jake's eyebrows lift. "Don't be an ass. We haven't time. Put it down." Suddenly, the *Carruthers* bucks, throwing Cook, his bone-thin wrist smashing down on the worktop, sending the knife sailing into the water. Cook's face disassembles, his mouth opening in a silent wail, and he falls to his knees, the water lapping morosely at his waist.

"We won't make it off this boat."

Although Harry now believes this might be true, it's a shock to hear it spoken, as if the words make it truer. He wades over to Cook. "Look, we'll stay together. The fore house is in good shape, far as I can tell, and the men will be waiting for a bit of what you got gathered up there." He points to the swaying canvas sack. "Now, we have to move because the storm is going to take all this aft-section. You understand that, Cook. Jake and me won't go without you, and none of us stand a chance if we stay."

Cook stares uncertainly at Harry until resignation comes over him, and he wearily staggers to a stand. "Stay close," he hisses. "I'm not so steady on my feet."

Harry smiles encouragingly, wanting to ensure Cook won't balk. "All of us will be fine."

Jake now looks curiously, calmly at Harry, his gaze landing squarely on the lie; it's not at all sure that they'll be fine but strangely, Jake seems either oblivious or indifferent to their prospects. He shifts the sack on his shoulder and the three push through torrents of boarding water.

They brace themselves against the flow, hands flattened to the oak-panelled wall. Water will be pouring into the cabins and common rooms, thinks Harry. Knee-deep by now in the cabin he shares with Jake. He has nothing of value, nothing he cares about except for Kat's tin, and he imagines it being swept out, carried on violent currents, tugged down into an indistinct black. "I'm going to get my duffle bag," he shouts to Jake. "You carry on with Cook."

The laker is pummelled again, and she leans profoundly. Jake is dripping, his teeth bared. "No bloody time for scavenger hunts."

A surge of despair rises, followed by acquiescence – *let it go* – the voice inside says. Jake is well ahead of him now, almost to the deck and Harry pushes his thighs hard through the rising water to the open air, where Jake turns, scowling. "Cook, you got to loop yourself on with your safety," He mouths the words, and then he jabs at his belt, where his safety is unhooked and ready for use. Cook, flummoxed, pats at his coat with his free hand and shakes his head *no.* It's clear he hasn't got a safety line. Peering longingly in the direction from which they've come, Cook curls himself into the metal companionway.

Harry is behind him and inside the passageway when the first wave hits, Jake on deck, somehow managing to stay upright. In the pause before the next wave, Jake shouts, "I'll fix him to me."

Harry shakes his head. "I'm the bigger man," he hollers, "I'll take him."

Jake hesitates and then motions for Cook to step out. He is moving quickly, fastening himself on, and then he turns to Harry.

Harry's fingers are stiff with cold, and it takes a few moments to free his safety. "Try and come a little closer", he says holding it out and sliding toward Cook who stands, terrified and clinging to the shell of the aft house.

There is no time. When the wave hits, the *James Carruthers* pitches downward, and Cook is violently thrown. He lands hard on the icy deck and slides toward a hatch cover, and with the next toss of the boat, he slips further still. His leg catches in a loose cable, the cable twisting it horribly. They can't hear Cook over the wind, but they see the pained gape of his mouth and his eyes are inhumanely wide.

They crawl on their hands and knees, flattening themselves to the deck. They are almost to him. Harry counts the waves: one . . . two . . . and then the inevitable monstrous third devours them. When the water retreats, it has taken Cook with it. All Harry can think of is that they've been failed by others – that men like Wright, like Jake, had seen this coming and led them out here regardless.

Dragging himself to his feet, he turns to Jake, who remains prone and reduced to a pile clothes, featureless except for the white face, the eyes fixed on the spot where Cook was. Harry feels suddenly enraged, seeing him. "That man shouldn't have been on this boat," he bellows, his voice lost to the wind.

A hand emerges from the heap, Jake rising to his knees as he gropes and then clasps a narrow fending pole. Bewildered, he pulls himself to a stand, his eyes not straying from the place Cook disappeared.

Jake is barely recognizable now and Harry must squint to bring him into focus. The snow has collected in his hair, and his coat is encased in a thin layer of ice. It's as if Jake has been instantly crystalized, that his heart has stopped beating, that there is no blood in his veins.

Thoughts go around and around, and with them a growing certainty that he's been cheated. A scorching heat moves through him now. He won't see Flo again, he'll be lost to this bloody lake. Another parting, another forever parting, which he could do nothing to stop. His chest is painfully tight, his face on fire, and he no longer recognizes Jake as Jake but as some other thing. "You selfish, selfish bastard," Harry wails. In this moment, he can give Jake no name, just *you, you, you.*

It's as though Jake has been utterly erased, his features buried behind a sheath of white. Lurching toward him, Harry takes an enormous swing, Jake's figure not shifting or dodging, but rather remaining rigid as standing stone. His punch catches mid-centre, moving through the give of Jake's coat, and beneath it, finds Jake's belly. Jake doesn't make the slightest move toward defense. He absorbs the blow, bends over, gasping, straightening, the covering of ice sliding off his cap and shoulders, the snow shaken away to reveal the simian face. His eyebrows lift in surprise. The boat bucks and rolls but remarkably, Jake makes no effort to hang on.

With his punch delivered, Harry is spent. He slouches, against a ventilation stack, an unexpected relief flooding through him. He sees Jake turn slowly, stiffly toward the lake, his arms free and lifting. For one horrifying moment, he waits for Jake to take flight, to disappear over the side, seeing clearly for the first time that this is what Jake wants.

"For Christ's sake, take hold of something, Jake." Tears run lavishly from his eyes and are taken up in the pummelling spray. He reaches out to Jake to secure him, to repair the blow he's delivered, knowing it was undeserved and yet strangely grateful to Jake for receiving it.

A wave breaks, and this time he topples back, pulled by a force he can't have imagined. He slams hard into something unmovable, his head cracking. A great rush in his skull and then nothing but cold black.

~

Harry had been filling the animals' water reservoirs when Kat came into the shed.

"Harry."

He turned and saw her in the open doorway, her clothes old-fashioned and more formal than the ones she wore in her workshop, and her thick pale hair was pulled into a tight knot. She held a travel case in one hand, and in the other, the leather valise that carried her tools: the powders and brushes, the ribbons and hooks, the liniments and ointments.

Her face was grave, her colour drained. Even when he'd seen her at work, immersed in silence, Kat was brightly alive, as luminescent as if she held the moon inside. Now, her pallor made him think of the little dead boy, the child's blue lips, his infinite quiet, the awful stillness. Harry had the inexplicable feeling that she might die. "Are you sick, Kat?"

"No, not sick." For a moment, she'd looked away, as if searching for the words. "I've come to say goodbye."

The mink were rattling their enclosures, chattering, protesting. She looked over at their cages, a slight wince around her eyes, and then she gazed at Harry. "How much longer before these will be culled?"

"What?"

"It seems like they know," she went on. "All the noise they make. It must mean something."

He shook his head, not understanding her. "They're just hungry."

Nodding, still fixed to her own thoughts, she said, "Don't you see, Harry? They're hungriest near the end because Connor always runs out of food." She'd given Harry an imploring look. "What's coming for them is easier than this. They aren't really living."

Harry put down the leather gloves he'd been using to reach into the cages. Her strangeness was unsettling. And her clothes, her hair – he'd wondered if she was travelling for work, laying-out a corpse in a far-off town, maybe down in the city.

"You're going somewhere? For how long?"

She'd taken in a breath, as if preparing herself for the answer. It would have been hard for Kat to hurt him. "I don't know. I'm not sure when I'll be back."

"Not sure? A week? A month?"

She'd said nothing, studying him, as if gathering his image so that she could keep it close, like she might a token or a treasure. That's when it dawned on him; she was already grieving for him. "You aren't coming back," he'd said, stunned.

Strain pulled at the corners of her eyes, around her lips, but she'd kept her voice even. "Folly has sold the business. The new man who is going into the place will do all the work himself."

If that was all there was to it, there was no reason for her to go and no obstacle to her staying. "Just ask him to keep you on. You know everyone around here – there won't be a problem."

She firmly shook her head. "He has no use for me."

"Well, there are other places you could do your work. Goderich, maybe. Or find something else to do. You're good at so *many* things, and you could stay here with us – help with the mink."

"You'll be off playing lacrosse somewhere before you know it, Harry." She was unconvincing, her voice too low. She stood, holding a piece of herself back from him, a pain or an intention. "You *have* to go, when the time comes. You must."

He could see that whatever was unfolding, he wouldn't be able to change it. Frantic now, anger pushing its way in, he thought she wasn't being fair, deciding to go away. "You've always been here, Kat."

"A very long time. Since your mother died, anyway." Her words broke over him and fell to the ground at his feet; the pieces that had led her to this, the signs that, like a small child, he'd not seen; the crackling tension between Kat and Connor, Kat stricken and crying over the dead boy, and the countless times he'd watched Connor turn away from her. Beneath it all was the obscenity of the furrier's visit, and Connor's face when he emerged, panting, from the shed.

In Harry's mind, a picture of her disappointment and Connor's failure coalesced, growing truer, shaded more darkly. A few feet from him, Kat still held her bags, her face frankly anguished. There remained an unstoppable current of love between them. The loss he felt as he watched her go felt ancient, as if it had been entombed inside of him for longer than memory. He would have been devoured by it if hadn't have been for his gathering fury with Connor.

For a long while, he'd waited in the yard for Connor to emerge from the house. He wouldn't go inside and look for him. He hadn't wanted to share the air with Connor, he hadn't wanted to stand in the same room.

When Connor finally came down the steps, he was harried-looking, with his cap pulled low and his collar up despite the September warmth.

Harry strode toward him. "What did you do?"

Connor stopped, cocked his head, and studied Harry. He looked toward the shed, as if he'd find Kat still there. "She talked to you, then."

"Of course, she did. She wouldn't go without saying goodbye." Harry paused, his breathing almost pained. "She wouldn't go unless you wanted her to go."

Connor shook his head dismissively. "You don't know what you're talking about."

"I *know* Kat." The mix of despair and anger had begun to burn his lungs, his throat.

"She'd made up her mind. I couldn't do anything to stop it."

"I *know* you did nothing, what you always do, except when it comes to yourself."

Connor turned and looked at the road in bewilderment. "She only told me today that she was leaving."

"But you knew she had to be out of Folly's, that the new man wouldn't keep her on. She must have told you all that before today. You could have helped her, given her a place with us here. The words were circling around and around the anger, not lighting on it, the feeling of betrayal beyond what he could say. "You might as well have sent her away yourself."

Connor studied the ground, his eyes shifting over the patchy grass and the thistle. "It wasn't going to work, Harry. That's all."

"What does that mean?"

As he looked down at his father, he saw the narrowness of him, a bent wire, a man ill-equipped for freight. For a brief moment, there was a glint of recognition in Connor's eyes, a closely guarded shame, and then Connor shook his head as if to rid himself of it. He stared belligerently into the distance. "It's between Kat and me."

The exclusion in his words had cut him. The loneliness he felt had brought on rage. He wouldn't understand until later what he'd done then – that he'd put his hands around Connor's throat. That he'd squeezed, and howled and cried, making sounds he never knew a person could make.

It was Rob McNeil and his son Donald who peeled him off Connor, the two having come to ask for Harry's help with threshing. Donald was as big as Harry and just as strong but even with McNeil's help, he'd had difficulty prying Harry's hands away.

Once freed, Connor fell to his knees, gasping, but none of them paid him much mind. "What's all this, lad?" McNeil peered into Harry's face, his eyes piercing and sharp, but Harry hadn't been able to speak. He went into the house and filled a bag with clothes. By the time he came out, Connor had disappeared and only McNeil and Donald remained.

"We've given your father some water and sent him into the drive shed for a bit. You can sort all this out later. You'll stay with us until things cool down between you, Harry." McNeil said, his voice stern.

Harry was sixteen, almost a man, and yet he felt the obscurity of the orphaned.

"There won't be any sorting. Not now".

~

He'd walked down the laneway, leaving the McNeils to puzzle about what they'd just seen. With each step he felt he was following Kat, that he'd see her waiting for him where the lane met the road, but when he got there, the road was empty.

He took the way to Kincardine, thinking that Macey would know where Kat had gone. Macey would help him figure out what to do next, how he might find her. On foot, the journey was long, Harry burning-up on the inside, his boot heels leaving divots in the road, his head never lifting.

It was early evening when he got there, the harbour quiet and golden. Seeing Harry in the doorway of his fish shack, his bag slung over his shoulder, Macey sighed. "Walked all the way, I guess. Your boots are awful dusty." Harry had begun to cry, Macey pulling him inside, pointing at a chair. "You must be hungry." Macey shared a meal with him and gave him place to sleep that first night. He didn't need to ask about what had happened. It was like he already knew. "Your father's an arse," he said to Harry the next morning, "but maybe with time..."

He'd been cold to any talk of Connor, then. "Do you know where Kat went to, Mace?"

Macey shook his head. "If she wanted you to know she would have told you." Macey studied him closely. "Look, Harry, it wouldn't have been possible for you to go with her. It's for

the best. Kat wouldn't have wanted to hurt you for the world. You have to know that."

He eyed Harry's bag. "I don't suppose I can't talk you into going back, talking it through, giving him a chance to do better. He can, you know. Do better I mean."

Harry shook his head.

"And lacrosse? Those fellows from the league are going to be back looking for you."

"No, Mace." There would be no more games now, he thought stonily.

Macey gave him the name of a friend, the master of a mail boat out of Cleveland. He'd pressed Harry with money for the fare down and some extra to live on once he got there. It was near the end of season and Macey explained that Harry was to find a rooming house for the winter, look for jobs. There was building going on in Cleveland. Industry. He'd secure something that would suit. As soon as the ice was gone from the Cleveland harbour, he was to find his friend and the boat, and tell the man Macey sent him.

~

There is an impression of lift and fall, the sensation of warmth. Light seeps through his eyelids, flickering and speckled with red. When he opens his eyes, Jake crouches next to him, his brow deeply lined, his lips flaking. His long arms wrap around shins, his swollen fingers locked as if to keep himself in place.

They are in the games room, Harry on his back, a kerosene lamp swinging on its hook on the wall. Why are the lamps lit? His memory lags and then catches him; the storm, the on-ship electrical wires had been taken out by the ice and wind. Now, all modern light has been extinguished.

He breathes, wriggling his toes and fingers. There is a great weight on his chest and when he looks down, he finds himself under a sodden pile of woollen coats. Dizziness and a sweep of nausea break over him and he closes his eyes against these, drifting. When he comes- to, Jake is exactly where he was, sitting close by like a sentinel. There is a great stir of emotion seeing Jake planted there. A mix of gratitude, worry, the deeper, truer pull of affection.

When he levers himself up on his forearms, it's as though an elephant sits on his skull. His mind sluggishly and painfully sorts through the events on deck, the pieces coming back in a mash. "You brought me in."

Jake's eyes are ringed in vivid red. "Thought we'd soon be following Cook." A grim smile, a sagging shoulder.

Harry is hit with a new wave of sadness remembering Cook. "Did we lose more besides?"

Sighing, Jake surveys the room. "Three. Captain ordered the portholes boarded, so the boys unhinged doors from the fore cabins, dragged them out on deck and went to work, but they got swept out. They were tied on, mind, but the rail broke. Waves took the doors, the men, the whole damn mess." Jake rubs his face vigorously as if to revive some spark of vitality in himself. "Some of the aft- structure still hangs on but most of it's gone. We tried with Cook, Harry."

It's an effort to absorb this news. Three men, four including Cook, out of a crew of twenty-two. It seems impossible.

And then another memory emerges, himself, monstrous with outrage, the wind turning him inside out, the blinding slashes of spray, and beneath it all, bottomless, shapeless despair.

He grins ruefully at Jake.

"Christ, Jake. I took a run at you." Remembering what he'd done to Jake, he's astonished, horrified, but there remains that strange relief inside now. Something in the violence of the weather had emptied him like a pocket rid of its coins, the money spent and gone, and he's lighter for it.

Jake is sanguine. "Weather like this does weird things," he shrugs.

Harry stares at the blank porthole. "Dumb as a bag of hammers to try that on you. All I can say is I'm sorry for it."

"I've taken much worse and given it." He is over-ridden with tremors. Nerves pull cruelly at his face and his boot taps erratically, mindlessly. Harry can see that Jake is so worn down he can barely contain the haywire signals in his body. He won't be able to go on working the lake boats if the movements get much worse, Harry thinks, watching him. Something in Jake is close to running out, the strange brightness in him a kind of alert, like a flare he sends out. He remembers now, seeing Jake face the storm, transfixed by the roiling water, not combative, as Harry once thought, but full of a fierce longing.

~

There is the sound of a crash, and then the stench of kerosene. When Harry cracks open his eyes, two of the crewmen are on their feet, furiously stamping out a burning oil lamp that has smashed to the floor. Next to him, Jake is slumped against the companionway, his gaze flat, no fire in him now.

Harry tries to calculate how long he was drifting in and out, but the obscure grey light in the portholes tells him nothing. He wants to imagine himself off the boat. He wants to go forward to a time when his feet strike solid ground. He tries to imagine the remaining crew walking down the *Carruthers'* gangway, their boots ringing on the boards.

"What will you do, Jake, after. You won't get back to fighting, will you, or managing a club?"

At first, Jake seems to want to shrug off the question but then he draws closer to it, his brows furrowing in thought. "Something happened a few years back that I think I need to answer for." His chest heaves, his breathing deliberate as the boat pitches and lurches beneath them. "I killed someone in the ring. I landed a punch that went bad."

Harry takes in what Jake said. "Doesn't that happen sometimes? It must be a risk that people take when they box."

Adjusting his balance, Jake shifts his body to better ride out the bucks and rolls, his face twitching, his jaw tightening. It must be a terrible effort, Harry thinks, to reach for stillness when your body screams for fight. "You could say that, but there was money involved this time. He was supposed to take me out in the second round, and I was to stay down. We were both being paid for the match to go that way. I don't know why now, but I couldn't go through with it, it seemed so important not to lose." He lowers his forehead to his clenched hand, rubbing it furiously against his knuckles. "I overpowered my punch to make sure I brought him to ground. He must have had a crack somewhere in his skull, like what you find in a teapot. The man wouldn't know it's there and no one else could know, just by looking at him. They find things like that after, when they cut a man open." Jake's face dissembles, guilt contorting the features like fissures in shifting ice.

"Is someone looking for you?"

"Likely. The people who wanted a payout for a fixed fight will be. And the police too if they have any idea of what went on. The fact that I left town that same night and never went back in the ring looks bad."

"Couldn't you go to another place where they don't know who you are?"

Jake grunts. "Boxing world is small, but you know what's not? The syndicate who paid me to fix the fight in the first place. They have a way of finding a man and making him pay."

Harry studies him, seeing the bind. "How will you answer for it?"

Retreating now into silence, Jake tucks himself away again, his eyes closed. Harry pulls himself up further and leans against the wall, the solidity of the wood steadying him. There are others in the games room. David sits round-shouldered, wet and shivering, his sketchbook balanced on his bent knees. He looks like a boy, huddled by himself like that. The hand that holds the pencil rests on the page as if too tired to hold itself up but remarkably the fingers move still. On the opposite side of the room, Leaps Levine braces against the pocket door, his face drawn down like a man at the ready but asleep on his feet. Four other men sit on the floor in various states of wakefulness. One man has his arm around his mate, his head tucked into the other man's neck in an abject gesture.

There is a commotion at the door, the sound of boots scuffing the floor and then a deliberate clearing of a throat. Captain Wright lumbers into the room, dripping, his moustache slicked down over his upper lip. There is a florid look about him, as though his heart is pumping too hard. It's clear he's been out on deck, surveying the damage. When he sees Harry sitting up, he smiles warmly. "Darling, you've decided to join us after all."

Wright's attention is like sunshine. "Thank you, Captain. I'm all right."

Wright nods enthusiastically. "Now, lads," he says, a new seriousness descending. "We've had some tragedy on board this morning. Terrible losses. Good men who will have their tributes and their memorials, rest assured. They *will* be remembered. But before we can give them that, we have to press on. We know where we are," he smiles broadly, "because it's wet and we haven't run a-ground, but to be honest, no visual contact with shore is possible with the snow. I suspect many of the lighthouses and even lightships will have been taken out by this wind. It's true, we've not seen anything like this before. I wouldn't believe it unless I'd seen it for myself. Seas and winds like these -" He shakes his head slowly, a bewildered look passing briefly over his features. "But we've got Ross and there's none better. We're having to go on by *feel* as much as anything. Soundings are difficult in seas this wild, but we'll keep trying. This laker, this *boat*, won't take care of herself. She'll need some prompting and we're going to keep her nose away from the shoreline until we find a place to settle in. I'll need you all ready. Rotation for duties in the engine room. No one attempts to go near the aft house, what's left of it, for any reason."

Harry thinks about his few belongings, Kat's tin in particular, swept out into the lake; he can't muster sadness about it. Strangely, it doesn't seem to matter. Wright goes on: "And I'm sorry for this. We must board up whatever potential breaches we can think of, so some of you will have to risk going back out on deck with more doors and paneling. Leaps is going to make sure you're tied on to something more reliable than those damn rails. Christ, the safeties and rails are the first thing

that will be refitted this winter, I promise you, boys. Now, who will go out again? Leaps here (his hand on the tall man's shoulder, a gentle squeeze of the fingers, a smile) will keep an eye."

Two hands shoot up, one of them Jake's. Seeing them, Wright lights up. "Fine then. There are a couple of crowbars in the companionway, lads. Have at the paneling. There are hammers and nails and metal spikes too for covering as many potential breaches as you can but focus especially on the wheelhouse. If we lose the ability to steer her, we're in trouble. Good, *good* lads."

"Jake," Harry says, his voice kept low. "You haven't got it in you, not after Cook. Stay back, for now anyway."

Jake's expression is unreadable. "I'll be all right." He heaves himself to a stand.

"Now before you go," Wright goes breezily on, "I've got a slug for you. *All* of you. Medicinal, you understand." He turns to Leaps, a grim magician who pulls a jug of rum and a tin cup from under his coat. They'd planned this carefully, this care that they now take with the crew. Leaps solemnly wrenches the cork from the top of the bottle with his teeth and then ceremoniously pours rum into the mug, passing it among the men.

Woozy and sick again, Harry lies back down, feeling the boat fighting and bucking beneath him, the *Carruthers* a lone animal surrounded by wolves.

18

Sunday Morning
Huron Shore,
The Road Home

"That your truck back there?" Connor asks the boy.

The boy nods dolefully. "Dad's."

"What you doing sittin' stupid here in the snow?"

"Don't know. Just thought I'd sit." The boy's teeth are chattering. He is plump, his eyes set deep behind fleshy cheeks. The crusting red from his wound is startling against his skin.

"You been out here for long?"

"It was dark when I crashed. I felt like I walked a long way. Long enough."

"You can't just sit. You'll freeze. You best come with me. Can you walk?"

"Nothing wrong with my legs," he says dully. "Walloped my head good though when I hit that animal."

Many times, Connor has seen the lad working in the field with his beefy father, the boy stout and slow, slapping at his trousers, looking up at the sky as if to distract himself. There had been something of a reluctant labourer about him and he was compliant and placid, lumbering around after his father. Now, looking closer at him, Connor sees fragility there, about the hump of his shoulders, the softness of his mouth.

He holds out his hand, the boy taking it, heaving himself off the branch almost sadly. "You're Connor Darling. Just the other side of McNeil's."

"That's right," says Connor, trudging back to the horse and gesturing to the boy to follow.

As if seeking refuge, the boy stands stolidly by the horse's shoulder and looks up at the wagon. "How are we gonna pass, with that branch in the road?"

"I'll have to pull it away with the horse and rope," Connor says. "I'll tip us in the ditch if I try and go around."

The boy nods and blinks. "Don't want help with that, do ya?"

Connor laughs, thinking of the boy struggling with the weight of the rope, his feet unsure in the snow. A round little snowman. "Nope. You go on up and put that sheepskin over you."

The boy's eyes light up. "Won't say no."

Connor busies himself with unhitching the wagon. He brings out the heavy rope from where it lies coiled with the tools and then trudges back to the branch. After winding the rope twice around the narrow end, he knots it, and then secures it to the horse's harness.

He glances up at the boy buried to his chin in the sheepskin, relief and embarrassment pressed onto his delicate features. "That's what the rug's there for," Connor calls up. He pushes hard against the horse's shoulder, smacking him on the rump with his good hand, and the animal reluctantly moves in the direction of the lake. The snow is deep, in places coming well past Connor's knees and his coat feels thin without the sheepskin to protect him. The fallen branch slides away from the road and Connor undoes the rope and stows it.

After the horse is harnessed to the wagon again, Connor climbs up to the bench, the boy sitting motionless beside him. The boy looks pale. Blows to the head can be a worry. Kat told him a story about a man kicked in the skull by a cow. The man, thinking he was no worse for wear had driven himself to his cousin's wake an hour away, gotten drunk with relatives, laughed and cried, only to fall dead on the ground by nightfall. Connor's eyes sweep over the boy's face. It's difficult to see the wound, the blood having spread like a map across his wide forehead. He rests his hands on the boy's round cheeks, and with a gentle tug he brings his head close. After some careful inspection, he finds the gash. It doesn't look deep, and it appears to have stopped bleeding.

The boy, who has been patient, reaches for Connor's injured hand, and holding it in his own he frowns down at it. "We're a pair," he says, nodding at the deep and livid cut. "That don't look good at all."

Connor grunts and hesitates before slipping his hand away. "I'll take you home. It's not too bad, your scrape. Could be worse."

When the boy blinks, Connor sees that he is crying. "It doesn't hurt, does it?"

The boy swallows. "No. But I killed that bull. And I smashed up my Dad's truck. He's only had it a few months. First farmer in the county to have one. I'll catch hell for it when I get home."

"What were you doing out with a truck anyway on this kind of day?"

"Grandparents over by Ripley need help with their cows."

"There was a lot of fog earlier," says Connor. "And you said it was still dark."

"Cows still gotta get milked. And Grandpa's no good since he had a stroke."

Connor is quiet. He imagines that the boy goes every day to help with the milking. "Your dad couldn't have driven over there?"

"My job's grandpa's cows. Dad takes care of ours." It is expected of him. He would have gone regardless of whether he'd been told.

The boy looks frozen in fear. "I'll be up to my ears in trouble for not taking better care with that truck. It cost an awful lot."

They drive on in silence, the horse slow, the boy's weight heavy against him.

~

"What's your name?" Connor asks the boy.

"Jack." The boy's teeth have finally stopped chattering and the warmth of the sheepskin seems to have revived him. He peers at Connor, his eyes small and clever.

"You're Harry's father." Not a question.

"Yes."

"Where is he?"

Connor doesn't answer. He thinks of Mace taking him to task not long after Harry left. They'd been drinking beer together in the Kincardine Hotel.

"He seems to think I drove Kat away. It's like he believes that I threw her to the gutter."

Macey regarded him closely. "You didn't exactly go down on your knees and ask her to stay, did you? She'd took a lot on your behalf, and you were happy to let her. Harry probably felt she deserved more."

Connor grunted. "Kat made her choices."

Macey had laughed but not unkindly. "What choices she had."

"Well, it was between me and her anyway. Nothing to do with the boy. And I couldn't have explained it."

Macey eyed him, shaking his head. "You're a sorry bugger, you are."

Connor squinted down into his amber-coloured beer. "Harry wanted to be out on his own, same as me at that age. He's likely getting on with things, as he should." It had rung hollow, even in his own ears.

"That's a good story," snorted Macey. "For Christ's sake. Write him a letter and tell him you want him home, that you made a mistake. I'll make sure he gets it. I've an idea where he is."

But Connor hadn't written a word, and he'd never asked Macey where Harry had gone. It was better, easier, he decided, not to know.

~

"Harry was very good at football," Jack is saying, "and lacrosse. There are trophies in the glass cabinet in the hallway at the school."

"He was good at games."

Jack nods in agreement, his chin poking forward, a look of admiration spreading over his soft features. "I'm not good at any games. I wish I was but I wheeze when I run."

Connor smiles slightly. "Not much of a driver either, are you?"

"Nope. Just learned earlier this fall. That's when Dad got the truck."

Valerie Mills-Milde

The wind savagely rattles through the slats in the wagon and threatens to pull it apart. Jack tugs the sheepskin over his head and then, blinking into the storm, he emerges from it a few moments later, clutching it tight beneath his double chin. Connor is reminded of the turtles he used to see near the Darling farm. The farm had not been too far from the St. Lawrence River and in an effort to forage, the turtles would awkwardly drag themselves over the dusty ground.

"Does Harry live with you still?"

"No."

"You farm them animals that look like rats, don't you?"

"Mink. I farm mink. They're not rats."

"I *know* they *aren't* rats. You farm them for their fur, right?"

"Why do you ask so many questions, Jack?"

"It's cold out here. And blowy. And I'm in for it when I get home. I'll probably get the strap. I'm just trying to take my mind off things I don't want to think about, I guess."

For a few moments, Jack is quiet, as if pondering what waits for him at home. Then he peers at Connor. "Mink are likely a good idea. People are wearing fur coats made from mink, or at least *rich* people are. You'll make money."

"And you are an expert in the fur business, Jack? Or on the wardrobes of the rich?"

Jack shrugs, taking no offense. He is clearly used to derision. "It only makes sense. How many farmers have mink fur 'round Bruce County? Not a lot of competition."

"*Pelts*," Connor corrects him. "Not fur. Not until the furrier gets a hold of them."

"Pelts," Jack repeats, thinking carefully about the word. "Like trappers catch."

Connor sniffs and then mutters. "Not much call for mink up in these parts. Hard to find buyers."

"But there are rich people down in the cities who want to wear it." Jack's voice is rising, the words tumbling out. "You just got to find the right people to sell the fur to. I mean the pelts. You should load up your wagon and go down to the cities. Toronto, Montreal. More luck there than here."

Connor feels himself ease into the boy's company, warming to his enthusiasm for the mink, his shrewd but simple business sense.

"Maybe you'll be a businessman, Jack."

"I like lessons. Maybe I'll be an accountant."

"You'll make a better accountant than a driver."

Jack looks at him earnestly and then laughs, the sound coming in short childlike bursts. Connor chuckles and then frowns into the snow twisters that dance across the road. Not far off is his own laneway but he will have to go further to get the boy home. The gusts are intensifying, kicking up great sheets of white and Connor can only trust the horse to find the road. His eyes sting. Jack's eyelashes and eyebrows are ice-covered, and Connor knows that his are the same.

~

He took the wagon and the horse when the farm was sold, the same wagon on which he and the boy now sit.

On his last day at the Darling farm, he, Sophie, and his sisters were absorbed in their own private sorting. Sophie and June would be staying with Sophie's brother in Hudson, although Sophie was non-committal about what they would do there. They'd have money enough, Connor thought, Connor having given her most of the proceeds from the sale of the farm. Anyway, he believed that it wouldn't be long before she would go back to Carey.

"Carey's in Montreal, I guess," he said flatly over the last meal, "near your brother."

Sophie's face was tight. "You sold to that manager at the woollen mill, Connor, that man who Ethan never trusted. We would have stayed here, together, and you would still be looking after things, but that's impossible now."

"You mean I should have sold to Carey." He shrugged indifferently. "I would have left anyway, even if you stayed here with him."

She put down her fork, her eyes searching her plate as if there was an answer in the largely untouched food. "You could have kept trying, Connor. Another woollen mill, or something else along with the sheep. Ethan wanted you to have it." She looked up, her expression hurt, contemptuous. "You sold it out of spite."

He blinked. It was true, he'd nearly choked on the prospect of Carey owning the place, smugly lording himself over them, and so yes, he made certain Carey wouldn't have it. But there was a deeper rift between himself and Darling Farm that had little to do with Carey. He would never make as good a sheep man as Ethan had been, and he would feel himself a disappointment.

Connor glanced at Sophie, the sight of her still galling, the idea that Carey had been allowed on the place – Ethan's place – still sour in his mouth. He wouldn't allow her to see one more inch of him than was necessary. "This place doesn't suit me, that's all."

He'd arranged for a cab to take June and Sophie to the station and now, standing on the lane, June hugged Dot fiercely. It seemed to Connor that June had become an adult overnight, a depth of knowing deep in her blue eyes, a seriousness coming over her. "Goodbye," he said to June, but she said nothing, her chin strong as she climbed up into the cab ahead of Sophie, her eyes still on Dot. Sophie had a foot on the step, and she turned for a moment, their eyes locking. She'd regarded him strangely, an uncertainty in her eyes, as if trying to decide about him. In the end, she'd pulled herself up and closed the door.

With the cab out of sight, Connor turned toward Dot, who was to take up a live-in position with her employers in town. She stood stony and still on the bottom step of the porch, her anger boring a hole into his centre, fusing with his own, sickening him against himself. And then silently, she picked up her small suitcase and began walking.

"Wait. I've got some money for you, Dot." He'd wanted to give her a small sum, something to secure her.

She shook her head, saving herself from words, or at least wasting none on him.

"All right then," he'd snapped. "We'll just say goodbye if that's how you want it, Dot." Watching his strange and remote sister leave, he'd felt an unexpected surge of sadness. Many times, he'd given in to ridiculing her, relieving some knot inside of himself, but now it was terrible to see her lonely form – the bird-like shoulders, the slight stoop under the weight of the bag, her hair pinned unsparingly, painfully to her scalp. Her suffering was clearer to him then than anyone's had been, before or since. A piece of him leapt up and ran behind her, like he was her shadow, or she, his.

He couldn't wait to watch her reach the main road. He'd gone inside to retrieve his things and by the time he'd loaded the wagon, hitched the horse, and then driven the length of the lane, she'd disappeared. He'd felt giddy with release, and with it an urgency to go while the early autumn sun was still high in the sky.

~

"Your hand is bleeding," Jack observes. "There's blood all over your clothes."

Connor's wound has opened again, the cold causing it to sting. He pulls it closer to his chest, out of Jack's sight.

"You ought to wrap it," Jack says sagely.

Connor nods. "I haven't anything to wrap it with."

Jack blinks up at him. "I do. I got a cloth in my coat pocket. Mom gave it to me to wrap the biscuits grandma always sends back, but I never saw grandma this morning because of the crash." Connor is thinking about how he likes to hear the boy chatter. "And it's clean. Mom wouldn't give me a cloth that wasn't," Jack says like an old mother hen. Jack solemnly takes the cloth from his coat and then placing Connor's hand on his knee, he winds it around and around Connor's hand, tightening it until it is firm. The pressure stops the sting but not the throb, which is loud and dull in his ears. Connor looks at the bandaged hand, a surge of feeling rising through him, his breath catching painfully. It is suddenly strange to not be alone on the road. Something in him tears open, as if along some hidden seam.

"You don't look well," says Jack, frowning.

"You don't look so good yourself," Connor smiles.

"This is turning out to be an awful storm." Jack is peering owlishly at the road. "Much, much worse than I thought it would get. Worst I've seen in November."

"And you've seen so *many* Novembers, Jack."

Jack nods as if this were true. He is still regarding Connor, his face old, like an old man's face, furrowed and fretful.

"Will the truck be all right, out in the snow and wind?"

Connor shrugs and sniffs, his eyes narrowing harshly. "Likely. But one thing's for sure. Someone's bull is certainly dead."

"Don't remind me." Jack remorsefully shakes his head. He turns away, peering absently out into the whirlwind of snow.

"Don't take it so hard," Connor says, shifting himself on the bench, his back now stiff. "I think you crashed near the Creston place but no matter. Might be McNeil's beast. Whose ever it was — they'll see the storm as well as you and me. They'll understand about the road and the fog earlier. And now the snow."

"Dad won't understand." Jack is shaking his head mulishly. "Bulls are expensive. I can tell you exactly how much a bull like that would bring at market."

Connor gives him a sideways look. "Bet you can."

"We'll have to pay it back, at least Dad will have to."

Connor is thinking that Jack's father should be glad to have Jack home, his head not crushed, his arms and legs still intact. He should be glad to have his smart boy there to tell him the market value of his livestock. If he must pay for the bull, that won't be the worst thing that can happen. And if it is McNeil's animal, McNeil is soft on the inside, as he was with Harry. At the thought of Harry, Connor is hit squarely by a wave of unmistakable grief. He has never said so to anyone, but Harry has become an ache, a phantom limb, and the wish to have him home sits squarely on the wagon bench between himself and

the boy. He wonders suddenly if that was what Kat felt for the unborn baby and he blinks into the storm, sorry if it was.

"Will you know your lane when we get close?"

Jack nods. Before long, he points to the left, where the dark outline of a large maple emerges out of the blowing snow. Connor pulls the horse off to the side of the road. "Not going to risk trying to get up your laneway," he says, "in case I wouldn't be able to get out. What I need now is a sleigh instead of a wagon."

Jack stares at him and then clambers down from the bench. Connor waits for him to walk up the lane, but he plants himself by the horse, his hand against the animal's neck.

"Would you come with me? Just to the door? Might be easier on me if you're there too."

"Jesus," Connor says, unable to imagine himself as comfort to the boy let alone protection. When he looks down into Jack's face, he sees something stalwart in the expression, some evidence of trust.

"All right. Just to the door. I got to get back."

Jack nods sagely. "For the mink." The sheepskin is drawn up over his chin, the edges of it hanging down into the snow like a monk's cowl. He begins to peel it off and hand it back to Connor. "You can keep that," Connor grunts. "A reminder of your fun with Connor Darling." Jack lights-up, looking surprisingly pleased.

Taking the horse's reins, Connor loops them over the gatepost and then pushes through ahead of Jack. Jack must run to stay close, and twice he slips heavily and then rights himself. Connor helps him up and the boy threads his arm firmly through Connor's. "You could come inside. My mother's good with cuts. She could look at it for you. You might want tea." His eyes burn bright and warm. Connor doesn't say anything, just lets the boy lean in as they make their way through the wind and then around the house to the kitchen door. The storm feels voracious now, as though it aims to eat them.

Standing on the threshold, Jack tugs heavily on Connor's arm and Connor staggers. It isn't the weight that almost topples him but an unexpected grip of sadness. He looks down at Jack's stoic little face. "I can't stay, Jack. I have to get back. But I'll tell your father how bad it was on that road and that the accident happened because it was too hard to see what was right in front of you. It would be too hard even for a grown man."

Jack nods and then opens the door, and light spills from the kitchen onto their boots. "Go fetch your father, Jack," Connor says, not stepping in but rather standing where he is, the bandaged hand tucked inside his coat like something precious.

19

Sunday
The James Carruthers,
Between Heaven and Earth

Harry is sliding in and out of his dreams, his head throbbing, the muscles at his neck tugging like claws. Strange, in the midst of pain, he thinks of his mother, whom he never knew, and then he thinks of Connor. Had Connor ever really loved her? He conjures a spring day, Kat and he crouched together by the creek. He might be six or seven and Kat is cutting pussy willows with a sharp paring knife, the freshly cut stalks strewn over the cool ground. She takes one from the bunch and gives it to him so he can stroke its soft grey bud.

"My mother died when I was very little," he says with a solemnity that isn't really his, but is rather in him, in the daydream, the weight of it there in his chest.

"Yes, she did. People can die at any time. We should remember that, and we should prize people while they're here. We should pay attention."

"Why? Why should we pay attention?"

"Because later, we might wish we did and that wishing cuts deeper than grief."

Harry becomes worried then.

"Did I prize my mother?"

"You were not much more than a baby, but of course you did."

He feels a stab of great sorrow, as one does in dreams, even though the sadness doesn't always seem to belong.

"And Dad. Did he?"

"Did he what?"

"Prize her?"

She touches the pussy willow buds with her fingertip and looks up at the clean blue sky. "Maybe he did. I don't know."

He's distressed, thinking that his mother died feeling she wasn't cherished. He tries to remember her face, but it is Kat who looks at him now.

"But *you* loved her, Harry. And she knew that, right up until the last breath."

"So she was prized?"

Kat smiles at him.

"I'm sure that she was."

~

The warmth has gone from the games room. Six men remain, all of them from the engine room crew. They sit against the wall, mindlessly holding tin cups, their faces black, their arms trembling with fatigue.

The *Carruthers* strains and pitches and groans. One of the men catches Harry's eye.

"You all right, Darling? Captain said to keep an eye on you."

Harry feels queasy still, but his head aches less than it did earlier. He nods. "Where is everyone?"

Shrugging, the man rolls back his head and rests it on the firmness of wall behind him. Exhaustion pulls at the folds of his face. It's a wonder he can keep himself from sagging to the floor completely. "Some of 'em giving relief with the engine, and others trying to board up what they can."

"The engine holding?" Harry asks. It is hard to tell over the storm, and he can't hear the sounds of the engine.

The man doesn't nod yes or no. "Great bloody wave came astern, flooded the fantail and took out the skylight in the engine room. Lost Rogers. Swept up into the boiler, right in front of our eyes. Poor bugger never stood a chance. Coal bins knocked over. God-awful mess. Chief told us to rig a tarp so we could keep throttling her, protect the engine from more boarding. Bitch of a thing to try and secure a tarp in this, the wind snaring it and whipping it 'round. Fred here just about lost a hand when a tie-down got wrapped 'round his wrist." Harry steals a look at Fred Lancaster whose hand is swathed in a bloodied bandage, his face a deadly white. "Once we got the tarp secured, Chief told us to get some rest in here. Sent your friend Spence down, and a couple of others, to take our place."

"Jesus." Harry says, thinking of Jake. "I could go down there, to the engine room, give some relief."

"Might come to it. But you look pretty green and that's a nasty gash you got, Darling. Let's wait on what the Captain has to say."

Fighting back a wave of nausea, Harry levers himself to standing and the throb immediately returns to his head. Steering and navigating will take all of Wright's attention now. Wright isn't likely to come to the games room any time soon, if at all. Surely, the time for speeches to the remaining crew is over.

"I'm going to the wheelhouse. See what I can do."

The man stares at him, apparently without comprehension. "Do what you must, then," he mutters. "Not sure it's going to matter now."

Lurching, Harry makes his way into the passageway, and then to the stairs that will take him to the navigation room and the wheelhouse. Progress is slow, his body careening between the starboard and port bulkheads, back and forth like a shuttlecock. He pauses, thinking of Flo as he catches his breath. They had watched a game of badminton played in the park on top of the bluff. The players wore white, and the grass was very green. Flo's head had faithfully turned back and forth, following the action, and he remembered in that moment, he felt a great swell of love, as though a damn had broken.

He hears the assault of water against the hull. So far, all of the portholes in the fore house either hold or have been successfully shuttered with planks and no water has come in. The cabins he passes are ghostly and dark. His head spins, all sense of the present brought down to the pure effort it takes to stay upright, to keep from being sick over his boots. For a few moments, he suffers a kind of blindness and screws his eyes shut, wondering if when he opens them, he might find that it is a clear autumn day after all, and that the water is blue and shining as they sail serenely into the Midland Harbour. He will get a train from Midland to Toronto, he thinks resolutely, and then he'll make his way to Goderich. To Flo, who is his beacon now.

If he makes it off this bloody boat, if he can keep his fear from swallowing him whole, then there won't be anything to be afraid of again. Harry pushes himself along the passage, past a smashed lamp, an abandoned, sodden coat, and finds the staircase, and hand over hand, he pulls himself up.

Valerie Mills-Milde

~

Ross is literally lashed to the wheel. Harry's never seen a wheelsman fixed to the helm before, but he's heard, in big seas, the weight of the man is needed to keep a ship on course. *Not a ship*, he reminds himself. *A laker.* He thinks of Macey then. Macey, talking about the tugs, the steamers, the lakers – a myriad of boats in and around Kincardine, not a ship among them. Harry has never seen the ocean before, although some of the men he has crewed with have. Some have sailed from England and Scotland into Halifax, or New York. Some say they've seen whales and icebergs, but he wonders if any of them have been in a blow quite like this.

Ross doesn't look at him. He has his eyes pinned to the enormous compass, every few seconds his gaze breaking to peer into the wall of white outside. His eyes are dark wet pools, the lines spidering out from the corners. Wright is beside him, lending his size and strength to the wheel when needed, no sign of fatigue in him.

"Correct, Ross. Correct now by three points south-west."

After a few moments, Wright squints down at the compass. "She's pushing too far east and she's having trouble correcting. We'll end up on a beach, broken up in a farmer's field. We'll buckle on impact." Wright moves quickly to the communication tube and hollers down a throttle instruction.

The *James Carruthers* peaks as if on a snow-covered mountain and then descends, the wheelhouse window going from white to black as she lumbers down the backside of the wave, her nose buried in a trough. Wright turns to Harry and eyes him with concern. "You shouldn't be moving, Darling. You look bad." Harry can't reconcile this strange show of care with

Wright's hard-minded choice to make the trip. His head begins to pound, and he takes a breath to steady himself.

"Thought I might be of some help."

Gripping the great wheel, Wright throws his weight in with Ross's, both men straining now against the boat's roll. "There, she's corrected a little," he says to Ross, his hand on the man's shoulder. "That's the way."

He turns to Harry again, swiping at his moustache with wide fingers as if to put it to rights. His lips turn reflexively upward in a habit of good humour. "Why don't you pry off more of this nice wood panelling, Darling? Can you manage that, do you think? Take it down to my bloody bathtub – get some kerosene from one of the lamps and start a fire. Then call the lads in to warm up. At the very least, it might take the chill off. Might add a bit of cheer." His eyes dance as he looks at Harry.

"Is there anything else, Sir?"

"Poke your head out on deck, will you? Secure yourself first, mind, and get Leap's attention. I want all hands in my cabin, around that fire, unless they are in with the engine. No one is out there in this. What hasn't been boarded-up will just have to stay that way. We're not losing anyone else, you understand, don't you, Darling? That means you too, lad."

The *Carruthers* is climbing again, cresting, and Wright turns to the communications tube.

Harry leaves them half-crawling down the stairway, making his way to the exterior door that leads to the deck. Before opening it, he ties himself to the companionway railing, testing the hold, and then he pushes it, the wind a battering ram against him.

He can see nothing at first, just lashings of snow, black water teeming down. Far off, he can just make out figures lying flat against the deck, their hands gripping a hatch cover. He shouts and hollers until a head pokes up. It is Leaps' face, long and ashen. Harry waves his arm, beckoning Leaps to come back. He can see now a phalanx of safety lines that lead to the fore house, all of them attached to a giant cleat. Leaps waits for the boat to climb and then pulls himself to a stand, tugging himself over the slanted deck until he is close to Harry.

"Captain wants all hands inside," Harry shouts, "save those in engineering."

Leaps stares at him, grimacing. He seems to be taking in this instruction, weighing it carefully.

"He wants you to bring them all in now."

Leaps nods, a momentary look of either relief or resignation crossing over his features, Harry can't tell which. He turns back toward the men, hesitates until the boat begins to descend, then inches his way to where the men still cling to the hatch cover.

It takes a long while for the men to make their way to the fore house. Ice-covered and stiff, their movements are improbable, unnatural, like men who live somewhere between heaven and earth.

20

Sunday
Goderich Harbour,
Bells, Whistles and Lights

Flo rises early, long before the light, a restlessness climbing into her limbs, tension coiled in knots at her shoulders. The night hours had been a mix of strong gusts and eerie calm and there were moments in which she could feel the bones of the old house shifting. Somewhere between sleep and wakefulness, her thoughts found Harry. He stood on an unlikely boat, a tiny vessel, tubby and sweet like a child's toy. The storm raged around him but somehow, the sturdy little boat didn't tip, instead riding the waves almost fancifully, as buoyant as a cork. Harry was oversized, his eyes searching the shore, his expression eager and unafraid. She stood just beyond where he could see, a great rope tied around her waist, and the rope stretching unseen beneath the lake's rowdy surface and secured to the wee boat by a ring. Flo had not for an instant doubted that she had the strength to hold the weighted rope, and so she steadily pulled, hand-over-hand as she'd seen the dockworkers do, certain that he wanted this from her, sure that he was asking her to bring him home.

She wakes in a surge of relief, remembering that Harry is on a train. In the next few moments, her mind works out the puzzle of his location. A layover in Toronto as he waits for another train that will carry him to Guelph? Or is he in Guelph already? Probably not yet on the final leg of the journey to Goderich, but surely close now. She's almost giddy, thinking of his return, a girlish anticipation stirring, causing her skin to flush.

When she swings her bare feet to the floor and stands, she feels a return to herself, like water poured into a bottle, the bottle capped, tucked into a bag for safekeeping. *He's on his way, this much I know, and the when doesn't matter.*

There are drafts in the room that snake around her ankles, and there are sounds – an assault on the windowpane, the lake pounding at the shore. The horn at the harbour's end bellows forlornly. Peeling back the heavy curtains, she peers into the street, the halloed light from a streetlamp revealing a slew of white.

She is already dressed when there is a knock on her door. Her landlord, Mr. Cray, stands in his green housecoat, his hair on end, grey stubble on his unshaved chin. A fastidious man, and proper, his expression is vaguely apologetic, great shadowy saddlebags beneath his eyes, and there are extra creases in his skin. Cray, a retired military man, is a widower. He'd climbed the stairs from his apartment below, his feet in slippers, and now he lightly wheezes. She's never seen him in anything but a white shirt, a suit vest, and pressed worsted trousers, and the unusually careless presentation raises an alarm. "Morning, Flo," he says, handing her a cup of tea. "Forgive the early intrusion. The boy from your office, Ted, was just down at my door. He says you're to get in quick as you can. Seems it's been an active night and you're needed." As well as her messenger, Ted is the harbour master's son and the harbour master would have rousted Ted from his warm bed, sent him tearing around the town, if not on his bicycle, then on foot. The boy will be wild-eyed, almost gleeful with adventure. As she thinks about him, a bell begins to ring – the bell on the town hall, which is rung for parades and celebration, but which now rings with a more dire message. Not for the first time she thinks that progress is slow here. The clamour of the bell is unnerving, and she quashes irritation that there are so few telephones in the town.

Mr. Cray regards the hard frown in her expression and nods toward the window. "It's a call for the volunteers to convene," he says in the way of explanation. "Strong backs needed along the shore." He sighs and then straightens, his old military bearing finding him again. "They'll be gathering in the square."

Mr. Cray has a heart condition that prevents him from overly exerting himself, and Flo sees that he's disappointed he won't be part of a shore party. "What are they looking for?"

"Boats, mostly. We can hear their whistles, even some shouting, but we don't see them. And this blow is fixing to get worse. We'll need to be ready."

Flo sighs and hands him the untouched tea. She reaches for a coat.

"You'll need something heavier than that," he says. "A winter weight, if you've got one."

Of course, she thinks. *Autumn has departed and winter has come.* "So much has changed in twenty-four hours," she says, smiling at Mr. Cray. She goes to the wardrobe and pulls out her wool serge coat, a felt hat, and a tall pair of boots. She roots around in the coat pockets and finds a pair of leather gloves. He'd said they'd be looking for boats, mostly. *Boats.* She bites down on her lip. Since Harry appeared in her life, when she thinks about lake boats, she thinks of him. As she

leaves her apartment, she puts a hand on Mr. Cray's arm. "Thanks for the tea," she says, "even if I didn't have time. I'm sure I'll be ready for some later today." He gives her a neat military nod, happy to be of some use. "I'll have something ready for you to eat so you won't have to cook. Let me know when you're home. It doesn't matter the time."

Flo steps out onto the street, pulling her collar up high against a vicious mix of snow and sleet. The cold bites her skin and almost immediately her eyes sting. The falling temperature has begun to harden the slush into uneven hollows, and although she sets out at a good pace, she must be careful not to slip. Looking up, she sees that the wires still hold although they sway horribly in the heavy gusts. At least the messages can still go through, she thinks, but what might happen when the ice builds?

~

The lights are on at the station and the stationmaster is behind his large oak desk, his expression owlish. "Hello, Flo. Glad you came. There are messages ready to go out." He hands her a stack. "And the printer has been clacking away in there. You'll have quite a job waiting for you."

She undoes the buttons of her coat, the air in the station fuggy and thick. "Trains are still running, are they?"

"For now," he says, "but after a few more hours of this, who can say." She registers this. No sense in expecting Harry to arrive today then, she thinks, resolutely casting aside the low hum of anticipation that has filled her all morning. Perhaps tomorrow, with some luck.

Ted is perched on a stool in her office, his face pinked from the wind. He springs up expectantly when he sees her.

When he stands close, she can smell the lake on him, snow, and the clean scent of soap. "You got some messages for me to run 'round, Miss Flo? Dad says we are going to have a day." He grins and quite suddenly she thinks of her brothers, their lean frames and voracious appetites, their insatiable greed for fun. They are men, of course, but she's grateful to still think of them as the boys they were. To have memories that she has strung together, binding them to her despite the miles and the years that have come between.

The stationmaster has set out oil lamps in case the wires go and they are suddenly swept into darkness. "Light those lanterns, Ted, while I check the printing machine. There will be lots of work today. "She eyes him as she slips the cover off her typewriter. "Have you eaten anything? You can't go speeding around in a storm without something in your stomach."

Ted earnestly agrees. He has always proven himself to be a hearty eater. "Dad spent the night at the harbour house and Mom had me run food down to him earlier. We shared it together."

"Your father's worried."

Ted shrugs. "He told me we've had lots of storms in November. He said it's to be expected." He sniffs and rubs the cuff of his coat across his small rabbity nose. He keeps his excited eyes pinned to Flo's. "He also says that this blow is fierce, maybe the fiercest he can remember, that the wind is at sixes and sevens and that it isn't behaving normally."

She peers at him, trying to understand what he is saying about the storm. The people here show a mix of acquiescence and pessimism about weather generally, but today there is also alarm. Sitting down she frowns at the messages that have come in over night. The printing machine had indeed been busy and long ribbons of tape now hang in a desultory way from the table. Streams of dots and dashes. She gathers the paper up and then sets out her trays, *personal/domestic, commercial/regular, commercial/urgent, other/urgent,* and readies herself to translate.

The first message she transcribes is from a Cleveland shipping company. It informs the local representative that an inbound laker is expected to be late in arrival because of the weather that struck Lake Superior Friday and Saturday. She sets it aside for Ted to take to the harbour offices. There are several more like it, most originating from ports along the upper lakes. Once she has typed and then sorted the official messages, she hands them to Ted. "Tuck them safe in your bag, Ted. Come back as soon as you're done," she tells him. "We'll do the personal ones next."

In the short time she's been in the office, more messages fly off the line, the machine hammering and ticking. After an hour or so of intense concentration, she stands, stretches her back and goes to the window. The gloom has barely lifted, and in the mix of heavy snow and sleet, the passing carts and horses appear as phantoms. Gusts rattle the windows of the station, and she can hear the lake, roaring inconsolably at the base of the bluffs.

~

By late morning, she's given all the incoming messages to Ted for delivery, and several telegrams have gone out over the wires. There are more reports of worsening conditions on Huron and finally, at 11:00, a message comes in from the Meteorological Service in Toronto: "STORM WARNING: *Ports Georgian Bay and Lake Huron. Indication of probability of gale force winds."* Flo sighs. That seems like closing the barn door after the horses have bolted.

"Ted, have they put up the gale force flags in the harbour?"

Ted shakes his head. "Storm flags. We don't use the ones for gale. We don't need them."

She looks at him waiting for more explanation but evidently, he doesn't have one. More acquiescence, she thinks, sighing. She hands him the message. "Take this to your father right away, Ted. He'll want to put out the gale flags today."

Ted stands for a minute, his eyes curious and bright. "They won't see flags from the water now, Miss Flo. Not in this. The lighthouse might help. And the horn too, but the wind might carry the sound off."

"Can they see the lighthouse when it's like this?"

He shrugs. "Depends on the snow."

No visibility, she thinks. No ship-to-shore for most of the boats, except for a handful of the American carriers. It suddenly comes very clear. They've lost touch with the people on those lake boats. She peers out the window, looking for a break in the sky, a lift in light, but finds none.

~

The silence in the telegraph office is startling.

Earlier in the afternoon, the electric lights had flickered and then gone out. Continuing to sort messages, Flo kept one eye on the printing machine, half-expecting it to miraculously sputter to a start but it remained obstinately silent. She'd never felt like doing violence to her equipment before, but with a terrible sense of urgency pressing down, she'd come close to tossing everything out the window. The moment passed. There would be no hope of transmitting messages anyway, no chance of the downed poles being resurrected any time soon. She's given herself over to the reams of printed communications that arrived before the power failed.

Ted has just torn out of the building with the last delivery. "Only those few, Ted," she told him. "There won't be anything more going in or out now. You might just as well get home." He stared at her for a few moments. "I'll want to help dad after," he said. "Shore patrol." He was practically vibrating with excitement.

"Must you do that?" She had alarming images of him being swept into the lake and engulfed by the waves, his child-body as flimsy as a paper doll. "Stay back from the water's edge," she said sternly. Perplexed, Ted took off his cap and rubbed at a red-tipped ear. "Don't think I can do much patrolling from a distance, Miss Flo. Water's got to come into it." She could see that nothing would keep him from joining his father and the others.

Now, alone, she blows out the lamps, the office instantly descending into gloom. There is nothing left for her to do here, the place untethered without operating circuits, the station bereft without trains. Earlier, a message came in regarding a fatal trail derailment further south and soon after, all the trains stopped running, the rails too clogged with ice and snow for passage.

With her coat on, she does a quick tidy of her desk, pausing at the New Haven, a slight and unprepossessing instrument, as familiar as a shoehorn. Sliding off her winter glove, she rests her finger on the brass key, the polished metal quickly warming to her touch. For a moment, she thinks to take the instrument with her, but then without the wires, it's voiceless. Strangely, she thinks of Terry Eldridge. "It makes no difference," he liked to say poetically, "how a message goes – on wings, or hooves or over the wires. It's what goes out, the message itself that matters." How Terry did wax on. And she hadn't entirely agreed with him, even then. What of intention, that peculiar spark, the most vital part of any dispatch? The most human part, the source of both hope and disillusionment. She thinks of what had gone on between she and Terry, the misdirection, the bits of himself he'd left out.

She imagines the lake boats entombed in the weather, the irreparable separation of the men from the shore. Without any clear thought of what she should do, she closes the door on the office, and makes her way outside of the station.

On the street, she is met only by ghoulish streamers of snow. The sky is dark and heavy. Through the murk she makes out figures with hurricane lamps, a stream of bodies half-running toward the harbour. They shout to one another, their words flattened by the wind. Pushing her way, she catches up to the last one, a man she doesn't know, who looks at her strangely from beneath a fringe of ice-encrusted hair. "Best get home, Miss. Awful wild down there."

"Is this a shore patrol?" Her tone is unwavering.

He nods, gesturing with his eyes to where the bluffs are barely visible. "There's a story goin' round that whistles have been heard coming from the harbour. Someone thought they might have seen a flare, 'though it's impossible to see much in this."

Flo nods and the man turns and humps along, Flo following, lifting the hem of her long coat as she walks through the track made by the others. Closer to the bluff, she catches

sight of the water, an enormous writhing black thing, splintered by row upon row of frothing crests.

The man waits. "You want to go back? I'll take you, Miss."

"No," she calls back. "I'm fine." He studies her and then moves on, making his descent to the beach. The wind presses hard against her thighs as she walks. From the top of the road, the harbour is difficult to make out. She can't believe the reach of the water, the furious waves overtaking the docks, pummelling the wooden boards. Refuse from damaged boats, fish shacks, repair sheds, all of it strewn over the snow like untidy bundles of twigs. Figures stand well back on the beach, coats drawn up around faces, hands pushed helplessly into pockets. They turn in small circles, as if to take in the full scope of the disaster.

The forces of the elements burrow in, her ears humming now, the storm more felt than heard. It's difficult to know where she is because nothing looks as it should. The harbour master is there, a compact, neat man directing small groups up and down the shoreline. He holds a large bullhorn but doesn't use it, gesturing instead with his arms. Strung around his neck is a pair of metal binoculars.

When she gets close enough, she presses her hand around the sleeve of his coat.

"Flo!" His face registers the surprise. He leans toward her so that she can better hear. "Do you want Ted?" She can see Ted along the shore, darting back and forth, his movements faster, brighter than the others. He wears a vibrant red cap that makes her think, improbably, of a hummingbird.

"No, I have no work for him. I've come to see if I can help. What is it you're doing?"

He studies her, the lines in his face deepened by the excoriating wind. His eyes are bloodshot. The weight of responsibility sits heavy, she can see. "We're hearing whistles and bells," he hollers. "And one of the lads here thought they might have seen a flare. We think one of the freighters is just offshore, trying to make its way in."

Flo stares out at the twisting water, just as the others do, as if willing the laker to come into sight. Peering into the veil of grey, she sees nothing.

"There must be something we can do."

"We're going to try with the lamps," the harbour master says. "The boats might catch sight. At least they'll know to stay off the beach."

The harbour master holds up his lamp, swinging it widely, and the shore party soon does the same. As Flo watches the lamps sway and flicker in the wind, she sees the message in them. A warning, but not an invitation. The lamps would help the boats see where they should not be, but it won't help them find the mouth of the river. Then there is a spark, like a match striking phosphorous. *Light*, she thinks suddenly, *can be used for a more exact purpose.* Taking the harbour master's lamp from him, she holds it up, passing her hand in front of the glass at intervals.

"Take the lamp for me. Up, like that. And keep it still." She takes off her scarf and straightens it to make a wide band, then lifts it up and down, creating breaks in the illumination. "You see? We can use code. What if you could give me the coordinates for this harbour and I transmitted them, like this, with the lamp. Would that work?"

He looks puzzled. "One small lamp? And with those seas and the snow, I doubt it. Besides, they would need to know their own coordinates for that, and I doubt they do at this point."

"All right, but even without coordinates, I could show them where the harbour is. Something to steer for, anyway. What if we make a line of transmissions? The message can be carried from one lantern to the next, as far out as we dare put someone. I can start the transmission, and the other lamp operators can simply follow me, each in turn. If we were each to have a bit of wood, we could hold the lantern in one hand and use the object in the other to blot out the light. "

He is looking grimly out at the lake, weighing her plan. It sounds desperate, she knows, and probably sadly insufficient but no more so than what they are doing.

A high-pitched whistle pierces the storm's roar, and she stares, riveted. "There *is* something out there," she calls out, her hand on his coat sleeve again.

He frowns, his neck thrown forward as he peers even more keenly at the heaving water. "The wind's carrying the sound toward us. Hard to know how far out it is." He places his binoculars to his eyes and sweeps them back and forth. "Nothing." He pauses, then nods. "All right. You'll have to work out the signal, Flo. I remember some Morse myself, and a couple of these others out here will too, especially the ones who have spent time on lake boats. Why don't you try and signal HARBOUR 500 YARDS EAST. We'll space the lamps on a diagonal behind you, so that the lights lead them in." He leans down and picks up a bit of galvanized tin and hands it to her. "This the kind of thing that might work? I'll send Ted around to find what we need."

~

Before long, twelve figures hold lamps, catercorner to Flo, spaced in intervals from the beach to where the shoreline gives way to the Maitland River. Flo quickly makes her translation on the back of a receipt fished from the depths of her pocket. She looks at the series of dots and dashes, weighing how to make the signal succinct and clear. She won't repeat *harbour* each time, for the sake of brevity. She frowns. The entire message will take longer than she wants because the others down the line will need to mimic each release and blanketing of light.

The wind and the sheets of snow make the task difficult. She begins with the first letter, "H", creating four pulses of light, and then she holds the light steady for three full counts. The lantern closest to her follows. After seven counts, she moves on to the second letter; *dot, dash.* Seven counts. Then R, then B, until the word HARBOUR has been signalled. She moves on to 500 - *dot, dot, dot, dot, dot.* Then YARDS - *dash, dash, dash*, and finally EAST - *dot,* pause, *dot, dash*, pause, *dot, dot, dot*, pause, *dash*. She waits a full minute before beginning the sequence again, resting her aching arms, her eyes sweeping the beach where the lanterns twinkle, on-off, on-off, like a fall of stars. And then she goes on, precisely, repeating the sequence of coordinates, the scrap of metal raised and lowered, raised, held, lowered. The others are doing their best to replicate her signals, although a couple of them have mixed up dashes and taps. She hopes they will get better with practice, that they remember to count precisely. She hopes that they will hold the light for long enough.

The whistle comes again, but it seems further away now, and calculating the distance makes her frantic. It comes again, and again, finally barely audible and then it is utterly silenced. Her eyes are pained with the strain of searching and without realizing she has reached the point of surrender, her tears flow. She turns to the line and waves her lamp back and forth and then reluctantly puts it down.

The harbour master sets his down too and the others follow, all except Ted. A diminutive bright figure, he hurls his lantern back and forth in extravagant bursts, his left-hand pointing. Flo blinks into the driving snow, toward the harbour. To her astonishment, a light emerges, and then the ghostly outline of a boat. Not a laker, surely, but a smaller vessel. It is shrouded in ice, and it bucks and rolls in the enormous swells. It is struggling to make entrance to the harbour. She picks up her lantern, sending the code, her signals quick and emphatic and soon there is a bright line of flashes coming from the shoreline as they all resume their work with the lamps. As the boat pushes past them, an improbable light lifts and lowers, lifts and lowers from its phantom deck and Flo answers it by resolutely raising her own.

Later, the captain on the provisions boat *McBride* would say that he had no idea where the mouth of the Maitland was, or if he was close to Goderich harbour. His boat was damaged from the high seas and taking on water but unlike the larger lakers with their narrow mid-sections, the *McBride*'s stout design stopped her from buckling when caught in the troughs.

It was the signals, he said, that drew him and his crew of three into the exact place. It was the code that he instantly recognized.

~

The shepherding of the *McBride* to safe harbour gives the shore party renewed determination and they continue with the lanterns until the cold and wet creeps so far into them they can barely stand. The harbour master finally trudges over to Flo, gently taking her lamp from her. She sees the resignation in him before he utters a word.

"It's time," he says finally. "We've heard nothing for hours and what was out there is long since gone. With luck, to another harbour."

She nods, knowing he is right. She searches the lake. What little daylight there had been is quickly draining, leaving only a great, pained emptiness. The harbour master waves the shore party toward the town and they follow, walking in pairs, their steps heavy. The snow has filled the harbour road and Flo finds she must take the harbour master's arm to help her through the drifts.

Ted catches up with them, his lamp swinging. He is blue about the lips and his face is drawn.

"Do you think they sailed further south?" he asks his father. "Maybe Sarnia? They could make safe harbour there."

He squeezes the boy's shoulder with his hand but doesn't look at him. Perhaps he wants to spare Ted the full force of his feeling. "We won't know until tomorrow."

21

Sunday
The James Carruthers,
The Captain's Bathtub

Harry alone disassembled the millwork in the captain's quarters, the other men too exhausted to be of any help. As he thrust his weight against the crowbar, he'd felt a terrible wrenching. The finishing nails, set deep in her wood panels, screamed as board after board fell away. It was all backwards, a betrayal to tear her, to devour her in this way. And yet he was strangely ruthless in the work, his arms burning with a thwarted purpose, his eyes swimming with tears as he did the only thing he could think to do.

What were they to do but try and stay warm? They made a fire in the captain's bathroom, a meagre blaze hissing in the cast iron tub, a pile of jagged oak trim and paneling lying on the floor next to it. The panels burned, the varnish making plumes of reeking smoke. Leaps, coughing savagely, rigged up a rudimentary chimney using a couple of tin pails, the bottoms punched out with a crowbar.

The fire draws slightly better now, but despite Leaps' chimney innovation, they sit in a funk, the air rancid with wet coats, kerosene. All of them have taken a good dose of rum and eaten some of the peaches from Cook's sack. Cocooned in the bit of heat from the fire, sleep stalks them, pulling eyelids and chins down low, heads bobbing off chests. One of the men, Bruce Clarke, hums a tune although the others seem too drained to join him.

~

Harry's head still throbs, the surge of energy he'd felt earlier now gone. His coat is scratchy on his skin. Strange, in the fug of the captain's cabin, he feels his father very close. Like plucking a glittering stone from a slag pile, he snatches an impression, or rather a memory, lost to him for years. He had been playing at fishing in the creek when he was four or five, a basswood branch for a pole. Losing his footing on a bit of ice, he slipped, and his feet had been swept from under him, the frigid water filling his eyes, his nose, his ears, and then his body went numb. It was as though he had fallen down a well, no up or down under the water, no light or dark. Only fear, and a vast and terrifying separateness.

He doesn't remember crying out, but Connor heard him. Harry felt himself being hoisted, then embraced in his father's wiry strength. He gazed up at Connor's face, angled and chalk-white with worry. He's surprised, thinking of this now, and it's as though he is inside Connor's scratchy woollen coat again, next to his father's warmth, Connor's chest heaving against his skull.

~

Harry opens his eyes and see's David, his expression unreadable. Occasionally, David pulls out his hand from under his coat and inspects his fingers: they are raw and swollen-looking, the knuckles an alarming blue white.

"You all right, Dave?" Harry reaches toward him. "Those fingers look like they could use some attention."

David gives him a wan smile, but it's Leaps who answers. "He's got frostbite. Out there for too long." Leaps throws another golden bit of trim into the sputtering fire. Of, course thinks Harry, most of the men had pitched their gloves overboard. The leather is useless, even punishing when wet.

David tucks his hands under his armpits, his arms crossed protectively at his chest, his head tilted to the wall. What will happen to him, to his gift, if he isn't able to hold a pencil?

"What were you doing out there? All flattened to the deck?"

Leaps gives Harry a long look, his eyes heavy-looking and drained of colour. "A hatch. Hatch number three wasn't closed right. We tried to fix it, but we couldn't. Mechanism was iced-up." He shrugs. "Too late to do any good anyway." Leaps watches the fire, his expression unreadable. He grunts, clearing his throat. "Water's already boarded the hold through that one hatch. She'll start to list soon."

Harry stares at him. "The bilges and pumps?"

"Clogged with ashes and coal. "

"But if we list too far."

"We'll roll." David flatly and quietly finishes Harry's sentence.

A wave of sickness takes hold. Harry buries his head in his knees, thoughts wheeling and catching: *Hatch 3.* He and Jake had been charged with closing it. They thought they had. They had checked the seal, gone to see if the winch mechanism had stopped – a signal that the closure was complete. It had seemed all right, but in truth, he'd had a moment of uncertainty, a suspicion that the system hadn't functioned properly. He remembers how he told himself and Jake that it *was* closed. He'd shored up certainty, willed himself away from what perplexed him.

He sees it then, the way a person can turn from knowing, peeling away from himself and becoming two parts, islands within, one willfully denying the existence of the other. If it can happen in a mere moment, it can happen over a lifetime too, a person pressing on even though bits of himself have dropped along the way. Abandoned parts. And if that happens, there is a hollowness inside, a big hole in which feelings slosh and spill and sicken.

When he looks up, Leaps is watching him. If there is any emotion in Levine, Harry can't see it.

"And the men in the engine room?" Harry asks, his voice low.

Leaps eyes turn back to the thin flame. "No one's goin' across that deck again unless it's to get off the boat. We'll see those men when we get to safe harbour."

~

At around three in the afternoon, something changes on the water. The movement of the boat is altered. It is no longer up and down, but more of a rocking, off-kilter gait, a lilting swagger as if she's drunk.

"I'm going to find out where we are," says Leaps evenly. He sighs, raising himself up, pulling himself to the door. David watches him, his eyes huge and penetrating. He manages to dump out his sketchpad from deep inside of his coat. The cover is warped but inside, many of the pages remain dry. Wordlessly, he takes his mouth to his jacket pocket and with his teeth, he pulls his pencil from it. He slides the pencil between his second and third fingers, the fingers extending and squeezing together but unable to bend. His hand hovers over the page, the lead touching and then moving over the paper as if the pencil has a life of its own. Harry watches, fascinated, calmed by the rhythmic motion of the hand, the confidence and precision in the small movements. He is drawing the boat now, her nose against an enormous sea, but inside one of the portholes, there are the silhouettes of heads – lightly shaded orbs that tilt one to the other with abject tenderness.

Harry looks around the captain's quarters at the circle of faces, all of them depleted, all of them frail. Even while he wishes he knew these men better he's grateful for them. Quite suddenly, he thinks of Connor. Connor who is probably lonelier on shore than Harry is now. He hadn't seen his father, really, just bits and pieces of the man, and what Harry made from these is woefully thin. Harry feels a gentle surrender to sadness then, for Kat, for his mother, for all that is known and unknown in that space between he and his father. He supposes that this is what forgiveness is, although he hasn't any idea anymore of what needs forgiving.

~

The *James Carruthers* has started to list badly to port. They can feel the sustained slope of her even as she heaves. Her belly will be filling with water, the load shifting, the weight of her impossible to keep afloat for much longer. None of them says this out loud. Instead, they watch David, still remarkably adept, adding their features to the faces in the porthole. The men are recognizable, a long forehead here, a pronounced jaw there. Wright and his improbable moustache.

And then a shaking takes hold, a sustained rattle, the metal of the great hull, the bulkheads, clanging and shrieking.

David gazes at Harry. "That'll be the engine," he says quietly. "And the sound of the hull, coming apart."

When Leaps comes back, they all strain toward him.

"Lost a blade from the propeller, lads." His face is deathly calm and there is a kindness in his tone that Harry has never heard before. "The wind is wheeling about, one minute coming from the south-west and then swinging north again. The seas are a complete mash-up. Ross thinks we're not far off Goderich, but he can't be certain. No light sightings. The lighthouse might well have been taken out in this – and the soundings are no help at all. But Ross has a nose for these things. He could be right."

At the mention of Goderich, there is a moment when the last ragged scraps of hope in the room grow fragile wings, lifting to hover over them. Harry is taken up with the idea of Flo. He feels a hint of giddiness, or is this pure fatigue? Perhaps they will make it into safe harbour after all. Perhaps Goderich is just a stone's throw, and the *James Carruthers* will find the river, push through to the harbour where they will tether her, then leave her.

"Captain's going to have to turn her, boys. You know it will be tricky but it's the only way." He sighs, "You have to understand she's crippled now, and she'll be broadside to the seas."

They all are likely thinking the same thing. If the cargo were to shift any more, she won't be righted. "What can we do?" asks Harry. "Is there anything?"

"No, Darling. Not unless you're inclined to pray."

Some of the men blink. David gazes down at his drawing, his head cocked, a look of satisfaction settling over his features. "Harry, there's a bottle inside my coat. Could you pull it our for

me?" Harry crawls over to Dave, and pulls out an amber-coloured bottle, the cork attached with a hinge. "Tear that picture away from the pad." Harry pulls away the drawing from the sketchpad, and Dave says, "I'll take it now, Harry." Using his palms to roll it first, Dave inserts the paper into the bottle. He corks the bottle with his teeth, pushing it with his elbow to make sure it's snug. His eyes meet Harry's. With fingers that are more like claws, he closes the sketchbook. His gestures are tender and shot through with pain, and he shuts his eyes and waits.

~

Leaps Levine leaves them and climbs back to the wheelhouse. He will convey what is happening to them after the laker's turn is complete. They are to be ready at a moment's notice – anything might happen now, he says dully.

They feel the *Carruthers* begin the turn to port, the engine straining horribly, the list growing worse with the waves that now brutally collide with her exposed side. She sways, the men scrabbling to cling to whatever they can. And then the water is boarding, travelling in streams down the passageway, finding the captain's quarters, eddying and swirling around the tub's elaborately clawed feet. What isn't tied down rolls forward into the stream – boots the men have taken off to relieve their swollen feet, a pair of wire-rimmed glasses, a photograph in a silver frame.

There are the sounds of crashing infrastructure; the entire wheelhouse has likely come down. Rivets pop in rapid succession like gunshot in the fall, and then the bulkheads give way and there is the terrible sound of steel buckling. The torrent of water in the cabin grows more voracious, forcing the exhausted men to drag themselves to a stand. The fire goes out, the lanterns smash and fall into the water, bobbing like Chinese lanterns. Soon, they are almost in total darkness except for one remaining hurricane lamp that Harry plucks from its hook on the wall.

Another change. Eerily, it feels like the boat has stopped all forward movement. There is just the awful side-to-side pitch and roll. Every man there knows what this means; she's caught in a trough, unable to complete the turn. Missing one of her propeller blades, she won't have enough push to climb out. Leaps is wading back through the water, looking like he walks on stilts, the captain stoutly pushing his way behind him.

"Is Ross not with you?" Brian Clark is a particular friend of Ross's. He'd served with Ross on many trips across the lakes.

"Still at the wheel," Wright answers. "Trying to get her out of the hole. I'll go back and relieve him, soon as we're done here. We've lost the top of the wheelhouse, lads. Blown clean off. You're for the lifeboats now. All of you. I know what you're thinking. Those lifeboats are lashed aft. You think they've been torn free by now, but one's still there. I've seen it. Now, it'll be a walk for you, boys, to get back but you'll tie on and secure yourselves. I've called down to the men in the engine room, what's left of it. Closer for them. They'll wait for you."

Harry sighs, grateful to hear that at least some of the engine crew are left. He's quite sure Jake will be among them, shakily poised on the brink, for now, a reluctant survivor.

"We're not far from shore. If you look hard enough, you might even see." Wright points to port, his thick finger digging into the air, his jaw pushing out a grin as if he can see land even now. "Don't lose heart. Follow Leaps. You do exactly as he tells you." He looks at each of them directly, his blue eyes bright and glowing. "You're a great bunch. The best crew I ever sailed with. Quite a thing, staying with her as long as we did."

There isn't time to think about what he is saying. They file solemnly past him, staggering and lurching as the boat rocks grotesquely, each man taking Wright's broad hand in his own.

Harry is last: an extra squeeze in the grip, Wright's gaze direct, unfaltering. They stand with the torrential flow of lake water at their waists. All of Harry's earlier resentment of Wright, his anger with Wright's choice to take the laker out, despite what he knew, has gone. What has taken its place is the outsized and beguiling force of Wright's belief, no matter how misguided, and the unfailing warmth of the man.

For a moment they are caught in a reluctance to pull apart. Harry thinks of the hatch, of the mistake he's made; the hubris to think a job was done when it wasn't. He wants badly to relieve himself of dark fragments, to pass them over to Wright who seems ample and generous and kind, and for Wright to pass them back, to make the pieces fit again.

"It was me who made the mistake with the hatch, Sir."

Wright studies him, the pouches beneath his eyes like great puddles, lines feathering out as if Wright is sinking beneath his own skin. From somewhere in the centre of the boat, there is the sickening sound of twisting metal and Harry knows that the back of the *Carruthers* has finally broken.

"Lots of mistakes were made. More than enough to go 'round, and as long as we're in the business of accounting, as long as we're brave enough to see what it is we've done, it was me that took her out despite the warnings. Me that wanted all of her before I left the boats for good." It is difficult to say whether Harry sees regret in Wright's face. There is certainly sorrow there, for the parting from the boat, from the men, from whatever his life had been. "Don't cripple yourself with this business about the hatches, Harry Darling." Wright claps him on the back. "Go get your arse onto a lifeboat. Get yourself home."

Harry looks ahead to where the men who trudge through water form a frail ligature. He follows the line and then turns, just in time to watch the captain ascend the watery stairway – a great orange salmon fighting its way upriver – to where Ross will be waiting to be relieved at the wheel.

22

Huron Shore, Find Him

It is after mid-day but the black cloud and the heavy snow have absorbed almost all light. Snow has piled in against the mink shed and now only the roof is visible. As Connor drives up the lane, he can make out the vague outlines of buildings – the small and broken-down barn, the plain clapboard house.

The horse, its energy spent, is labouring with the wagon's wheels, which frequently jam and lock. Froth collects at its satiny muzzle. Connor clambers down from the bench, thinking what to do, his mind wheeling away, his feet pinned by his own weight. *Tend the horse*, says a voice, quietly encouraging, the sound of it like Ethan's. Drifts hunch against the barn door and he uses the shovel from the waste pile to dig his way through. The horse, eager to get inside, drags the wagon a few steps before Connor can undo the hitch and rub down its chestnut coat with a soft rag. The animal quietens as Connor whispers, *settle now, settle*.

The water trough, deep and angled, has a skim of ice and Connor breaks it with the handle of an axe. He scoops oats into a feed pail and then puts down fresh straw. His movements are slowed by a foot-dragging reluctance. *Too much*, he thinks, imagining the mysterious onslaught of winter, and the mink, scurrying and pacing in their pens. He leans his head into the horse's neck and rests it there, the warmth of the animal moving through him, loosening his limbs, sleep threatening to overcome him where he stands.

The mink still dig at him. He thinks of the remaining offal, deep in the root cellar and under the dump of snow. *Get on with it*, he tells himself, peeling his body away from the horse. He'll need the shovel to free the cellar's trap door of snow, the cellar not meant to be used in winter months. He would have moved the feed to the barn, if only he'd known. He steps out again into the seemingly endless storm. *The world is turned inside out*, he thinks, and the result is less an unleashed fury than a measured, intentional pummelling. For a terrible moment he wonders if he has *earned* this ravaging weather. Shrugging his way into the gusts, his thoughts screw down and harden. The storm shouldn't be happening, not this early in November, not before the mink have been culled.

~

It takes him a long while to clear the trap door, the wind fighting him, threatening to tear the rough planks from their hinges. Inside, he lights the hanging lantern, and clutching it with stiff fingers, he descends. The cellar is frigid, the usual scent of fish tamped down by cold. He peers around and eyes the barrels, remembering that not much of the offal remains now, just the bit that is left from McNeil, and what there is will have to be softened before the mink can eat it.

McNeil's generosity is still a mystery to him, a focus of suspicion. He goes to the barrel that contains the remaining offal, slides off the lid and peers down at the frozen contents. More than half empty. The wind is racing across the open hatch, whining like a dying animal in the bush – a fox or a

rabbit. It occurs to him that there won't be enough for all the mink. How many times has he stared *this* down – the margin between fruition and failure, the entire business with the mink hanging by a hair? Each time, obstinacy has taken hold, and something beneath it; a persistence that has been a kind of self-battery. He imagines himself, hurling again and again at the allusive hope of a profit.

What had he hoped for, really? To emerge from the contest his own man? The truth is, he's never come close, because of the setbacks and the ball-ups. He thinks back to the furrier who came years before – a woman from the States, her coat shining in the muted light, her blue scarf at her throat, the gold jewelry twirling on her wrist. She'd come to evaluate the mink, *his* mink and he'd felt it was his moment, somehow.

When he led her across the yard and into the mink shed, Connor couldn't have known that earlier, he or Harry had failed to slide the latch on a pen and that one of the animals had managed to free itself. He couldn't have foreseen that the escaped mink would dart from its hiding place, behind the wooden shelves, and tear at her hand as she bent low to inspect a cage. He recalls how, at first, she regarded the limb, as if it didn't belong to her. Groaning, she used the silk scarf to awkwardly bind the wound, the blood seeping, turning the blue silk crimson. It was horrifying to watch the woman, blanched and panting, slide down the wall in shock. Not knowing what else to do, Connor cornered the animal and caved in its small triangular head with a wide-bottomed shovel.

After the furrier drove away, Connor saw Harry watching, his face pinked, his eyes enormous, and for a moment, he wondered if Harry had seen the violence in the shed, although surely that wasn't possible. Everything had unfolded beyond his view. Still, God knows what the boy had made of the dismal parts he witnessed, the woman leaving hollow-eyed as a ghost, Connor near sick against the mink shed wall. (He hates to think of the furrier now – her silent departure like a hammer of judgement coming down.) Finally, he cleared away the dead mink, burying it and the bloodied scarf behind the shed, and after, spewing-up over the grass where Harry couldn't see.

She hadn't returned, of course.

He's run out of options. It's obvious that he will have to cull some of the animals now, reduce their numbers and ration the food for the ones that are left. The inferior coats – those that are dull or still sparse – he can chuck or perhaps sell to a furrier as seconds. Blinking, he scoops all the offal from the barrel and a thought comes to him: sheep *would* have been easier. He laughs out loud. Why had he thought they wouldn't be, all those years ago when he ordered the mink from down east? At least the bloody sheep graze, they drink from the muddy pond, they stupidly, docilely trot to the barn when the weather turns. (Of course, there are predators to look out for – the lambs must be watched over. Ethan had taught him that. Ethan ever the shepherd.) On the day she went away, Kat stood in his kitchen, just inside the door, her bags soft at her feet. "You always run out, Con. You can't make it stretch." The mink had been particularly vexed, screaming, squawking, Harry in the shed, doling out what he could. She was frowning as if she was seeing him now from a distance, like she was trying to take the full measure of him. She'd seemed all at once older, or perhaps just tired.

"What's this, Kat?" His eyes traveled to the carryall, and the worn bag she used for her trade.

"I'm pregnant and further along than I was with the last." Her voice was level. There was no outward show of emotion, her intention and concern securely wrapped around the fragile life she carried.

He'd swallowed down, his throat tightening against him. "You've known a long time?"

She nodded. "Before Folly told me he was selling."

"And you didn't think to tell me," he said sourly. He'd regret this later, the puny tone in his words, the lack of grace.

"I could see it wouldn't make a difference."

He'd been stunned, and also caught-out. He gawked. "You might have tried me, Kat."

Her face tensed, her eyes searching his, doubt passing like a shadow across her features. "I've had years of yearning for a child. Constantly, since I lost the first one. I waited, thinking you might be with me in this, that we would find our way." She frowned. "Maybe I should have given you the chance when I found out, but honestly, I was tired of trying."

His mind jumped at the possibilities. He felt a hopeful rise of determination, a glimmer of possibility. She should stay. There was room enough in this house. They'd manage fine, the baby, Kat, and him. And Harry would go off with the league for a time but would come home, and they would be all four together. The vision, so shimmering and bright, fell away then, and it was Dot that he saw, the dark cut of her, the straight back as she walked alone down the lane of Darling farm. Who was he to hope for anything? He was swept up in a sense of terrible inevitability, and with it his words became jammed in his mouth.

"I could help," was all he managed.

Her expression settled into smooth resolve. "I'm fine on my own. I always was."

When she turned, she said, "I'll have my goodbye with Harry." She'd put her hand on the door as if to push it open. She paused, tilting her head a fraction so he could see just the length of her face. The last glimpse of her.

"I won't tell Harry about the baby, Con." He'd not thought about Harry. "He'll want to come with me, but he should be with you. This will be a blow to him. You'll *have* to take care."

He'd remained slumped in the kitchen for a long time, watching through the window and then, after a few minutes, Kat left the shed.

~

Connor's legs feel heavy and taking the single pail, he shuffles to the bottom of the cellar stairs, the world a clotted grey above him. If the cellar door is blown closed, the snow will surely cover it, and the weight will be too much for him to lift. And if the storm goes on, if there is no end to it, the snow will just get deeper and he'll be trapped. The horse, the mink, they will die and so will he. In a few days, perhaps a week, someone will come looking. Macey, likely. Bloody loyal, Mace is, his affection unearned and inexplicable. In Connor's exhausted state, the idea of Macey makes him wet-eyed, a lump swelling in his throat. Mace will look inside the minks' cages and see Connor's neglect which is now a mystery even to himself. A perversity like picking a scab with a rusty nail. He can't say why he's let the place go, why he's just put in the barest effort, getting a meagre trickle of profit back. Perhaps he has expected nothing more grand, more lasting than this. Shivering, he tightens his grip on the pail and climbs the steps, the snow hitting him full in the face, and then he turns in the direction of the mink shed.

The storm has blotted out all sound, devoured it, changed it to one sonorous howl. It is strange, he can't hear the animals once he gets close. Strange because he's always heard them, their terrible scratching and clamouring. He wished for their silence often, longed for a world without their complaint. Now there is reckoning in the quiet, a gathering tension in his throat and chest.

After entering the shed, he shuts the door. Holding up the lantern, he takes a few steps forward, the shadows of the pens making dark stripes on the walls. And then in the gloom he thinks he sees Harry, a warm presence, the bulk of him an instant reassurance. He lifts his lamp and the shadows shift, the impression of Harry disappearing. But of course, he can't be there. It must be that the time spent with the boy on the road has raised up Harry in his mind, like some sort of visitation. Connor has never been much of believer. Perhaps he is going mad. He's missed the boy so much, and he admits it now with only the whine of the wind as witness.

Where is Harry? The unasked question tunnels through him, illuminating the cavernous space inside where Harry should be. And then it occurs to him: he could go to Macey, tomorrow maybe, when the roads have cleared. Macey will give him the answer because Macey has known all along. When Connor finds the boy, he'll tell him that he's sorry about Kat and he'll try to explain what it's like to live inside of his own shadow, afraid of his own son, afraid of Kat, terrified of what they would see in him.

He thinks of Kat, how she stayed for all of those years, holding a wide and generous space for him to climb into, waiting for him to do it. *Remember, Harry, how she illuminated everything around her, enlivened all the grey? You do remember, Harry, because you loved her.*

The silence in the shed is unearthly. He moves forward, sweeping his lantern over the pens, and then he sees what's happened. The water has frozen in the shallow reservoirs; the animals are on their sides, reduced to dark lumps, their eyes black and piercing. Their bodies, so still, show the press of their bones. They've perished, every one. How is it possible, in so short a time? He feels a burst of anger, his foot kicking out, hitting nothing. The anger quickly ebbs and is replaced with raw remorse: the animals were half-dead with starvation, with no reserves to survive this freeze.

He stares blank-eyed at the row of pens. From the far end, he hears a faint sound, a scratch, a bit of chatter. He swings his lantern past the grim sight of the dead mink and holds it close to the larger pen, which is kept against the wall. From inside, two of the animals peer out at him, their heads sunk low, their bodies pressed together. He'd forgotten that he'd put the two in there to mate – the king and the queen from which the forthcoming litters would come. He looks at the water reservoir and sees that by some strange occurrence, the water still beads into glistening droplets. The combined warmth of their bodies has kept the water liquid, or maybe it's just good luck. Placing the pail overtop of the lantern, he softens the offal, and then, opening the top of the pen, he scoops all of it into the bowl. Instantly, the animals burst into frenzied feeding. He watches them, transfixed, amazed by their agility, their hunger. For a moment, he feels relief, the losses of the others overtaken by this new wonder.

Valerie Mills-Milde

He can start again with these two, but it will take months if not years. Besides, he has no credit left with anyone. He can muster not a shred of resolve to continue. No bloody good at this, he says under his breath, wheezing out a laugh. No better than Jack is a driver. Well, if this is the end then there is no point in holding onto the two that are left. He crouches low and studies them, his admiration growing. There is a gathering force of feeling – a balling together of regret and sadness and from it an intention forms. He picks up the cage and labours with it past the quiet pens and swings open the door. Putting his face into the wind, he drags his coat around himself. The snow drives at him, horizontal now, frenzied, and every trace of familiarity is swept away.

His boots fill. Carrying the animals is harder than it seems, his injured hand throbbing, the cage awkward as the animals inside dart and scrabble. Strong little bastards. He stumbles, the feeling of falling seductive, almost relieving, and at the same time, there is a terrible protest from the mink as the cage dives into the snow. He staggers up, hefting the cage, his face streaming with tears now. Ahead, a line of trees emerges from the bush, skeletal and cold. The pound of the lake is like a drum from the west. The surge of feeling inside seems to clench his lungs, his breathing pained, a ragged sound to it. *Christ.*

Inside the woods, the trees sway and moan. The stream won't be far. He feels it like a pulse. Standing, panting, he peers into a furious white nothingness. He's thought many times of freeing himself of them, killing them long before the killing would be profitable. The impulse to bring them here, to this determined little stream, witness their escape as they bob and swim, lithe and certain, is new to him and utterly convincing.

Connor walks a few more steps and then the stream is there, before him, and he drops to his knees, breathless and exhausted and giddy. His heart rises as he opens the door, the animals rushing out, no hint of fear or hesitation. Just a certain greed for life. He lies back in the snow, great heaving sobs pulled from him.

23

Sunday
The James Carruthers,
A Lifeboat

On deck, the men tie themselves on and cling to anything they can find, and then they crawl toward the lifeboat. From all directions, water thunders at the floundering *Carruthers*, sometimes seeming to retreat and then rushing in, the gigantic waves changing in shape and form. A narrow view of sky above the watery troughs, a thin light seeping through felted cloud, unending lashings of snow. Nothing is recognizable to Harry, no feature on the boat or in the lake. The port railings are completely submerged, the *James Carruthers* a long sliver of icy-glass protruding from a seething blackness. She seems much smaller than she was. The lake is relentlessly pulling her, and they perhaps have only a matter of minutes. There should have been panic but Harry feels a steady presence of calm. He looks around at the other men, each prepared to finish this. Nothing left for them to do now but go over the side, make for shore. Wouldn't it be something if he found himself close to Kincardine. He'd try to make it to town, and then to the harbour. Macey will be there, inspecting, making an inventory of the damages. He'll tell him about the storm, the men he'd crewed with. Mace will understand all of that – the camaraderie, the sentiment he now feels for the boat. Harry's sadness about

Wright. And then Harry will make the short journey to see Connor. He will shake Connor's hand, the residue of Wright's warmth still there on his skin. Peculiar old Connor. Connor will be perplexed, but that won't matter because Harry will let the water close over what's in their past, all the ragged and confounding bits and pieces will slip away. After all, there's blame enough to go around, he thinks. Around and around and around, and it must stop somewhere.

He'd told Flo once how Connor had never wanted help with the culling of the mink. "I'm happy he didn't, but I've wondered why. Even when I was in the shed helping with chores, standing right next to him, he was all sealed up in himself, like it was me that made him uncomfortable."

Flo looked at him, rooting out what was at the centre of things, the hurt still there. "Maybe he intended to keep that awful business from you," she said pragmatically, "since he hated it so much." Yes, he thinks, seeing the intention in it, the care.

He will go to Flo. He sees himself boarding the train, ready for the short journey. The idea is so real, so certain, there is no need to follow it to its conclusion. He might as well already be there.

He can just make out the outlines of the men from the engine room, lashed on to the starboard railing and inching their way along. Leaps is there, head and shoulders above the rest, a phantom, his coat thrashing in the gusts. In one hand, he holds a flare gun, and every few minutes, he holds it high over his head and shoots.

When finally, all the remaining men converge at the lifeboat, Leaps clambers to the highest point on the tilting deck. He turns to them, his teeth bared, the bones of his face protruding through the drawn skin. Not a phantom now, but more of a dark angel, ushering something in, witnessing a passage.

"We'll right this boat and put on the life vests. Then we'll load the boat and lower."

Harry knows that the lifeboat lowering system on the *Carruthers* depends on men willing to operate the davits and wrap the fall ropes around the bollards, to slacken off the sisal falls as the boat swings down. Two men at least and one to oversee their efforts.

"I'll need a man for the bow fall and man for the stern," Leaps is yelling, his voice flat. Crawling, Ross reaches around Harry, his one hand clutching the rail and the other held up. "I'm here, Leaps. Put me on the bow."

Leaps gives a short, solemn nod and from deep inside the cluster of men who'd come from the engine room, Jake muscles himself forward.

"I'll take a line."

Jake has a look of finality on his face, the look of a decision made. Something inside of Harry turns and drops. *Not Jake.* Leaps and Ross are lowering the lifeboat to the deck, and the men press themselves to it, plucking life vests from under the seats, awkwardly closing the fastenings. There is something childlike in the big, padded vests, reducing them all to toddlers. Harry grips Jake's arm as he moves past, then peers into his friend's creased and coal-streaked face. "You're just doing penance, Jake. It won't help. What's done is done. I'll stay with you, give a hand."

Jake is momentarily fierce, his expression set in a scowl before the muscles give way to violent shivers. "Don't even think of staying back. After the lifeboat's lowered, we'll climb down with the Jacob's ladder, and you wouldn't manage that, Harry. You're weak as a bloody kitten since that knock on your head."

Harry can find no words. The Jacob's ladder will thrash against the hull, and the men, clinging to it, will either be thrown into the water or crushed. Jake won't make shore. There is never a moment's doubt about this. Harry won't see Jake again, or any of the others who stay with the laker.

A glitter has leapt into Jake's eyes. "It's all right," he says. "Go." He shoves Harry toward the lifeboat, but in the last moment, he tugs him back, pulling him close, his arm thrown carelessly around Harry's shoulders. "Loneliness can make a man selfish. I should never have asked you to come." The words are lightning quick, and in an instant, Jake is on to the man behind Harry, bullying him forward, his hands rough on the man's back.

The lifeboat looks as fragile as an insect. The men climb over the slatted sides, some with a look of terror, others deadened, too exhausted or cold to show fear.

"*In*. For the love of Christ, Darling." Leaps is still busy with the davit, Ross and Jake winding the fall ropes around the bollards. Harry half-dives over the side of the boat, taking up a seat just behind Brian Clark, focusing on the density of the man's fanned back.

Leaps is waiting to spot the next cresting wave before giving the order. Once he sees it, he yells, "lower away!"

"All right then, lads. Hang on." Ross and Jake work in unison, the pulley on the davit hoisting and then swinging the lifeboat to starboard where it clears the rail, and then for a few moments, the tiny boat and the men wag horribly in the wind.

Valerie Mills-Milde

They wait for the approach of the enormous swell. And then it's upon them, the crest racing beneath the lifeboat like a horse, the boat riding its back down until the wave reels away. Beside them, the *Carruthers* rolls, and Harry fixes his eyes to the paint on her hull, remarkably smooth and unmarked. He recalls how new she is. Barely broken-in. He thinks of Kat. "Everything falls away, Harry," she once said, "But we keep going. We tuck our past inside, thinking it doesn't show but it's written on our bodies, in our words, in who we love and who we leave." Connor is his past, his mother too, although he can't remember her. And Kat. She is the best part. Spray drives in hard, swells breaking over the boat's sides and making a kind of curtain. He wipes the sludge of water from his eyes, and then he sees them, far off in the distance: an improbable slurry of lights. They appear and vanish and then appear again. He is both astonished and unsurprised. Watching them, Harry's thoughts are no longer with his past, or even what waits for him, but rather what hums like a steady charge beneath his breastbone. He closes his eyes and visualizes the current inside travelling, finding its way to Flo, lodging in the deepest places in her. They are end-to-end now, their circuit complete, and these moments, brief or not, are everything.

He looks up. Water completely eclipses the sky and makes the world slate-coloured, and the strange lights have not returned.

"Ready to bail," Farley hollers from the bow.

He is focusing on the back of Brian Clark's life vest, seeing the man's shoulders jump each time the lifeboat jerks. Despite the violent motion, Harry feels a strange sense of peace. Perhaps it's the bang on his head that he took on deck. Perhaps he's dreaming. Another lurch, this time just affecting the lifeboat's bow, now all the men tilting forward, their heads on their knees. The bow is near the water. Harry grips while knowing no hold could be strong enough. Somewhere above them the *James Carruthers* gives out a groan.

A sudden jerk. The bow fall rope drops free and whistles past them into the black, leaving them awkwardly suspended like a pen in an inkwell, man piled upon man, the lifeboat swinging horribly.

Harry lifts his head. They are not far from shore, just as Wright said. Certainly, he can feel it there, even if he can't quite see it. And then he does see something, an intermittent glow, like blinking eyes, bright, then brighter. The lifeboat shoots bow first into the hard curve of lake, piercing that watery underworld with Harry held fast by that strange and faithful light.

24

Tuesday
Huron Shore,
Heart's Desire

The train station is busy, the rail lines finally cleared of snow. Inside, Flo stands by a streaky window, her overnight bag in her hand. The air is fuggy and warm, but she doesn't think to undo the buttons of her coat.

A group of newly arrived passengers wordlessly file past, bewildered, lost, limp with exhaustion. They form a loose knot around the stations' bulletin board. The stationmaster has pinned up a notice which gives directions to the area hotels and guest houses. There is a frank admission that because the capacity of the county morgue has been maximized, several temporary facilities have been made operational to meet the current need. The whereabouts of all the morgues are listed. And then, finally, *"Those seeking information about missing crewmen should make their way to the harbour offices where the boats' crew rosters can be confirmed."* Fingers trace these final words, eyes narrowing to better see. Flo imagines that many will hold onto "missing," keep it close, not think about the morgues until they are resigned that here is nothing else left for them to do.

Volunteers wait quietly in the reception area, ready to direct people. Mr. Cray had been one of the first in Goderich to lend his services, escorting arriving family members to various locations. A reassuring presence, Flo thought, for people who moved ghost-like, through shock. Before she'd left the apartment this morning, he made her a package of food and then walked with her to catch her train. "I'm sorry, Flo, about your missing friend." He'd frowned down at his boots and then held her eye, his sympathy direct and unwavering. "Your boy Ted told his father and his father let me know. If there is anything I can do."

She'd given him a quick smile. "I'm all right." They walked along silently and then she asked. "Do you think there is any chance?" Of course, she knew the answer. She needed to hear it though. There was no point in cradling faint hopes or living in an imaginary world, one where Harry would somehow walk off an icebound laker, the shambling smile on his face, his eyes a sunny August blue.

~

Yesterday had been Monday and Flo spent the entire morning in the office waiting for the telegraph poles to be resurrected and the circuits to be repaired. The outgoing box was overflowing with waiting messages, and soon customers lined up at the counter. Ted dumped a stack of documents on her desk, collected from around the harbour earlier. "You're to send these first thing. When you can, that is," he said, a little apologetically.

She'd tensed, evaluating the pile-up of work, and then fixed her gaze on Ted who stood close, restlessly fiddling with the frayed strap of his messenger bag. He was clearly looking for more to do, and she decided to harness his energy. "Ted, see if Ruby would be willing to come in for a few hours once the wires are up. And when you get back, you can help people with their messages. And take their payment." She'd handed him a paper with the rates marked. Ted was young to be handling money. It was company policy that messengers weren't supposed to do that, but he would catch onto it quickly, and he looked very pleased.

When Ted returned, she was free to begin typing the messages in preparation for sending. At mid-day, the telegraph lines were humming again, and Ruby arrived soon after, slightly out-of-breath, a glint of excitement in her eyes. She walked directedly over to the printing machine, now nattering away without a pause, reams of messages pouring in, all requiring translation from code.

"You do that for a bit, Ruby, and I'll get a start sending the outgoing ones," Flo said, sighing appreciatively and nodding at the printer,

With the New Haven now before her, Flo felt instantly settled. Earlier, she had set aside the urgent or time sensitive messages for priority. There were newspaper dispatches to Toronto, Montreal, Cleveland, Chicago. And the harbour master's missives – his notifications to the shipping companies, an itemized accounting of what, thus far, had been discovered along the area's shoreline; life vests marked with the name of a laker, a ship's bell, planks of wood, and the bodies of course. Scores of them.

She put her finger to the instrument's key, the brass soft and firm against her skin, and then, as she had done hundreds of times before, she immersed herself in code. Soon, the articulated sounds coalesced, becoming lithe, fluid, passing through her to travel along mile after mile of high-strung wire.

She barely looked up until around 3:00 P.M., when Ruby placed a *Please Be Patient* sign on the counter. Ruby scooped Ted, an arm around his shoulders and steered him to a picnic basket in which she had placed ham, thick slices of bread with butter, and four perfect apple tarts. Flo put the kettle on the stove to make tea. They took the basket and tea to the back, behind the station, and sat on the little stoop, sharing the old blanket from the office cupboard.

"All anyone wants to talk about is the storm," said Ted brightly, wiping his mouth with the cuff of his sleeve. It was a relief to have Ted there, chattering in the dull damp air, both women quiet, weighted with the work still ahead.

~

Just after the train to Guelph pulled away from the station, Ruby took Harry's last telegram from the print machine. She translated it from code and typed it up on telegraph paper. She'd stood looking down at it for a long time before walking it over to Flo.

"Flo," she said quietly, her hand on Flo's shoulder. "It's for you."

An unplanned outbound job working the James Carruthers sailing Thursday. Will catch first train from Midland. With you very soon. Can't wait. Unceasing Love. Always. Harry.

Flo stared in disbelief, and then read the message again thinking it was a mistake. He was expected today or tomorrow by train. Had Ruby made an error in translation? And why had it arrived so late? Even with the lines down for a few hours, this should have come Friday, or Saturday at the latest. A terrible turbulence took hold in her body then, a flailing creature under her ribcage. What if there had been a delay in transmission at

Valerie Mills-Milde

the other end, an operator's oversight? Or had Harry given the message to someone else to send – that sometimes happened - and for whatever reason, the person hadn't sent it right away. The truth tunneled its way in. She recognized the name of the lake boat from a dispatch they'd received earlier which listed all the vessels presumed lost. The *James Carruthers* had been among them.

After Flo read the telegram several times, she'd placed it on her desk, next to her instrument. She continued to work because she didn't know what else to do. Ruby went to see her baby and then came back an hour later, putting her arms around Flo before she'd even taken off her coat. "Go home, Flo. I'll be happy here for the rest of the week. The baby is fine with my sister, and I can nip home now and again and let Ted keep watch here."

Flo eyed the stacks of waiting messages, the skeins of tape that cascaded from the print table. "It's too much, Ruby."

Ruby took her firmly by the shoulders, her hands warm and sure. "No, it isn't." She turned to her desk, straightening it, restoring her telegraphy machine to its exact spot, according to her preference. When Flo hadn't moved, Ruby's voice became stern. "It's all right, Flo," she said, "I've missed this, you know. Something about this business gets under your skin. Take your time – we'll manage. I've contacted C.P. to see if they'll send up some help."

~

"It was the *Carruthers,* wasn't it, that the lad was on?" Mr. Cray asked earlier as they walked the slushy street on the way to the station. "I think it's very unlikely that anyone survived." The response was kind and dignified, with a military precision.

Exactly the answer she expected from him and probably what she needed. Besides, she knew in her heart that Harry was gone.

"You're going to identify your friend, if you can find him?"

"Yes," she said simply.

That was her intention. She'd learned through the telegraph office that debris from the *Carruthers* was washing up on beaches in the vicinity of Kincardine. Bodies had been found, some wearing lifejackets that bore the laker's name.

"He had no family, then? No one else to help with this?"

Flo shook her head. "None that he was close with." She'd felt a sudden wave of sadness. If it had been one of her brothers instead of Harry, there would be family, neighbours – she herself would travel that distance back home. And it was in this moment that it came to her, definite and sure, as though it had been specially delivered to her, a message sent and received. She would find Harry's father. *This* is what she would do for Harry.

~

Her train is late but that isn't surprising, given all the disruptions of the last two days. After it finally pulls in at the Goderich station and disgorges its passengers, she walks to the platform and climbs into the car. It will be a short trip to Kincardine. As she takes her seat, she sees the blank faces of the other passengers. No one looks up.

The man across the aisle has his newspaper open, the headline visible: "Woman Telegram Operator joins search and rescue effort at height of storm in Goderich." She'd felt annoyed by the article when she'd first seen it at the station earlier. Now, she thinks only of the telegrapher who had taken down the story, the taps and spaces she'd made, the quickness of her fingers on the keys as the words streamed onto the page. The story is hyperbole; the shore party and the line of lamps sending code straight into the heart of the storm, the running boy, the fortunate provisions boat that miraculously made it into harbour. But what of the missing parts of the story, she thinks. The boats that were too far from shore, or the boats that were already broken. There were so many who were beyond reach of her lamps. If she were to tell the story of the rescue effort, she would want to tell the whole of it.

The grief of the many losses, as many as three hundred, some reports say, is too new to allow for blame. The individual accounts haven't yet emerged, and the investigations, identifications, the gathering of accounts, have only just begun. But Flo knows that there were failures. Watching the passing lake from the train window, its surface eerily calm, she feels a sickening throb of anger. The futility of all the deaths is inescapable. There shouldn't be incentives for captains to deliver their loads in bad weather. And all lake boats ought to be equipped with ship-to-shore communications. Ridiculous that they were reduced to storm flags and people waving lanterns – there are telephones and radios and automobiles now. The doomed lakers, some within a hair's breadth of shore, might just as well have been one-thousand miles at sea for all the good anyone on land could do them.

It is this that makes her heart break. The men cut-off from safety, from love, in all that darkness. She closes here eyes, the train swaying and rocking. Over her years as an operator, there have been so many sad messages, each carrying an imperative; *come closer, know this, remember.* How many like those will be sent over the next days, the sorrow carried by electric currents, criss-crossing borders, circling the lakes, around and around and around. There will be an outcry now, in the shadow of devastation. There will be a demand for modernization in communications, for more precision in weather forecasting.

Her own loss is a private knot of sorrow. She thinks of Harry's last message to her and wrestles with it, wanting to change the text into the promise of seeing him again. But the message is unalterable. She chooses instead to fix herself to its essence, to the vow she finds there: *With you very soon*. Stop. *Can't Wait*. Stop. *Unceasing Love*. Stop.

And then that last word that held everything. *Always*. Harry had always meant to come back. It had been his heart's desire.

When she arrives in Kincardine, she gathers her bag and along with many others, steps out of the train. The small station is quickly overwhelmed by the somber and jagged stream of people. She moves toward an older woman in a black dress who holds up a sign: "volunteer here to help."

She takes a breath, unsure of what direction she should ask for, uncertain where to begin. "Could you tell me the way to the boats?" she asks. There had been the friend, the fisherman at the harbour. Macey, wasn't it? Macey would be down at the docks, sorting out the mess the storm delivered. He'd want to know about Harry too. After all, Harry loved him.

~

At the harbour, a man piling debris for burning points Macey out. "He's the big fella over there," he gestures, "working by his boat, *The Grace.*" Macey is laying out bits and pieces of rigging, assessing the damage. He moves slowly, as though his bones are tired.

"Hello," she says when she is close. He looks up, his eyes focusing, trying to place her, his hands suddenly still.

"I'm a friend of Harry Darling. Harry told me about you. Macey, yes?"

Macey instantly grins, hearing Harry's name. He enthusiastically wipes his hands on his trousers and holds one out to Flo. "That's me. Is Harry with you?"

Taking his hand, she looks into Macey's face, lines running from the corners of his eyes, his cheeks wind roughened. She holds his gaze, not pausing or flinching. "Harry was on a freighter called the *James Carruthers*. It didn't make harbour."

She can tell by his stricken look that he knows about the *Carruthers*, and that he is aware that there are lakemen's bodies washing-up on local beaches. Everyone in Kincardine would know that by now, especially those who make their living on the water. For a few moments, she thinks he will fall where he stands, an enormous tree going down. Finally, he takes a deep breath. "Poor lad. Not a chance in hell."

Flo feels a fresh blow, hearing him say it. "I've come to ask for your help. Will you take me to his father? He should know about Harry."

Macey rubs at his face and then gazes at her, bewildered, the mess of his friend and his friend's son, such an anguished tangle. "You know they haven't spoken…"

"Harry told me."

He frowns, regarding her more carefully. "You were close, then. I mean, you were his girl."

She gives a small smile. "We were close."

His eyes travel over her face. He turns, kneeling, taking up his lines and rigging. "When Harry loved someone, there was no mistaking it."

Stepping closer to Macey, she crouches down, her eyes watching the thick fingers labour with knots. She can see the tears now, just at the corners of his eyes. "I'm sorry, Macey. He told me you were always his friend, and his father's friend too. That's why you should come with me. He'll hear it better with you there."

Macey stares ahead, saying nothing, and then with a determined grunt, he stands. "We'll take my cart. It's just up the hill. But Con might not welcome a visit – don't take it to heart."

"I'll take my chances."

Nodding, Macey closes his fish shack and then leads her away from the harbour. "You know what the fallin' out was over back then, I suppose?" He says, half-turning.

There is a long quiet as she follows him up the hill. "It was over Kat," she says simply. "He thought his father was cruel to her."

Macey thought about this for a moment, helping Flo into the wagon and then heaving himself up after. "Cruelty is one way to look at it. Or he's thick as a stump. Connie never seems to know what's best for himself, or anyone else." He gives her a chagrined look. "And, you know, Kat made her choices too."

They drive on for a long way. Suddenly, his face contorts. "I'm the one who put him onto the bloody lakers, you know."

"He had to be someplace," she says without hesitation, "and it's how we met. Harry came in off one of the boats, thinking to send a telegram. To you," she says. "He was thinking of coming home."

"He never sent it."

"He would have. He just needed time."

25

The Bottom of the Well

For a long time, Connor lies on his back in the snow, arms spread-eagled, his eyes on the leaden sky. He thinks about the animals, how swiftly they'd disappeared, how eager they were to be gone. He is strangely content to remain motionless, to feel his body sink down, to feel his heart slow and his body numb. If this is the way death is, it isn't so bad. Was this how Essie felt, in the hours before? Of course, Essie had Harry, snuggled in close. And what about Ethan? Had Ethan seen him standing by at the last?

In this enveloping cold, there is little want left in him. Just shadows, and he could let himself go now, and hope to find Kat there, at the end, her hands tender on him. Surrendering to his watery dreams, Connor sinks deep into the murk, but then, remembering Harry, he feels himself yanked back to the stream. There's just one want, the only one. He *wants* to find him. Sleep finally claims him, and as it does, he fastens himself to the idea of Harry.

~

He wakes in a blank darkness. The wind has dropped and snow slips from the limbs of the pine trees overhead. The temperature has warmed slightly to something just about freezing. He can hear the stream and thinks, with contentment, that the animals will likely be miles from here now.

He sits up, the smell of the evergreen and snow sharp in his nostrils. He has no idea how long he's lain there but he is stiff and wet and very, very cold. Holding on to a small sapling he raises himself, pushing off the snow that clings to his chest and thighs.

A pinkish light is just beginning to climb the sky in the east, and seeing it, he is brought to tears. All he can think is *sorry, sorry, sorry.* For what, he isn't sure, but the sentiment feels real, like the bottom of a well when the rock finds it. He stays like that for a long time, his hand holding the fragile sapling, and then he turns and makes his way back to the unlit house.

<h1 style="text-align:center">26</h1>

<h2 style="text-align:center">Altered Light</h2>

There is a knock, and the sound of Macey's voice burrowing its way through.

"Con. Connie – I know you got some coffee in there for me. Been a helluva few days." It is several moments before Connor can decide whether Macey is real or imagined. He stares down at his hands, his continued existence an unfathomable mystery to him. He half-expected to go the way Ethan had, an unrecoverable sinking, the cold stopping the heart, but here he is, he thinks sanguinely, resurrected.

"I looked for you in the mink shed," Macey is saying through the door, "I saw 'em, all lying in their pens. Awful sorry, Connie." But Connor feels only relief as far as the mink go, a burden lifted.

It's dim in the house, and impossible to know the time of day, especially with the one window still boarded-up. He should fix it, he thinks, but then remembers he hasn't got putty. Macey knocks again, this time more softly, as if he knows Connor is right there, at the kitchen table, as if he might be able to hear Connor breathing. "Look, someone's here that wants to have a word." His voice holds a certain gravity. "I think you should let us in."

Heaving himself up from his chair is a herculean effort. Once he opens the door, he finds Macey standing on the stoop, bigger than life, his face a torment. Behind him is a small woman with dark eyes. Her gaze is steady with intent. Chestnut eyes, sturdy-looking build, thick richly coloured hair that makes downy wisps at her temples.

"Come in," he sighs, and they come in together, the woman opening her coat, taking off her felted hat, sliding off her gloves despite the chill in the room. Her head is poised, as if she listens to a sound he can't hear.

Blood is oozing through the kerchief that is still wrapped around Connor's hand, and Macey eyes it. "Christ, what happened? We'll have to do something with that. But first, mind if I get the stove going? What about some tea?"

Not waiting for an answer, Macey's turns his back and rummages through the cupboards. The woman speaks, her voice cutting cleanly through the fug in the room. She tells him that she is a telegram operator, a friend of Harry's. Hearing Harry's name, he feels a sort of quickening. "Is he here?" His eyes search behind her, as if he might find Harry there.

"No", she says, and he sinks again.

He longs to put his head down on the table and sleep. She watches him, he can feel it, his hopelessness, his surrender. With a small movement, she straightens her back. There is a flinch around her eyes, a flash of pain, and with it comes a look of renewed purpose. "Harry was lost in the storm," she says. "He was on the *James Carruthers.*"

Macey has placed an old wooden tray on the table with Essie's teapot and three mugs. He sits in his chair and slides his eyes dolefully over the boarded window.

Connor doesn't understand what the woman has said. "Mace? Does she mean this blow, what we've just had?" He hasn't thought of what he's experienced in the last days as a storm. Storms are vast, heartless. A storm has no human face.

Where he's been is deep inside of anguish, in a tunnel, the world shrunk down by weather, ghosts for company. Not only ghosts, he reminds himself. There was the boy, Jack, flesh-and-blood-Jack with him on the snow-shrouded road, the boy chattering away beside him. And the mink, the last two living ones. He remembers he carried them to the stream and watched them greedily slip away. As nasty as the little bastards could be, in escape, their joy was boundless. He'd been alone then, lying in the snow, in the heart of that cold with only fragments, shards of glass, and beyond him, everything breaking.

No, he knows nothing of what happened on the lake.

"What's the *James Carruthers*, Mace?"

Macey rubs at his swollen-looking eyes. "You've not been following it, Connie. A bulk carrier. She went down somewhere nearby. Several lake boats are lost, their crews gone."

Connor stares. "You don't know he was on it, and even if he was, maybe he made his way back in." He desperately wants Macey to leave and take the woman with him. He wants to sink back down into the murk of dreams, to freeze, or starve or just to sleep forever.

Macey shakes his head. "Con, he sent Flo here a message just before boarding her."

No one moves, no one says a word. He is as stiff as bailing wire, brittle as wood fall.

"There won't be survivors off those lost lakers." Macey's voice is deep, tethered to certainty. Stirring herself, the woman operator pours tea into Connor's mug, and after she gives it to him, she touches his hand. "Now, I will tell you what I came here to say." He feels her willing him back to the moment, to look at her.

When she tells him that Harry intended to come home, that Connor had been there, in Harry's thoughts, her words fly right into his centre and find the bereft and empty places. Cradling himself, his fingers dig down into the flesh of his arms, the gash on his hand breaking anew. A choking sadness floods him, and to keep himself from drowning, he starts to keen. There are words but they are secret, unknowable even to himself and he rocks back and forth like a child. Later, Connor won't remember this moment precisely. What he will recall is a great falling away, bits of himself peeling off, vanishing until he emerges as if naked.

The three are joined by an invisible push of feeling, Flo and Macey waiting for him to exhaust himself. The sound of blood rushing in his head is deafening, a great surging wave, and when it recedes, it is Flo's voice that he hears. "We'll go together to the morgues, to look over the faces," she says finally. "Maybe we'll find him there, among those frozen men, and maybe we won't. But it's what we must do."

She stands and clears away the table, buttons her coat and then holds out her hand to Connor. Macey takes his other arm, and they step out into the day, a trumpeting sun finding them through a slit in the dark cloud, the warmth of it a shock after the days that have come before.

Acknowledgements

Over a period of four days in November of 1913, three distinct weather fronts collided over the Great Lakes, creating an extratropical cyclone that claimed hundreds of lives. Although the *James Carruthers* was one of the carriers lost in the storm, the reconstruction of her last voyage in *The Current Between* is entirely fictitious. In truth, little is known about her last hours. At the time of writing, her wreck, presumed to be somewhere at the bottom of Lake Huron, has never been located, an astonishing fact in the era of satellites and radar. Consequently, there remain enduring questions as to why the enormous laker, and several others like her, failed to make harbour.

William Wright was indeed the captain of the *James Carruthers,* a well-loved and by all accounts, affable character, known to many around the lakes. Any suggestions here as to his role in the fate of the laker is pure speculation and it is likely that hurricane-force conditions, the limitations of communications, and the insufficiencies in the lake boat's design would have overwhelmed even the most seasoned captain. All other characters in the novel are born purely from imagination.

The account of the rescue effort in Goderich is also fictitious, although several witnesses reported that flares were sited over the water on Sunday, and some heard whistles which they took to have originated off a laker.

Many people helped in both researching this book and writing it. However, any errors or inaccuracies are completely mine. Rob Ledingham was the first to share in my enthusiasm for the Great Storm of 1913, and together we made an early exploratory trip to the Bruce County archives. It was the start of a compelling stretch of reading and researching for me. Richard Bywaters generously supplied materials and resources from his personal collections of related history, and his interest in the project often kept me going when energy flagged. Bruce Kemp, author of *Weather Bomb 1913: Life and Death on the Great Lakes*, made time for me, sharing his extensive research into details of lake boat design, navigation, and in particular, deadly wave action unique to the lakes.

Several books were helpful in gaining an understanding of this extraordinary weather event and how it might have unfolded on the *James Carruthers*. A few of these are, in no particular order; *November's Fury: The Deadly Great Lakes Hurricane of 1913 by* Michael Schumacher, *The Wexford: Elusive Shipwreck of the Great Storm, 1913* by Paul Carroll, *Ships Gone Missing: The Great Lakes Storm of 1913* by Robert J Hemming. Members of the St. Joseph Museum and Archives were very helpful, as was information and exhibits found at the Huron County Archives, and the Point Clark Lighthouse National Historic Site.

The book, *My Sisters Telegraphic: Women in the Telegraph office, 1846-1950,* by Thomas C. Jepson gives a fascinating account of women telegraphers and the significance of their contributions to what was for decades a vital form of communication.

I was very fortunate to have worked with two phenomenal critique partners who set their literary gaze on various segments of this book. First, thank you to Michael Kaan for his keenly intelligent responses and intuitive insights, and Michelle Westlake for her astute and humane observations, and for her good-humoured encouragement. My gratitude, always, to Bethany Gibson who has an uncanny sense of where a narrative needs to go, and who's suggestions always speak to the heart of the work. To my first reader, Rob Ledingham, for contributions to historical details and nuances related to locale - I can't thank you enough. Peter Mills offered numerous suggestions and corrections around technical and nautical details and faithfully read two entire drafts of the novel, lending carefully considered and invaluable direction. I could not have written with any kind of accuracy or confidence without his suggestions. Hugh Dinsdale-Young supplied a vivid and harrowing account of what the launch of a lifeboat under such horrendous conditions might have been like for the unlucky crewman of the *Carruthers*. His description haunts me still.

Gratitude always, to Michael Milde, for reading, and for supporting a writer's preoccupations, even when not convenient. And finally, my heartfelt thanks to AOS Publishing, for carefully editing, designing and producing this book and for giving *The Current Between* a home.